LINCOLN

PROPHECY

Yvonne —
Thanks for your support.
Hope you enjoy.
~Carter

CARTER HOPKINS

THE LINCOLN PROPHECY

Copyright © 2016 by Carter Hopkins

ISBN: 978-1-5330-8560-3
First Edition: May 2016
10   9   8   7   6   5   4   3   2   1

ACKNOWLEDGEMENTS

I would like to say thanks to: my wife, Amie, who supported me throughout the long writing process; Emily Cassady for kindly reviewing multiple early drafts; and my awesome editor, Caren Estesen, for taking the time to teach me and help this novel come to life.

CONTACT THE AUTHOR

If you have any questions, thoughts, comments or critiques about this book, I'd love to hear from you. Please email me directly at:

thelincolnprophecy@gmail.com

Also, look for the next Michael Riley novel to arrive in 2017.

If this government ever became a tyrant, if a dictator ever took charge in this country, the technological capacity that the intelligence community has given the government could enable it to impose total tyranny, and there would be no way to fight back because the most careful effort to combine together in resistance to the government, no matter how privately it was done, is within the reach of the government to know. Such is the capability of this technology.

Senator Frank Church
August 17, 1975

PROLOGUE

November 26, 1864

Abraham Lincoln walked alone up the Grand Staircase holding a solitary oil lamp to light his way. Three and a half years of war had emptied the national treasury and, to save what resources remained, the lights throughout the White House were extinguished by this late hour. Reaching the second floor, he walked slowly down the faded red rug that ran the length of the central corridor.

The President's six foot, four inch frame cast a long shadow down the hallway as he passed his bedroom towards the east end of building. Though he was tired, Lincoln knew he couldn't sleep. More than half a million men had died in the struggle to preserve the Union and the promise of freedom that it held. But as the war dragged on, he had witnessed a new threat to the future of the country. Over time, he became certain the emerging force would one day eliminate the very freedoms for which they fought. Tonight, Lincoln knew he couldn't sleep until he had warned his brethren.

Nearing the end of the hall, Lincoln stepped into his personal office. The blue and gold patterned rug dampened his footsteps as he made his way towards the center of the room and the simple wooden table he had used as a desk throughout his Presidency. Setting the oil lamp on the edge of the table, he turned to warm himself by the fireplace.

As the fire grew dim, the weight of his conclusions sank deep inside and filled him with conviction. America will never be destroyed by outside forces. If the American people were to falter and lose their freedoms, it will be because we have destroyed it ourselves. It was his duty to warn the people about any threat to their nation – even one they had created themselves.

Turning from the fire, Lincoln stepped to his wooden chair and picked up the wool blanket that was hanging neatly over the back. He unfolded the blanket and draped it over his shoulders before taking his seat at the desk and pulling a sheet of blank paper from the stack sitting next to his pen and inkwell. A gas lamp, fed through a rubber hose connected to the chandelier above, sat in the center of the table. Lincoln adjusted the knob at the base of the lamp and a warm yellow light spread across the desk.

The President lifted his white quill from its holder and dipped the metal nib into the inkwell. For a long moment, the pen hung motionless over the paper as Lincoln closed his eyes and made mental edits to the words he felt compelled to say. He could hear the windblown snow tapping against the windowpanes across the room as he lowered the pen and began to write.

Executive Mansion,
Washington, November 26, 1864

Colonel William Elkins,

My dear Colonel

We may congratulate ourselves that this cruel war is nearing its end. It has cost a vast amount of treasure and blood. It has indeed been a trying hour for the Republic; but I see in the near future a crisis approaching that unnerves me and causes me to tremble for the safety of my country. As a result of the war, corporations have been enthroned and an era of corruption in high places will follow, and the money power of the country will endeavor to prolong its reign by working upon the prejudices of the people until all wealth is aggregated in a few hands and the Republic is destroyed. I feel at this moment more anxiety for the safety of my country than ever before, even in the midst of war. God grant that my suspicions may prove groundless.

Yours very truly,
A. Lincoln

As he set the pen back in its holder, a familiar voice broke the silence. "Excuse me, sir." The President turned to see the face of the White House butler, Peter Brown. "You want me to prepare your bed for you?"

Lincoln smiled. He knew precisely what his friend was saying. "Are you sending me to bed, Peter?"

"Oh no, sir. I wouldn't do that," Peter replied as Lincoln neatly folded the letter. "But I'll go ahead and prepare your bed anyway," he said with a raised eyebrow as he quietly left the room.

Lincoln stared at the folded letter and wondered if his words were enough to safeguard the freedoms purchased by the deaths of so many. Only time will tell, he thought as he placed the letter in the pile for the morning post. Then he turned off the gas lamp and stood before picking up the oil lantern from the edge of the desk and walking the long corridor to his bedroom. When his eyes finally closed that evening, Abraham Lincoln had no idea the words he had written would one day change his country forever.

CHAPTER 1

The man lowered himself to the ground and crouched in the shadow of a nearby oak tree. Leaning against the heavy stone wall, he gazed across the moonlit grounds of the estate and up to the mansion at the top of the hill. The darkened interior suggested no one was home but the man knew differently. He had chosen tonight precisely because he knew someone was there. The task before him could not be completed alone.

Staying in the shadows, he slipped through the formal gardens and up to the house. He reached the stone façade and peered around the corner to the back of the imposing residence. Across the central courtyard, an incandescent glow filtered through a set of ornate French doors and spilled out into the night. A brief smile crept onto the man's face. A username and password were all he needed to ensure the security of a nation, and the one person who held that secret was hiding somewhere inside.

The man crossed the courtyard and landed softly against the wall, inches from the frame of light streaming through the glass doors. He stood in the shadows to slow his pulse, and remembered the phone call that led to this moment.

"You and I have some things in common," the stranger had said. *"We recognize the significance of what happened on that cold night in November of 1864. We know the truth of Lincoln's Prophecy."*

The Prophecy. From the moment he'd heard it, the man had seen the world in a different light. Lincoln had saved the country once, and through his Prophecy, he called upon future generations to save it again. With Lincoln's words driving him to action, the man recruited like-minded people to his cause. Soon, they began to train and together they comprised a dedicated and formidable team. But to what end?

"I have followed your group closely," the stranger continued. *"I know that you understand Lincoln's call to arms and stand ready to act. And that is why I have gone to such lengths to find you. We both know the world will never be free if the path upon which we find ourselves remains unchanged. But I know something more – something that confirms The Prophecy is upon us and, if we do not act, confirms the end of our great nation."*

That night, as the stranger's vision unfolded, the man experienced a moment of clarity like a bolt of lightning. A single phone call from a complete stranger had brought order and direction to his life's work. When he was finished, the stranger asked a final question: *"Have you heard of the Sons of Liberty?"*

The Sons of Liberty was a band of citizens who led the resistance against British tyranny during the American Revolution. They became famous when they destroyed nearly 100,000 pounds of British tea by dumping it into Boston Harbor in what was now known as the Boston Tea Party. *"Yes,"* he had responded, *"I've heard of them."*

"Tonight, we become The Sons of Liberty. We will resist the tyranny that grips our nation."

"What do I call you?" the man had asked the stranger.

"Samuel. And I shall call you Isaac."

The rattle of leaves in the wind brought Isaac back to the present moment. Stepping to the corner of the doorframe, he crouched down and turned to look into the ornate interior. A quick scan indicated there was no one in the room. To be sure, Isaac took another look. The room was cavernous. Dark oak bookshelves packed with multi-colored volumes circled the room from floor to ceiling. Countless paintings and sketches hung throughout the library. In the back corner, a spiral staircase reached up to a second floor balcony that wrapped around the lower room and housed another full floor of books and art.

Overhead, a massive mural carved the entire ceiling in two. On the far side, a mixture of clouds and penetrating beams of the sun burst across the morning sky. Nearest to the door, a gigantic comet cut through the dark of the night. And in the center, a swirling tempest raged where darkness encountered light. It was where the sun and the moon met to fight the final battle for supremacy.

Shifting his gaze back to the ground floor, Isaac examined the magnificent carved-oak desk sitting just inside the doorway. And there, in plain sight on top of the desk, Isaac saw what he had risked everything to find.

The computer terminal appeared normal enough – a standard wireless keyboard and mouse, along with two wide-screen Samsung monitors. Isaac had been informed the computer was connected to a large server room in the basement. And hidden somewhere in the depths of that server was a file that would change the world. To get it, Isaac needed some help.

Just then, there was movement in the back of the room. A man walked in balancing a fresh cup of hot tea in one hand and studying a document in the other. He was tall and thin with long gray hair. His elongated face was punctuated with thin reading glasses perched at the end of his pointed nose. A thin smile spread across Isaac's face.

He stepped back into the shadows and waited as the man continued his slow path towards the desk. Nearing the doorway, mere feet away from Isaac's position, he set the teacup and document on the desk and settled into his burgundy leather desk chair - exactly where Isaac needed him to be.

Patiently, Isaac watched as the man placed his fingers on the keyboard and entered his username and password. Instantly, the login screen disappeared, revealing what appeared to be a standard Windows desktop. The final keystroke gave him everything he needed. The old man had unwittingly done Isaac's work for him. It was time.

Isaac stepped to the door and grasped the handle. With a gentle downward thrust, the well-oiled mechanism released without a sound. His heartbeat quickened as he slowly opened the door and stepped across the threshold. He focused with singular intensity on the back of the leather chair that concealed the old man from view.

Moving closer, he reached into his leg pocket and removed a garrote made of a thin line of piano wire strung between two cut broom handles. His heart beat faster with each careful step. Steadying his hands from the rush of adrenaline, Isaac twisted the handles to create a loop in the wire. With the man now in reach, Isaac slowly extended his arms. Looking through the wire loop, he visualized his target.

Suddenly, the old man turned and caught Isaac in his peripheral vision. The man spun in his chair as Isaac lunged and looped the wire around his neck. The man let out a short scream but Isaac pulled hard on the handles. The thin wire pierced the man's neck. He coughed and gasped for air. With a swift movement, Isaac pulled the handles tight, severing the man's throat.

Blood streamed down the man's neck as he looked up into the eyes of his assailant. Isaac knew that, only moments after losing its blood supply, the man's brain was still functioning. He wondered what final thoughts were running through the treacherous man's mind. Isaac looked into his eyes for signs of regret or remorse, but there was only fear and confusion.

He grabbed the old man's shoulder and pulled him roughly out of the chair. The body fell to the floor, coming to rest in a twisted position that could only be assumed by the dead. Isaac listened with satisfaction as the man surrendered his traitorous life with a slow gurgling breath.

Isaac pulled a two-way radio from his belt, "All clear."

"Three minutes," Isaac heard in rapid response.

Isaac rounded the desk and walked directly to the spiral staircase at the back of the room. He reached the second floor landing and immediately began pulling books at random from each shelf. The sound of books falling carelessly to the hardwood floor echoed across the room as he moved from one shelf to the next.

Minutes later, something stirred in the room below. Isaac drew his pistol from its holster and lunged to the edge of the balcony. He quickly searched the room through the sight of his H&K.

The sights landed on a man whose black military clothing and familiar face registered instantly. "Alexander!" barked Isaac.

Startled, the man turned towards the voice and instinctively ducked upon seeing the pistol. "Sonofabitch, Isaac!" Alexander said, regaining his composure.

Isaac smiled and lowered his gun. "Get to it," he said, motioning to the computer. "We don't have much time." Then Isaac turned back to the bookcases and continued his search. As he neared the far end of the balcony, he pulled a book that didn't move. Isaac stopped and faced the shelf. *Just as Samuel said,* he thought.

Kneeling down, he examined the length of the shelf. It certainly looked like all the others with its neat row of leather-bound editions. He carefully examined each book by pulling on the top of the binding. Finally, one moved. It was a copy of Mary Shelley's post-apocalyptic classic, The Last Man. Isaac chuckled, *figures.*

He pulled the book and felt the resistance of a latching mechanism. Pulling further, the mechanism released and the shelf swung open. An interior light flickered on and illuminated a hidden compartment. It was lined with red felt that was well worn from years of use. Inside, Isaac saw a line of neatly organized lab notebooks. He allowed himself a brief smile while he stacked the notebooks into a pile and returned downstairs. Settling into a leather couch, he spread his find on the parquet coffee table.

Alexander looked up from his work to see the pile of notebooks. "Just as Samuel said," he whispered in disbelief.

"You find it yet?" Isaac questioned impatiently.

"There's a lot of files but I've got a query running to get rid of the garbage. It's almost done."

Isaac sat back on the couch and opened a notebook at random. It was filled with handwritten notes that appeared to capture a stream of conscious from the old man's mind. Knowing he could make no sense of the contents, Isaac began shoving the notebooks in his black Kevlar backpack.

"It's not here," said Alexander, as Isaac stood and zipped his bag.

"What?" Isaac asked, incredulous. "It has to be."

"I've searched the entire server. It isn't here."

"You're sure?"

"I'm sure. Maybe it doesn't exist after all," Alexander speculated.

Isaac's eyes grew instantly cold. Despite all they knew, Alexander's faith was still weak. Everything Samuel had said about The Prophecy and tonight's mission had been true. The file must exist – if not on the server, then somewhere. "Let's go," Isaac ordered.

CHAPTER 2

Wake up with the Dunham and Miller show and remember to tune it in, turn it up and keep it on Sports Radio 1310..." Professor Michael Riley awoke and silenced the alarm clock with a reflexive slap. He knew the time but rolled over to look at the clock anyway. Confirming the ungodly hour, he let out a deep sigh and stared up at the ceiling.

In the dim light of the early morning hours, he could barely make out the cabin's thick beams overhead. He closed his eyes and lay there for a moment to feel the soft breeze of the ceiling fan on his face. Then, with a deep breath and a heave, Riley sat up and extracted himself from the firm grip of the mattress.

The hardwood floor was cool on his feet as he made his way into the master bath of his small, two-bedroom lake house. He had bought the house in the emotional haze of his wife's sudden death and, at the time, he had no intention of keeping the place. He just needed to get away from the crush of life in Washington D.C. and be alone with his grief.

Now, five years later, Riley still used the cabin to get away from things and, occasionally, to get some work done. Yesterday, he had given his last lecture of the spring semester to a room full of eager students at SMU School of Law. Exams were only two weeks away and Riley hadn't written a single question. So he'd packed his bag and made his way out to the cabin, hoping the isolation would focus his efforts. But first, he had to wake up.

Riley's eyes shot open as the cold water clung to his three-day growth and dripped from his face. He glanced in the mirror and was not surprised to see the mass of tousled dark hair, which he attempted to tame with another splash of water and a quick comb with his fingers. He patted his face dry and changed into his running gear.

The wooden screen door clapped to a close as Riley stepped off the back porch. He lifted the garage door to reveal the tailgate of his 1981 Chevrolet long-bed truck. The original blue and white paint was now spotted with what Riley described as a "tasteful patina." But to most people, it was just rust.

Riley ran his hand along the top of the bed as he passed by and opened the driver's door. He threw his hat and cell phone onto the blue vinyl seat and slid inside. Turning the key, which he always left in the ignition, the engine sputtered to life and Riley headed out towards Highway 205.

The highway cut through the surrounding farmland, which was planted with perfect rows of sorghum and corn. A mile down the road, Riley approached a bridge that spanned a broad irrigation canal. He pulled across the highway into the shoulder of the oncoming lane. Making a hard left, he turned off the pavement and onto a dirt road that ran down a short embankment before leveling off in a cornfield. Riley looped around and parked under the bridge by the canal. He grabbed his hat and tucked his cell phone under the driver's seat as he waited for the dust to settle. Then he opened the door and slid out into the early morning air.

Riley had learned the hard way that, once you turn forty, stretching before a run was no longer optional. He walked around to the back of the truck and looked out over the canal during his pre-run warm-up. With a final stretch of his calves, he eased into his morning run. He followed the dirt road, which ran about two miles along the bank of the canal and ended in a copse of native trees. The road itself, Riley guessed, was formed by years of farm trucks bouncing over the rough terrain until it was relatively tamed.

Riley had loved this stretch of farmland since the day he found it. In all the years he'd been coming here, he had never seen anyone along the road or tending to the crops. The isolation had always given him comfort and allowed his mind to roam freely.

On this morning, his thoughts wandered to the unpredictable chain of events that had taken him from his high-pressured life as a big firm lawyer in Washington, D.C. to the relative calm of a constitutional law professor in Dallas. His thoughts mixed with the rhythmic sound of his shoes contacting the grass and dirt. Then, *BANG!* The sound was startling and stopped Riley in his tracks. *BANG!* There it was again! *What was that? Sounds like a car door,* Riley thought.

Having never seen anyone down there before, he was unnerved by the thought of company. Through the morning breeze, he could make out voices, but couldn't tell what they were saying. Fearing it may be a farmer who might not like trespassers, Riley ducked into the cornfield.

Under cover of the tall plants, he stopped and listened. The rustle of the corn stalks in the wind made it difficult to hear, but he was certain there was an argument underway in the trees. His curiosity getting the better of him, Riley wove his way to the edge of the field, where the corn stopped and the trees began. From there, he heard the voices more clearly but a large pile of brush inside the tree line prevented him from seeing anything. They didn't sound like farmers.

Riley darted from the field and landed behind the brush pile with a thud. "What was that?" a voice asked. Riley's heart stopped.

"I didn't hear anything," said a second voice after a beat. "Give me a hand over here. We're almost done."

"Alright, alright," said the first.

Riley waited for the men to get back to their task before he edged over to look around the side of the brush. From there, he saw the corner of a black Suburban with the back doors open. Beneath the doors, he could see two sets of legs jostling as the men struggled to maneuver something in the cargo space. Then, one of the men began to back out.

"Come on, dammit! Get the other side," said the second man.

"I got it," reassured the first.

One of the men stepped slowly backwards, allowing the other time to get a better grip on the seemingly bulky object. As they cleared the back of the door, Riley strained to see what they were carrying. With a sudden collapse, one of the men turned and fell as the object slipped off the rear bumper and landed on the ground with a dull thump.

Riley's breath caught in his lungs as he tried to comprehend what he was seeing. Lying on the ground, in a crumpled and lifeless pile, was a man's body. His elongated face and pointed nose were framed by long gray hair. His unblinking eyes were staring directly at Riley, who recoiled back behind the brush pile.

"Dammit, Alexander!" boomed a voice. "You said you had it!"

"Sorry. He slipped!" responded Alexander.

"Well pick him up. We've gotta get this done."

Riley tried to calm himself. *Think!* He demanded as he looked around. The presence of the two men and a dead body made the distance to the cornfield seem impossibly far. He quickly decided the safest thing to do was to stay put until they left. He closed his eyes and focused on slowing his breathing, which had been accelerating on its own accord. His hands were shaking from an enormous surge of adrenaline. *You've got to calm down and you've got to see who these people are*, he convinced himself. Slowly turning back, he peered around the brush.

The men had recovered the body and were setting it down near a freshly dug hole. "Okay. Let's strip him down."

"C'mon, Isaac. We don't have to do this," said Alexander.

"Yes," Isaac said with a cold stare, "we do." Alexander saw there was no turning back.

Isaac looked down and studied the old man's face. Despite being thrown on the ground and dragged through the dirt to this deserted place, the man appeared perfectly at peace. Isaac found comfort in the man's expression, as if he was silently approving all that had happened.

Lifting his gaze, Isaac watched as Alexander sat down and untied the man's shoelace with a slow pull. With Alexander at work, Isaac knelt at the man's shoulders and began wrestling his arms from the suit coat. One by one, they threw each article of clothing into the crude grave until the old man lay in the dirt completely naked.

Alexander stood and backed away from the body, wanting little part in what he knew was about to happen. Isaac looked up. "What're you doing? Get over here and start at his feet," Isaac gestured with his head. "I'll start up here."

A mixture of fear and disgust gripped Alexander. He wanted no more of this. He wanted to leave the old man lying naked in the dirt and run, but Isaac's icy stare held him in place. Having little choice, Alexander knelt beside the body and reached for the lifeless foot.

Isaac grabbed the man's right arm and set to work. Starting at the fingers, he began methodically probing the man's skin. As if giving him a massage, Isaac worked his hands down the arm with slow, circular movements. Reaching the base of the arm, he continued into the man's armpit, across the chest, and down the other arm. With a determined look, Isaac shuffled around to the side of the torso. He glanced down at Alexander, who was working the top of the man's left thigh with a slow, pressing motion. "Anything?" Isaac asked.

"No," Alexander responded tersely, without looking up.

Frustrated, Isaac resumed his examination. With the same circular motion, he probed across the man's stomach and down the left side of his pelvis. Moving to the right side of the pelvis, he felt a hard knot just beneath the skin. "Hold on a second," he said as he gently pressed around the knotted area. Alexander stopped his search and looked hopefully at the spot on the old man's hip.

Marking the knot with his left hand, Isaac pulled a hunting knife from his belt. He placed the silver blade to the edge of the knot and pressed the tip into the man's skin. Carefully, Isaac cut a small, U-shaped flap around the knot. The severed skin appeared translucent in the morning light.

Looking inside, Isaac's eyes shone with satisfaction. He set the knife on the man's stomach and, with the flap held open, delicately pushed his forefinger inside until it made contact with a hard object. Probing deeper, he reached behind the object and pulled it from beneath the skin.

Alexander struggled to see what it was until Isaac lifted the object up over his head to examine it in the morning sunlight. It was a black rubber capsule about three-quarters of an inch long. As the capsule turned in Isaac's hand, he was astonished at the extreme measures the old man had taken to hide this tiny object from the world.

"Okay," Isaac said, "let's get him in the hole."

Alexander grabbed the corpse by the ankles and began dragging it to the edge of the grave. Isaac circled around the grave and retrieved a shovel. By the time he returned, the body was lined up beside the hole. Alexander glanced over at Isaac, who had sunk the shovel blade into the dirt pile. "Well, go on," Isaac instructed.

Kneeling down beside the old man, Alexander rolled the body into the grave. He watched as the old man spilled over the edge and fell to his final resting place. The image of the naked man's twisted mass burned into his memory.

With Alexander leaning over the grave, Isaac grabbed the shovel with both hands. Suddenly, he lifted the shovel and swung it over his head in a long arc. The blade glinted in the rising sun as it sped through the air. Isaac let out a guttural scream as he brought the shovel down hard until it connected with the back of Alexander's head with a sickening crunch. Instantly, Alexander's body went limp. Isaac cocked the shovel, prepared to strike again. But as he began his swing, Alexander slumped forward and fell into the hole, where he landed motionless atop the naked and butchered man.

Riley recoiled and waited motionless behind the brush. He could hear the scraping sounds of the shovel as it made contact with the dirt over and again. After what felt like an eternity, the scraping finally stopped. Moments later, he heard rustling sounds as Isaac dragged branches over to better conceal the grave. A car door slammed and the Suburban's engine roared to life.

Quickly, Riley scrambled back to the edge of the brush. As the rear tires began to spin in the loose soil, Riley just caught the first three letters of the license plate, GLH, before the Suburban disappeared in a cloud of dust.

CHAPTER 3

The black Suburban sped down the dirt road and out of the trees. Isaac was leaving the gruesome scene as fast as he could, but it wasn't fast enough. His eyes darted from left to right, looking for anything that might get him caught. He wiped the sweat from his face and looked down the road to the highway up ahead.

Alexander's death was unfortunate but necessary. On the night they found the notebooks in the old man's library, Samuel had ordered Alexander to catch the next flight to Washington D.C. and deliver the notebooks to Samuel's courier. Alexander met his contact and delivered the notebooks but then he made a mistake. Against Samuel's explicit instruction, Alexander had followed his contact back through the city and had learned too much.

The success of their mission required absolute discipline. Alexander had failed to obey orders and paid for it with his life. But the trip to D.C. was still successful. After pouring through the stolen notebooks, Samuel knew exactly where the traitor had hidden the computer file that would change the world. The next night, Isaac and Alexander exhumed the old man's body from the local cemetery. Just as Samuel had said, the capsule had been implanted beneath his skin. Now that they had it, they could complete the work Lincoln had begun more than 150 years ago.

Isaac pressed the accelerator to the floor. By now, someone had undoubtedly discovered the chaos of the old man's gravesite and the discarded casket. Just as certain, that someone had called the police, which meant Isaac was on borrowed time. Suddenly, the Suburban bounced violently as it hit a depression in the road at full speed, throwing Isaac forward into the steering wheel. He let off the gas and, as the Suburban climbed the short embankment leading up to the highway, something caught Isaac's eye and he slammed on the brakes.

What was that? His pulse quickened as he closed his eyes and focused on what he had just seen. With no room for error, he grabbed the gear shift and threw the car into reverse. Spinning the steering wheel as he backed down the embankment, the front end of the large SUV slid around. Isaac slammed the transmission into drive and tore back down the dirt road.

Nearing the bridge by the canal, Isaac threw on the brakes and looked out the passenger side window. As a cloud of dust passed in the wind, the outline of a blue and white truck appeared. "Shit," Isaac whispered. He had no time for this complication, but it couldn't be ignored. He turned the wheel and eased down the road towards the truck.

The Suburban passed a patch of tall grass and the truck came into full view. Isaac carefully scanned the banks of the canal. No one was there. Reaching across the passenger seat he pulled a pen and paper from the glove box. The license plate was clearly visible as Isaac uncapped the pen with his teeth and wrote down the number.

After double-checking his accuracy, he shifted the car into reverse and backed down the road. As the Suburban turned south on Highway 205, Isaac pulled out his cell phone and dialed a familiar number.

"Samuel," he said, "we may have a problem."

Riley sat with his legs pulled in tight and his back against the brush pile. Sweat dripped down his face and soaked through the collar of his white t-shirt. His ears were trained on the Suburban speeding over the rough terrain. As the sounds faded into the distance, Riley didn't move. Staying still had kept him alive.

Minutes passed and his muscles began to ache. Only then did he realize that his arms had been flexing his knees tight into his chest for what felt like hours. Now that the effects of the adrenaline had started to subside, the pain intensified. It took a conscious effort to relax his arms and drop them to his side.

As his body relaxed, his survival instinct flooded his mind with questions. What if someone's still here? What if Isaac parked the Suburban and is doubling back here on foot? What if he's right behind you?

Riley's head snapped around and he surveyed the cornfield. He could feel the pressure in his veins. His eyes travelled along the length of the field, carefully examining the narrow gap between each row of corn. Nothing.

Slowly, reason began to overtake fear. He had watched carefully. There were only two men at the scene – one of whom was now dead and buried in a crude, unmarked grave only yards from where Riley was sitting. The other had sped off with a goal of getting as far away from here as possible. Riley was alone.

He moved back to the edge of the brush pile and peered around the corner. He scanned the small clearing until his eyes hung upon a thin layer of branches and leaves that Riley knew was concealing the bodies of two men. Riley stared in disbelief and strained against the deadly images forcing their way to the surface. Moments later, he pushed the thoughts away and sprang into action.

Riley spun back behind the brush pile and coiled his body like a sprinter in the starting blocks. He raced from the trees and was into the cornfield in seconds. The leaves and stalks slapped against his midsection and raked his eyes. Riley reflexively threw his forearms out to protect his face as he sprinted down the perfectly straight row of corn. Though the dense vegetation slowed his pace, Riley knew he could cross the length of the field in under fifteen minutes.

Suddenly, Riley's foot hit a depression and he stumbled. Trying to regain his balance, he threw his leg forward in a wild motion, but it caught on a cornstalk in mid-flight. The momentum carried his body forward and Riley instinctively threw his arms out and turned his body to protect his head. He landed on his shoulder in an uncontrolled fall and skidded into the neighboring row in a cloud of dirt and debris. "Fuck!" he yelled, as he got to his feet and was off again before the dust had settled.

He was nearing the far end of the field where he knew the dirt road split and led down towards the canal where he'd parked his truck. He made a sharp left turn towards the road and picked up his pace. Hurdling row after row, he looked through the gap in his arms until he saw the outline of the road up ahead. With the road in sight, he cautiously slowed to a walk.

When he reached the edge of the cornfield, Riley knelt down to catch his breath and take in his surroundings. There were no signs of the black Suburban or the man named Isaac. There was only a peaceful dirt road running alongside a sunlit canal. The scene was so tranquil it was almost impossible to believe that not far from here, two men lay dead in an unmarked grave.

He looked towards the bridge. The tall grass beside the road swayed in the wind, allowing Riley momentary glimpses of his blue and white truck. Confident no one was around, Riley darted from the cover of the field. By the time he reached the dirt road, his legs were churning at full speed.

Arriving at the truck in seconds, he threw open the rusty driver's door and jabbed his left arm under the seat. Passing his hand over decades of dirt and debris, he made contact with the edge of his cell phone. He pulled the phone from beneath the seat and unlocked it with a quick swipe of his finger. Then he slid to the ground and dialed 911.

"911 emergency," answered a female operator with a thick southern accent.

"Yes. My name is Michael Riley. I've..." Riley paused in disbelief at what he was about to say, "I've just seen a murder."

"Okay, Mr. Riley. Is the assailant still in the area?"

"No. I don't think so. He's in a black Suburban and he just cut up one man and killed another."

"Okay, sir. Are you somewhere safe?" she asked.

"I think so. He's been gone for a while. I was jogging and came across them. They were arguing," Riley said, struggling to form a coherent line of thought. Then, his words spilled out uncontrollably. "There was an old man with long gray hair. I think he was already dead when they got here. They stripped him down." Riley hesitated at the horrific images flooding back into his mind. "They cut him open. And then one of the guys killed the other with a shovel!"

The operator remained calm. "Sir," she interrupted, "where are you now?"

Riley looked around. "I'm on a dirt road off Highway 205 on the north side of Rockwall. I'm under the bridge by the irrigation canal."

"Okay. I'm sending help right away. Please stay on the line," she said as she placed him on hold. The sound of Riley's breathing filled the silence and he struggled in vain to keep the images of the forest from flashing before his eyes. The silence on the line lingered for far too long. *What the fuck is so hard about calling the police?* Then finally, after what felt like an eternity, the operator was back. "Sir? Are you still there?"

"Yes. I'm here," Riley responded. "What the hell's taking so long?"

"It's okay, Mr. Riley. The authorities are on their way."

Something about the way she said "authorities" sat uncomfortably in Riley's gut. The discomfort passed as the operator launched into a long series of questions. While Riley was answering each question in turn, he hardly knew what he was saying. He had no idea how much time had passed when he began hearing the operator again.

"Sir?" she asked. "Sir? Are you okay?"

The haze that had descended on his mind began to lift. "Yes. I'm okay. Hold on a second." Removing the phone from his ear, Riley listened. "I hear sirens," he said, putting the phone back to his ear. "I've got to go flag them down or they won't find me." Riley hung up the phone.

CHAPTER 4

Riley ran down the road and up the embankment to the highway. Standing on the shoulder he began waving his arms overhead. Instead of seeing the blue and white markings of the standard-issue Rockwall County police car, he saw a Chevrolet Caprice followed by two large SUV's. All three vehicles were solid black with dark tinted windows. The only indications they were law enforcement vehicles came from the solitary blue light flashing in the windshield and a siren screaming from somewhere under the hood.

As the cars drew close, Riley motioned for them to follow and he ran back down the embankment. The vehicles arrived at the edge of the cornfield and stopped in unison. Dust was still hanging in the air when the driver's door of the lead vehicle kicked open and a man stepped out.

"Mr. Riley?" the man asked, circling the hood of the car.

"Yes," Riley said. The man was of average height and build with thinning hair and a dark suit and tie. This was no ordinary policeman. He was removing his sunglasses with one hand and fishing in his inside coat pocket with the other. By the time he reached Riley, the glasses were tucked away and a black leather case containing an identification card and badge had appeared.

"Mr. Riley? I'm Special Agent Coffman with the F.B.I."

Riley looked around. "F.B.I.?" he asked. "Where's the local police?"

"They're not coming," Coffman said bluntly while reaching into his coat pocket and pulling out his card. Handing it to Riley, he said, "The F.B.I. has taken jurisdiction over this case." Riley studied the card briefly until Coffman asked, "You want to tell me what you were doing down here?"

Riley felt a hint of accusation in the question. "I was jogging. I've been coming down here for years. I was just jogging." Riley said defensively.

"Okay. So you were running down this road," Coffman pointed over his shoulder, "and that's where you saw it all happen?"

"Yes. At the end of that road on the left," Riley pointed to ensure Coffman knew which fork in the road he was referring to, "all the way down in the trees."

"Anyone driven down the road since the assailant left?"

"No. No one's ever out here," Riley assured him.

Coffman stared at him for a long, accusatory moment. "Okay, Mr. Riley. Let's go," Coffman said as he turned swiftly back towards his car. "You can ride with me," he gestured towards the passenger door.

The terse conversation and complete lack of any opening formalities struck Riley as odd. He had never personally been involved in an F.B.I. investigation, but he'd studied them in-depth while defending white collar criminals at his firm in D.C. *Maybe they're waiting until we get to the scene. Then, another thought came to mind: Or maybe these guys aren't really F.B.I.*

Sitting in the passenger seat, Riley's skepticism began to fade. The car was filled with the computer monitor, radios, and other equipment one would expect to see in an F.B.I. field car. But how had the F.B.I. already taken jurisdiction of a case he just called in? He looked over at Special Agent Coffman and was about to ask, when Coffman said, "So, you've been coming down here for years, you say?"

Riley's head bobbed backwards as Coffman eased on the accelerator. "Yes. I have a small cabin not too far from here. When I'm out here, I come down to the canal to jog."

"What do you mean, 'When you're out here'?" Coffman asked.

"I come out on weekends and for most of the summer, but I work in Dallas and have an apartment downtown."

"Where do you work?"

"At Southern Methodist University." Riley braced himself against the door as the car bounced over a depression in the dirt road. "I teach constitutional law."

Coffman turned and stared at Riley. The agent's sunglasses had returned, so Riley couldn't read anything from his eyes. Coffman shifted his gaze back to the road. The accusatory look only added to Riley's confusion and he decided to just keep his mouth shut.

They rode in silence until they approached the tree line and Riley pointed through the windshield. "Right up there. That's where I first heard the sounds."

Coffman slowed the car to a stop and put the transmission in park. He turned to the passenger seat and leaned on the center console. "We're about to enter a crime scene, Mr. Riley."

No shit! Riley thought, but he kept it to himself.

"We need to make sure we don't disturb any evidence. So I'll ask that you stay with me as we walk the scene."

"Of course," Riley said. He knew all too well that even the best criminal cases could fall apart if the evidence was not properly preserved. The O.J. Simpson case sprang to mind.

"Then let's go," Coffman said as he opened the door and hopped out of the car. Riley got out and rounded the back of the car to stand next to agent Coffman. He glanced behind them and noticed the doors on the trailing SUVs remained closed. Riley squinted to catch a glimpse of the other agents but the dark tinted windows blacked out everything inside. "Alright then. Tell me what happened," Coffman ordered, regaining Riley's attention.

With intermittent questions from Coffman, Riley recounted the macabre story to the point where Isaac had hit Alexander with the shovel. "Hold on, Mr. Riley," Coffman said, lifting his hand to Riley's chest. Riley paused and Coffman whistled loudly, making a large circling motion over his head with his other arm. Instantly, the doors from the black SUVs sprung open and people began piling out in a flurry of activity.

The agents pulled large plastic cases from the back of the SUVs and began organizing their equipment. Within seconds an agent began driving long metal stakes into the ground between the cornfield and the bank of the canal. Another agent trailed behind, hanging yellow crime scene tape between each stake.

Coffman turned to Riley, who was studying the efficient movements of the forensic team. "Mr. Riley, I need you to walk me to the scene exactly as you approached it."

"Sure. Of course," Riley said, refocusing his attention. "I walked this way," he gestured and stepped towards the field. Coffman followed and looked back over his shoulder to confirm a full forensic team was trailing close behind. They traipsed through the field until they reached the tree line and the brush pile came into view.

Upon seeing the tangled heap of branches and leaves, Riley's breathing grew heavy and random images of the scene flashed through his mind: the shovel flying through the air, the man lying naked in the dirt, the knife blade piercing the man's skin.

"Mr. Riley?" Coffman asked. "Mr. Riley? You okay?"

"Yeah. I'm fine," Riley lied, wiping the sweat from his forehead.

"So you were behind that brush pile," Coffman pointed. "And where was the vehicle parked?"

Riley pointed to the spot. "Over there."

"Okay. And where were these men buried?"

Riley looked around the small clearing. "There," he said, pointing again. "Under the branches. I think he covered the grave with the branches right before he left."

"You think?" Coffman questioned, taking off his sunglasses to look Riley in the eye.

Again, Riley was alarmed by the aggressive nature of the questioning. "Well I didn't see him cover the grave. As I told you, I was hiding behind the brush. I just heard branches being moved around."

Coffman motioned to the forensic team, who had been listening intently to the conversation. Hardly saying a word, they spread out and got to work. One man ran crime scene tape down the tree line and across the dirt road. A photographer with a telephoto lens appeared and began shooting the scene from every possible angle. Others began setting up portable tables and work stations.

Coffman pulled a small notepad and pencil from his coat pocket. Flipping it open, he said, "Let's talk about the man who left the scene. What was his name again?"

"Isaac. And I think the man he killed was named Alexander. I have no idea who the third man was. I think he was already dead when he got here. He was old. He had a long face and..."

"Let's talk about Alexander and Isaac, Mr. Riley," Coffman interrupted. "You need to walk me through the whole thing again and focus on every detail you can remember about those two men. Nothing is insignificant."

Riley retold the story and, under the direction of Coffman's meticulous questioning, he recounted everything he could remember about Isaac and Alexander.

Coffman closed his notepad and moved to return it to his jacket pocket. "That'll do it for now, Mr. Riley."

Riley was stunned by the abrupt closing of the interview. They hadn't even discussed the old man. He opened his mouth to object when Coffman spoke.

"Oh, one more thing," he said, pulling the notebook back out and flipping to a fresh page. "I need your phone number and the address for your cabin out here and your place downtown." He thrust the notebook and pencil towards Riley.

Riley took the notepad and began writing. "You know," he said, looking down at the paper as he wrote, "there's more detail about the old man..."

Coffman cut him off. "I think we have enough to go on for now, Mr. Riley."

"Really? But I haven't told you all the facts. How can you have enough to go on?" Riley objected forcefully, handing the notepad back to Coffman.

"We got it, Mr. Riley. And besides," Coffman added as he verified the information and snapped the notepad to a close, "we know where to find you, don't we?"

Coffman turned to one of the nearby mobile work stations. "Agent Harper?" An imposing man with a military haircut looked up from his work. "Agent Harper, would you take Mr. Riley back to his car?" The agent nodded and walked around the folding table. He took a few steps towards Riley and then stopped to wait.

Coffman extended his arm, as if showing Riley the way to the door. "Thanks for your cooperation," Coffman said, dismissively. The F.B.I. clearly wanted Riley to leave, so he turned and left the scene with Agent Harper close behind.

CHAPTER 5

Movement on the video display caught John's attention. The monitor was one of a small collection of screens showing the perimeter of the Georgetown home. As the head of physical security, John spent countless hours staring at the same images from the external cameras. Since the lab rarely received visitors, the appearance of a man approaching the front door had John on high alert.

He watched the black and white image as the man descend the short staircase, where he stopped at the basement door and looked directly into the camera. The man was athletically built with dark hair and a beard. John instantly recognized him as Samuel's courier, Joseph.

Joseph entered a code into a keypad beside the door and John turned to watch a set of red and green lights beside the surveillance monitors. As an added security precaution, Samuel changed the code regularly. A green light would signal that the individual was still trusted and unlock the basement door. A red light would set off a series of security protocols and potentially shut down the entire operation. John watched the lights in anticipation.

Within seconds, the green light flashed and the buzz of the electric lock sounded. Joseph stepped into the secure antechamber just inside the front door. When the outer door's electric lock clicked into place, John pushed his heavy frame from the chair and rounded his desk to leave the tiny office.

He opened the door and felt a rush of dry, cold air that filled the remainder of the basement. The volume of high-powered computer equipment that filled the basement required constant air circulation to keep cool during operation. John navigated a long row of servers towards the front of the townhouse. At the end of the row, he crossed into a makeshift computer lab.

The servers, terminals, and accompanying technology were all state-of-the-art, but they were sitting on cheap plastic folding tables. A maze of network cables ran across the floor in all directions, connecting each terminal to the servers in the back of the basement. There was no overhead lighting and, with the windows blacked out, the lab was lit only by the glow of the monitors and four small desk lamps. Near each lamp sat a molded plastic chair, each of which was occupied by a technician hard at work.

In the chair nearest to John sat an attractive, middle-aged woman staring intently at her screen. John's arrival broke her concentration. She removed her designer glasses and turned with a swish of her long red hair. "Is it here?" she asked. Codenamed Sarah, the red headed woman was the group's lead scientist, and the fate of all her hard work depended on the answer to this very simple question.

"Let's hope so," John responded as he stepped carefully over a tangle of network cables on his way to the front of the basement.

The antechamber was windowless with vinyl flooring and thick, reinforced walls. Though he wasn't claustrophobic, the tiny, four-by-four room made Joseph uneasy as he watched the solid metal interior door. There was a familiar electric buzz and a click before the door opened, flooding the antechamber with cold air.

The mass of John's overweight frame partially blocked the doorway, forcing Joseph to turn sideways to get inside. John closed the door behind Joseph and listened while the lock clicked back into place. "You got it?" he asked, unable to wait any longer.

Joseph nodded. "Got it."

"Then let's go," John said, leading the way to the back of the lab.

Sarah watched as the two men approached her desk. "Do you have it?" she asked impatiently.

Joseph reached into his pocket. His hand was clenched when he extended it towards Sarah. She stared eagerly as Joseph slowly revealed exactly what Sarah had wanted to see. It was a small, black capsule. Her excitement was visible. Samuel had assured her that everything she needed was inside that capsule. It was the final piece of the complex puzzle she and her small team had been laboring to complete.

Sarah took the capsule from Joseph's palm and leaned back in her chair. She held it to the light and turned it to study the seal that circled the rubberized container. "Has anyone opened this?" she asked Joseph without looking up.

"No," said Joseph swiftly, knowing the price for disobeying orders.

Sarah lowered the capsule until it hovered just above the white plastic desk. She grabbed both ends with her fingertips and gently twisted them until the seal loosened and finally gave way. The container opened and a tiny, gray microchip clattered to the surface of the desk. Sarah carefully lifted the chip and leaned over to examine it under the yellow light of the desk lamp. It was a SanDisk four-gigabyte micro SD card, about one-half of a square inch in size.

"What is it?" Joseph asked.

"A flash memory card, which doesn't tell us much," Sarah responded, still examining the card closely under the light. "You can buy these anywhere."

She reached over to the neighboring table and retrieved an SD card reader. After plugging the reader into the back of her workstation, she slid the tiny card inside. Moments later an icon appeared on the screen, entitled *SanDisk SD*. Sarah moved the mouse so that the pointer was over the icon. "Well," she said, turning to John and Joseph, "let's see what all the fuss is about." Then she pressed the mouse button and opened the file.

CHAPTER 6

Riley woke when a beam of sunlight filtered through the blinds of his downtown apartment. He lazily opened one eye to look at his bedside alarm clock – 9:57 am. He never slept this late, but he'd stayed up half the night replaying the events of the canal over and again. And now, laying in the familiar quiet of his bedroom, he could hardly believe it was real.

Riley yawned and tossed the covers aside before sliding off the bed and onto his feet. With his eyes half closed, he shuffled slowly to the closet and grabbed a clean t-shirt. He was pulling the shirt over his head when he left the bedroom and entered the short hallway that led to the kitchen and the rest of the apartment.

Entering the kitchen, his mind returned to Isaac, Alexander and the old man. The entire scene was so bizarre that he struggled to make any sense of it as he went about making his morning coffee. *What was in that capsule? Why did Isaac kill Alexander?* Riley had no idea.

With the coffee brewing, he walked to the front door to retrieve his two daily newspapers. Years ago, he had canceled his subscriptions and attempted to read his news online. But he missed the feel of the paper in his hands and, within a week, the newspapers were once again arriving daily at his downtown apartment. To learn about the serious issues of the day, Riley read The Dallas Morning News. To keep up with the local gossip, nothing beat the Park Cities Tribune – a small paper devoted to life in the wealthy communities surrounding Southern Methodist University. As usual, both papers were waiting for him when he opened the front door.

Riley loaded the papers and coffee onto a wooden tray and headed out to the balcony, where he liked to sit and read while taking in the Dallas skyline. He was leaning over to set the tray down on the patio table when his eye caught a headline in the Morning News that shot a jolt of electricity through his body. He hung there, bent over the table while he read the headline again: *East Texas Man Found Dead in Rockwall.*

"Holy shit!" Riley exclaimed as he set the tray down much harder than he intended. He quickly rounded the table and dropped into the lounge chair while grabbing the paper from the tray.

He turned to the headline and dove into the article:

Rockwall, TX. *The F.B.I. recovered the body of a man buried off the shore of Lake Ray Hubbard in northern Rockwall County. The unmarked grave was found along side a dirt farm road located a half-mile north of John King Boulevard on Highway 205.*

The F.B.I. identified the man as twenty-seven year old Dennis Lavine, who grew up in Colmesneil, Texas, forty-one miles southeast of Lufkin. Lavine worked as a ranch hand in Colmesneil and was a member of the East Texas Militia, which attracts members from all over East Texas. Lavine reportedly failed to show up to work three weeks ago and friends and family had not heard from him since.

Sources say that Lavine had been struck with a blunt object and thrown into a shallow grave, where he was buried alive. The F.B.I., who have taken over the investigation from local authorities, refused to confirm the report.

Officials were alerted to the scene by a 911 call received early yesterday morning. The F.B.I. said the 911 tape is still being reviewed and will not be released until the investigation has come to a close. The name of the caller has not been disclosed.

"The investigation is ongoing," said Special Agent in Charge, Brinson Coffman. "We are pursuing all leads and will continue to do so until the individual or individuals are brought to justice. We have no further comment at this time."

When he reached the end of the article, Riley read it again. He began flipping pages of the paper at random and scanning the content. He scoured the entire newspaper but there was nothing else. He closed the paper in disbelief. The article's omissions were glaring. There wasn't one body buried in that shallow grave, there were two. And the article made no mention of the old man.

A familiar question ran through Riley's mind: What could possibly be in that tiny capsule that is so important?

Riley began to wonder if the answer to this question was the reason the old man's presence was not reported. Agent Coffman had focused exclusively on Isaac and Alexander during the interview process. The F.B.I. was holding something back, but what?

Riley poured himself a cup of coffee as the question turned in his mind. It wasn't unusual for law enforcement to hold back information about an investigation. But they had decided to release the name of Dennis Lavine – the man Riley knew as Alexander. *Why release one name and not the other?* The more he thought about it, the more questions he had.

With a sigh of resignation, Riley tossed the paper to the floor of the balcony. He had been thinking of nothing but the disturbing events at the canal for more than twenty-four hours. He needed to clear his head and decided a dose of local gossip might help. He leaned over to the side table, topped off his coffee and grabbed the Park Cities Tribune.

While the Tribune included legitimate stories from time to time, there were three issues that always received in-depth coverage: weddings, divorces and deaths. Riley slowly flipped through the pages, seeing nothing of particular interest until he reached the obituaries, where an article caught his attention: *The Life and Legacy of Christoph Varden.*

Renowned inventor, entrepreneur and local philanthropist, Christoph Varden, dedicated the first half of his life to making the world a safer place, and the second half to making it a better place.

Born in 1946, Christoph was the son of a British Royal Army doctor who was stationed in Wuppertal, Germany during the post-World War II occupation. The family moved back to London in 1949, where Christoph grew up and eventually graduated from Imperial College with a degree in mathematics in 1966. He then moved to Boston, Massachusetts, where he earned his Ph.D. in computer science from Massachusetts Institute of Technology.

Leveraging his work at MIT, Varden started MicroCon, a dedicated security technology company. With the advent of the internet and the rapid expansion of personal computing, MicroCon grew into the world's largest security vendor with customers ranging from banks, to hospitals, to government agencies. The company stayed on the forefront of security by following Varden's now famous maxim – To beat the bad guys, you have to think like the bad guys.

The application of this maxim led Varden to first develop innovative and powerful technologies to bypass or defeat computer security so that he could then build stronger defenses into his own products. Many have criticized Varden's methods, as they led to the creation of some of the world's most powerful computer viruses and hacking techniques. But experts agree these developments pushed computer security farther and faster than anyone could have imagined.

With MicroCon established, Varden moved to Dallas in 1992. For the next twenty years, he dedicated his life to a wide range of philanthropic endeavors. Varden built state-of-the-art computer labs in every Dallas public high school. He established the Varden Skills Center, where thousands of Dallas residents have received free computer training. He also donated millions of dollars to the preservation of natural wetlands around the Trinity River in south Dallas.

Christoph Varden was a unique individual who directed his astonishing skills to making Dallas and the world a better place. He will be greatly missed and never replaced.

Riley folded the paper in his lap and sipped the last of his coffee. He sat for a moment as he searched his memory for where he'd heard Varden's name before. Finding no answer, he collected the newspapers, threw them on the tray and carried everything inside. He had just enough time to shower and get to campus for his lunch meeting.

CHAPTER 7

R iley pulled into the SMU faculty parking garage and drove to his designated space at the end of the first row. With the oppressive Texas summer looming, he was always thankful for a place to park in the shade. He grabbed his bag from the passenger seat and slung it over his shoulder as he got out of the car. Leaving the garage, he crossed the narrow side street and onto campus.

Summer had not quite arrived and Riley enjoyed the unseasonably nice weather as he walked along the shaded sidewalks through campus. Typically, such weather would attract scores of students to relax outside in the law school quad, but with final exams only days away, the campus was a virtual ghost town.

Riley strolled through the law school campus towards Dallas Hall – the central administration building on the main campus of Southern Methodist University. A long, open mall extended out from the front of the building. At the far end sat a squat, concrete fountain where Riley knew his friend would be waiting.

He had met Amie Hawkins during his first semester at SMU. Amie was the chairwoman of the computer science department and had been working on an article about law enforcement's use of advanced surveillance technologies. Following the suggestion of one of her colleagues, Amie called Riley to see if he would provide comments on the constitutionality of the issues raised in the article. The meeting led to an academic partnership that had developed over the years into a deep friendship.

Riley was walking down the mall and saw Amie sitting on a bench by the fountain. Even from a distance, her long brown hair and olive skin made her easy to recognize. She was making notes on a stack of papers in her lap when Riley walked up beside her.

"I can always tell it's you," Amie said without looking up. "You're the only one I know who wears beat up old loafers like those." She stopped her note taking and looked up at Riley. As always, her dark brown eyes sparkled with energy.

Riley returned a smile and glanced down at his feet. "What's wrong with them?"

Amie shook her head and tucked the papers she had been working on into her shoulder bag. "You're hopeless," she said, standing up. "So, where to for lunch?" It was a rhetorical question, as they always went to the same place.

"Oh, I don't know," Riley responded airily. "Let's just see where we end up." They started walking back up the mall towards the law school. "I've got a story to tell you that you won't believe," Riley said. They walked along the tree-lined path and Riley began to recount the events by the canal. As he described Isaac and Alexander pulling the body from the back of the Suburban, Amie grabbed Riley's arm and yanked him to a stop.

"Shut up!" she exclaimed. "Michael, you must be joking!" When Riley looked back at her, she knew he was telling the truth. She had never seen him look so serious.

"It was terrifying," Riley said, looking Amie directly in the eyes. "But it gets worse." Riley waited as the gravity of the story registered in Amie's expression before they resumed their slow walk through campus. Amie listened in rapt attention while Riley detailed the removal of the black capsule from the old man's body, the murder and burial of Alexander, and the F.B.I. interview at the scene.

By the time he finished, they had made their way across campus. Amie stood in shocked silence as they waited for the traffic light at the corner of the busy intersection at Hillcrest Avenue. She was deep in thought when the light changed and Riley was forced to grab her arm and guide her into the street. When they reached the door of Peggy Sue BBQ, Amie was still silently analyzing the incredible story.

"Hey. You with me?" Riley asked as he reached for the door.

"Yeah. Sorry," Amie responded, emerging from her thoughts. "I'm just going over it in my head. I can't seem to wrap my brain around it. It's just so unbelievable."

They entered the restaurant and were seated in a green, vinyl booth by the front windows. The portly waitress dropped menus on the red and white checkered tablecloth. "Y'all know what you want?" she asked, smacking on a piece of gum. She'd waited on the couple for years and already knew what they would order.

"We'll both have the chopped brisket and iced tea," Amie said.

"Uh, huh," the waitress said, clicking her gum and turning towards the kitchen.

As soon as the waitress was out of earshot, Amie said, "Some of this just doesn't make sense."

"No kidding."

Amie leaned over the table and lowered her voice to a whisper, "How'd the F.B.I. show up before local police? And why would they avoid conversation about the old man? I mean, the whole story's crazy but cutting something from beneath that guy's skin? It's clearly what the other two were after. Why not ask about that?"

"That's exactly what I've been asking myself," Riley said with a sigh. "There was an article in this morning's paper about it. The F.B.I. only mentioned the discovery of one body – the guy's name was Dennis Lavine."

"Dennis Lavine?" Amie interjected.

"Yeah. I guess that's Alexander's real name," responded Riley.

"So he was using an alias," Amie thought out loud. "I'll bet Isaac is an alias, too," she concluded.

Riley hadn't thought of that but it made sense. He shrugged. "Could be. What bothers me is that I may have seen something about the old man that could help the investigation."

"Like what?"

"I don't know. Maybe nothing. But the F.B.I. wouldn't know because they didn't ask."

Amie paused for a few seconds to think. "Well, that agent gave you his number, didn't he? Why don't you give him a call? It'll probably make you feel better. There must've been a rational reason why they didn't want you hanging around the crime scene."

Riley thought about it and decided she may have a point. Preservation of evidence was always a top priority. A good way to spoil it was to allow untrained people to walk through a crime scene. "You're probably right. I have his card. Maybe I'll give him a call after lunch."

The waitress arrived balancing three beige plastic plates on one arm and holding two cups of iced tea with the other hand. Amie sat back in her seat just as the waitress unloaded the items on the table. "Y'all need anything else?" she asked, still smacking her gum.

Amie looked at her and smiled. "No, thanks. It looks great."

The waitress left and Riley reached for his tea and took a long drink. He felt much better having discussed everything with Amie. She was a friend and scientist with a methodical mind, and Riley trusted her advice.

They ate in silence for a short while until a question crossed Riley's mind. Amie was picking up her sandwich for another bite. "Did you know Christoph Varden?"

Her sandwich hung in mid-air. "More like I know *of* him. He's a pretty big deal in the network security field. I met him once at a conference but I wouldn't say I knew him." Amie took a bite. "Why?"

"I read an article about him this morning and feel like I've heard his name somewhere."

"I'm not surprised. He was pretty eccentric. You could have heard of him from any number of places."

"I guess so," Riley said, taking another bite of his chopped brisket. "But I feel like it was more specific than that." Riley thought for another moment but quickly gave it up. "Well according to the article, he seems to have put his money to good use."

"He really did. It's a tragedy his life ended the way it did."

The article hadn't mentioned how Varden died. "What happened?"

Amie set her sandwich down and wiped her hands on a napkin. "It was the strangest thing," she said, as she began digging in her bag for something. A moment later, she pulled out her iPad and swiped it open. She opened the browser and the screen flashed as the search page loaded. She selected the first news link and turned the screen so Riley could see.

Riley looked at the display and the color instantly drained from his face. There, staring back at him was the face of a man he had seen before. It was long and thin with a pointed nose and was surrounded by wiry strands of gray hair. It was the old man at the canal.

CHAPTER 8

The park bench at the tip of Dangerfield Island overlooked the Washington Sailing Marina and, across the bay, Regan International Airport. The bench was empty and warmed by the afternoon sun when Jordan Sloane sat down and looked out over the Potomac. The sounds of the marina filled the air – the gentle lapping of the water against the wooden piers, the distant ring of the channel buoy. Jordan breathed in the fresh air as she ate her lunch and waited for her phone to ring.

Overhead, the roar of a 747's twin engines shook the ground. Jordan watched as the plane continued along its glide path towards the southern runway at Regan. One day, she thought, her life would become too dangerous and she'd catch a plane to nowhere. She had multiple escape routes in place. Cash and passports of various nationalities were stashed in safe deposit boxes around the city. She had visualized her flight from D.C. to the point that it was now automatic. From where she was sitting, Jordan knew she could have a new identity and be on a plane in under an hour.

As the 747 touched ground, a phone rang at the bottom of Jordan's purse. The handset was cheap and, when today's conversation was over, she would drop it into the Potomac with all the others. She pulled the phone from her bag and flipped open the receiver. Only one man had the number, so she knew precisely who was calling.

"Preevyet," she said, in perfect Russian.

"Ms. Sloane?"

Jordan's heart stopped. The man's voice was not accented and broken as she had expected. It was formal, polished and American. Her first instinct was to hang up and throw the phone into the river. But if she did, she would never know the identity of the man who had somehow traced the disposable phone number directly to her. She made a quick decision. If she had to run, it was best to know whom she was running from. Jordan pressed the phone firmly to her ear.

"Who is this?" she demanded.

"I'm a fan, Ms. Sloane."

A what? she thought. "Who is this?" she repeated forcefully.

"I'm calling to congratulate you on receiving the Millennium. It was well deserved."

The Millennium Technology Prize was the rough equivalent of the Nobel Prize for applied technology. Jordan Sloane had recently returned from Helsinki, Finland where she was awarded the prize for developing advanced network security with artificial intelligence.

"As impressive as that is," the man continued, "I am more interested in your other work."

"What other work?" Jordan asked cautiously, sensing the conversation was entering dangerous territory.

"Your communications work at the Naval Research Laboratory."

Jordan was now on high alert. Instinctively, she looked across the Potomac to the small cluster of white buildings that housed the U.S. Navy's most advanced research facility. Her research, and the fact that she worked for the NRL's communications division, were both highly classified. Jordan didn't breathe a word.

"I know," the man went on, "that you develop technology that encrypts communications with the U.S. nuclear submarine fleet. While fascinating, even that isn't the most interesting part of your work. The most interesting part is what you've been doing with the encryption codes."

Jordan moved to the edge of the bench, ready to run in a moment's notice. If the stranger had her phone number, he had her location. The window for escape was closing fast. She had to find out what the man knew and, more importantly, what he wanted.

"What have I been doing with the encryption codes?" she prompted.

"You've been selling them," the man said matter-of-factly.

"That's ridiculous," Jordan protested.

"No need to get upset, Ms. Sloane. I am your friend. I appreciate your unique blend of talents, and I am willing to pay for them."

"Look," Jordan said through clenched teeth, "I don't know who you are but this conversation is over."

"Kazimir Bulgakov," the man said.

Jordan's mouth dropped and she broke into a cold sweat. Kazimir Bulgakov was an invisible man. He was a ghost. But he was a ghost that paid in cash. Their system was simple. When there was information to sell, Jordan contacted Kazimir through a classified ad in the Washington Post. The ad was always the same: LOST: BLACK AND WHITE SIBERIAN HUSKY NAMED NATASHA. The ad contained the latest disposable phone number, which Kazimir Bulgakov knew to call the following day at precisely 1 pm.

Jordan's team at the NRL had recently developed a new series of encryption algorithms, which meant there was highly valuable information to sell. The advertisement appeared in yesterday's paper and today, Jordan had located the isolated park bench at the tip of Dangerfield Island to await Kazimir's call. Instead, she found herself talking to a total stranger who knew everything.

"Interesting name, Kazimir," the stranger mused. "It means *the keeper and destroyer of peace.* Did you know that?"

"Yes," Jordan said. Time was running out.

"I want you to listen very carefully, Ms. Sloane, because this is important." The man paused to ensure Jordan's full attention. "I am your Kazimir now," he said. "I can keep or destroy your peace."

Silence hung in the air for a long moment. "What do you want?"

"I have a job for you."

Jordan thought through her options as another 747 thundered overhead. Perhaps she would be catching a plane sooner than she had expected. She visualized the nearest safe deposit box and the identity hidden within. But for the moment, she remained seated on the park bench. If she was going to run, there was no harm in hearing the man's offer. "If you know anything about Kazimir Bulgakov," she said, "then you know my services don't come cheap."

"Of course. You are the best. And you have shown a certain, shall we say, disregard for conventional boundaries, which is exactly why I have called."

"Who are you?" Jordan asked for the third time.

"You can call me Samuel and I will call you Sarah."

"Fine," Sarah said, knowing that codenames were a necessary part of the business. "But before you tell me what the job is, you'll have to tell me how you know about Kazimir and how you got this phone number."

"How I know about Kazimir and this phone number is precisely the reason I have called."

The story Samuel told was astonishing and, as the details unfolded, Sarah's skepticism faded. Though she sensed Samuel was not telling her everything, what he had revealed was brilliant. It seemed he had everything in place - everything except a chief scientist. Sarah knew the job Samuel proposed would be her last, but she was ready. Over the years, she had stockpiled enough cash to live comfortably for the rest of her life. With the money Samuel offered, she would live very comfortably.

"I'm in," Sarah said. Then she walked down to the edge of the water and threw the phone into the Potomac.

Now, months later, the memory of her first contact with Samuel played in Sarah's mind while she waited patiently in the Georgetown laboratory. The scene vanished in an instant when the results of her calculation flashed on Sarah's monitor. "I've got something here," she said, leaning in close to the screen.

Joseph was sitting on a stool in the corner of the lab and reading the paper when the silence broke. He looked over and saw Sarah staring at the computer monitor, typing as if she hadn't said anything.

Feeling Joseph's gaze, Sarah pulled her hands from the keyboard and turned deliberately in her seat. "Go get John," she ordered. Joseph hopped off the bar stool and walked hurriedly back towards John's office. Moments later, the two men emerged from the server stacks.

John felt a rush of excitement as he crossed into the lab. Samuel had promised him the contents of the memory chip would change the world. And now, after spending so many months locked away in this freezer, he was finally going to see for himself. He circled around Sarah's chair until the monitor came into full view.

The screen was covered with multiple open windows, each of which contained countless lines of computer code. As John studied the image, his excitement was slowly replaced with confusion. He wasn't sure what he had expected to see, but this certainly didn't look like something that would change the world.

"What is it?" Joseph asked before John had the chance.

Sarah turned her chair to face the two men. She took off her glasses and pressed the end of the earpiece to her bottom lip. "The SD card contained only one file," she said matter-of-factly, "but it's encrypted. So, at this point, we can't read it."

"Great." Joseph said, throwing his hands up in the air. "So we did all this for nothing?"

"Not exactly," Sarah said as she put her glasses back on and swung around to face her computer. With a few keystrokes, she quickly pulled up another window with lines of computer code that appeared to be generating all on their own. It looked like some sort of calculation was being performed.

"What the hell is that?" John asked, losing patience. "How do we read the damned thing if it's encrypted?"

"That's what's so surprising. The file's encrypted, yes. But the level of encryption is very low. And a genius like Christoph Varden would know that. So it looks like Varden only wanted to obscure the file – he didn't want it to be completely inaccessible."

"Bet he wasn't counting on someone cutting that thing out of his hip," Joseph quipped. Sarah and John turned and stared at him, clearly not amused.

"So what do you mean?" John asked, breaking the silence.

"There are different levels of encryption. If the level is low enough, then you can break it by simply trying every possible solution. Think of the combination lock you used back in grade school," Sarah explained. "If you had the time, you could literally start at 0 – 0 – 0 and work your way through every possible combination until you hit the right one. That type of code breaking is called a brute force attack."

"So what good is encryption if someone can just break the code?" asked Joseph.

"That's my point," said Sarah. "You can easily encrypt something so it can't be broken by brute force attack."

"So we're screwed," interrupted Joseph again.

"No. We're not," said Sarah with a hint of satisfaction. John opened his mouth to interrupt and Sarah's hand shot up to cut him off. "Like I said, Varden wanted to obscure the data, not make it completely inaccessible."

"So how did he *obscure* it?" asked John.

"He used 64 bit encryption." Both men stared at Sarah, waiting for further explanation. "At that level of encryption, the data is still susceptible to a brute force attack, albeit a more difficult one. We'll simply have to start at the beginning and work our way through every possible solution."

John was discouraged. "How long will that take?"

Sarah didn't hear him. Two recurring questions had risen in her mind: *Can Varden's program actually do everything Samuel said, and, if so, what did Samuel intend to do with it?* The questions turned in her mind and, as they began to weaken her resolve, she stopped herself. She was in this for the money. Plus, the project allowed her to satisfy her intellectual curiosity. She wanted to know whether Varden had somehow accomplished everything Samuel described. And she needed to know whether she was capable of making it better. Either way, Sarah told herself, she didn't care what Samuel did with the final product. She had almost convinced herself of this when John's voice broke through her thoughts.

"Hey," John said. "How long will it take to break the encryption?"

"It's hard to say for sure. It'll take a little time, but," Sarah nodded to the back of the laboratory and the vast computing power housed in the servers, "if we turn our machines loose on it, we'll break the encryption."

John stood in silence for a moment while he thought through what he'd just heard. "Okay," he said, clapping his hands together. "Then we'll leave you to it." John squeezed his rotund frame past Sarah's chair and headed back towards his office. When he reached the servers, he stopped and turned back to Sarah. "You sure you can do this?"

Confidence shone in Sarah's dark hazel eyes. "I'm positive."

CHAPTER 9

A mie watched as the color drained from Riley's face. Something was terribly wrong. She turned the iPad to get a better look. "What is it?" Amie asked, deeply concerned.

Riley was speechless. Upon seeing the picture of Christoph Varden the entire nightmare of the canal flashed before him.

"Michael. What's wrong?"

Riley blinked for the first time in a minute. "It's him," he said softly, hardly believing his own words.

"Him, who?" Amie asked. "Who is it?"

Riley's head was clearing and he spoke with more confidence. "It's the old man from the canal." Amie looked back at Riley, her expression a mixture of confusion and disbelief. "Christoph Varden was the man they cut open and buried in that grave," Riley said in a steady voice.

Amie knew from Riley's tone that it must be the truth, but she couldn't believe it. "You sure?" she asked.

"It's him," Riley said, pausing to think for a moment. "How'd they get his body?" he wondered aloud.

"That's what I was going to tell you. I heard he was exhumed by grave robbers."

"Holy shit," Riley said. There were too many pieces to the puzzle to make any sense of them. "What the hell is going on?" he asked. The possibilities were endless. But the fact that they now knew the old man was Christoph Varden gave some indication where the possibilities might lead.

Amie was thinking along the same lines. "With Varden involved, it certainly makes things more ominous, but it narrows the possibilities of what those men could have been after." They took a moment to silently speculate about the small black capsule and what might have been hidden inside. Amie spoke first. "You've got to call the F.B.I."

"They must've already known it was Varden," Riley responded, "which explains why they didn't ask me anything about him at the canal." Riley rubbed his temples with both hands and exhaled deeply. "But still," he said, reaching for his glass of tea, "I think you're right. If they know I've figured out who the old man is, maybe they'll want to ask more questions."

Riley drank the last of his iced tea and threw some cash on the table to cover the bill. They slid from the booth and walked out of the restaurant into the mid-day sun, where they turned back towards campus.

"There are only so many things that can fit into a capsule of that size," Riley speculated, half to himself and half to Amie.

"That's true," Amie agreed. They had reached the cross walk and were waiting for the light to change. "Could be as simple as a rolled up piece of paper. It could have almost anything written on it, like bank accounts or passwords."

Riley hadn't thought of anything that specific but Amie was right, which only complicated things. "I suppose it could be just an elaborate robbery," he reluctantly admitted. "Varden certainly had enough money to make it worth their while." Riley's intuition told him that Isaac and Alexander were not after money, but he couldn't explain why so he kept it to himself. The light changed and they stepped off the curb in unison to cross the street.

"You're going to call the F.B.I., right?" Amie asked.

"Yeah. I'll call them when I get home. Maybe I can make a little more sense of this before I get there."

They made it to the other side of the street and Riley turned to head into campus. Amie touched his arm. "You don't need to escort me back. Just give me a call after you've talked to the F.B.I. – unless you want me to call them with you."

Riley smiled. "No, that's okay. Thanks. I doubt there'll be much to report, but I'll give you a call."

"Okay," she responded, her tone laced with hesitation. Amie walked up the deserted sidewalk that led to the center of campus. After a few steps, she looked over her shoulder and said, "Good luck. And call me later." Then she rounded the corner and disappeared.

Riley let out a sigh and shifted the shoulder strap of his bag before he turned and walked down the entrance ramp of the faculty parking garage. He wasn't exactly sure what he was going to say to the F.B.I. and was formulating his thoughts when he reached his gray BMW. He popped the trunk and threw his bag inside.

He was turning towards the driver's door when something caught in his peripheral vision. As his mind processed the image, he knew something was wrong. He reached for the door handle and allowed himself a quick and seemingly casual glance across the parking garage. In that instant, his every fear was confirmed. Sitting just around the corner, and almost hidden from view, was a black Chevrolet Suburban. Riley scanned the license plate and his blood ran cold. The first three letters were clearly visible – G L H.

Riley froze, his hand resting on the door handle. But there was no mistake. With the cold chill spreading over his skin, Riley's body confirmed what his mind already knew. Isaac had found him.

Riley forced himself to think. The worst place he could be was a deserted parking garage. He had to get out of there. Without looking back at the

Suburban, Riley turned from his car and hurried out of the garage towards the safety of campus.

After crossing the side street, he looked over his shoulder. He half expected to see Isaac's athletic frame and blonde hair running up behind him, but there was no one there. Riley allowed himself a moment to breathe and take in his surroundings. He felt better being on campus but he still wasn't safe. The closest building was Storey Hall.

Riley crossed the parking lot behind Storey Hall and reached the far end of the building. Clearing the short staircase descending to the ground floor entrance, he pulled the door handle and darted inside. He ran past the heavy metal doors of the school's legal clinic and rounded the corner of the staircase.

Taking three steps at a time, he reached the second floor landing in seconds. He turned the corner and attacked the next set of stairs. Arriving on the third floor, he crossed the faculty lounge and ran down a short hallway lined with offices. Up ahead, the hall turned to the right and spanned the entire length of the building. Riley slowed his pace when he approached the corner and searched for his office door key.

He located the key just as he reached the door. Sweat dripped down his brow as he attempted to force the key into the lock. When it slid into place, he reached for the knob and heard movement in the distance. His nerves calmed at the thought of a colleague being nearby. He looked down the long corridor along the front of the building and opened his mouth to shout for help but the words caught in his throat.

A shadowy figure peered into the offices at the far end of the building. Riley stepped back from his office door so that he could see the length of the hallway. He watched as a man stepped out of a distant office and came into full view. The man turned to look into the next office but stopped short. Slowly, he shifted his gaze to the far end of the hall and directly at Riley.

When Riley saw the man's eyes, a torrent of recognition and fear surged through his veins. The man had an athletic build and closely cropped, almost white hair. It was Isaac. They stood at opposite ends of the corridor for a long moment. Watching. Studying. Each man waiting for the other to move.

The rush of adrenaline finally broke through and cleared Riley's mind. Keeping his eyes locked on Isaac, he reached into his pocket to get his cell phone. It wasn't there. A flash of panic. Riley quickly patted each of his pockets. Then he remembered. He had stowed the phone in his bag, which was now locked safely in the trunk of his car.

His mind raced for other options. For an instant, he thought of barricading himself in his office and calling the police but he knew the flimsy wooden door would never hold. He also knew there was no other way out of the third story office. There was only one thing Riley could do.

He took a deep breath and ran. Riley raced down the short hallway back the way he came. He passed the faculty offices in seconds and crossed the lounge near the top of the third floor landing. He grabbed the handrail tight to steady himself when he hit the top of the staircase. The sounds of Riley's heavy foot falls echoed down through the stairwell as he descended the steps three at a time.

At the second floor landing, Riley rounded the corner and kept running. Arriving at the ground floor, he skidded to a stop on the white vinyl tile.

He looked down the length of the hallway and, to his horror, he saw Isaac turning the corner from the opposite stairwell. The two men were once again at opposite ends of the building. This time, Isaac didn't hesitate. He was running towards Riley at full speed.

Instinctively, Riley took a step backwards to continue his escape but the heavy metal doors of the school's legal clinic blocked his path. He pulled one of the door handles and saw the mechanical keypad that allowed faculty and students to access the clinic after hours. The sounds of Isaac's footsteps rang down the tiled corridor as Riley reached for the keypad. Praying he remembered the code, he punched in the numbers 2-1-4 and pulled on the handle. The door released and Isaac let out a guttural roar. Riley jumped inside and pulled the metal door closed just as Isaac's hands slammed into the metal doorframe.

Riley watched through the door's small, reinforced glass window as Isaac furiously pulled on the handle. But the door didn't move. The automatic lock had reengaged the second Riley closed the door. Isaac let go of the handle and calmly lifted his eyes to the window. The men were standing just inches apart, separated only by the width of the door. Their eyes met. Riley's heart beat wildly in his chest. He felt Isaac's cold stare bore straight through him.

Isaac broke eye contact first. He stepped out of the window frame and Riley strained to see what he was doing. Then there was a heavy crash of metal on metal. Riley peered out the window and saw Isaac holding a heavy fire extinguisher over his head. He slammed the extinguisher down onto the handle of the metal door with another thunderous blow.

Riley was paralyzed as he watched Isaac slam the extinguisher into the door over and again. Knowing the door would eventually give way, Riley had to find another way out. He spun from the door. The office was filled with standard cubicles, flanked by offices and conference rooms on either side. A dim light filtered through blinds that covered the double-hung windows surrounding the entire space.

Riley looked over his shoulder and saw the door bending under Isaac's incessant assault. He darted down the center aisle of cubicles to the back wall, where he turned down a narrow corridor leading to the faculty offices. Passing the last office, he reached the window at the far end of the hallway. He pulled the blinds away from the window and jumped behind them. He flipped the lock at the top of the window and pushed hard against the frame. The rhythmic crash of Isaac's battering ram echoed again and again as Riley strained against the wooden window rails. With a final heave, the window gave way and a gust of warm spring air rushed inside.

Riley could still hear the sounds of Isaac battering the metal door when he stepped out of the window and into the grass of the central courtyard. Unsure where to go, Riley ran across the courtyard and down the sidewalk near the Underwood Law Library. Rounding the corner, he turned towards Hillcrest Avenue where he planned to flag down a passing car. When he got there, he saw something better. About a half a block away and lumbering slowly up the street was a city bus marked with the bright yellow paint of Dallas Area Rapid Transit.

Riley ran down to the bus stop in front of the law library. He waited nervously until the bus finally came to a stop and opened its doors. He took one last look over his shoulder. Isaac was nowhere in sight. Riley jumped on the bus and anxiously watched out the window until the doors shut and the bus pulled slowly away from the stop.

CHAPTER 10

Moments earlier, the clinic door flew open with a final crash of the fire extinguisher. Florescent light from the hallway streamed through the twisted metal door and carved a silver rectangle on the floor. Isaac stepped inside and closed the door behind him.

He stood in the entryway and listened for movement while waiting for his eyes to adjust to the low light of the room. Everything was still. Walking slowly down the center aisle, Isaac peered into each gray cubicle until he reached the narrow corridor at end of the row. Then he turned to search the next aisle.

Continuing down the next row, he heard a light clacking sound from somewhere in the room. He turned to locate the source of the sound. Looking down the narrow hallway that led to the faculty offices, he studied the window at the far end. The blinds moved in the breeze and clattered against the wooden window frame.

"Shit." Isaac ran to the end of the hallway and grabbed the nylon cord hanging from the blinds.

With a violent pull, the blinds flew to the ceiling and Isaac saw the window was wide open. Ducking down, he stuck his head out the window and quickly scanned the courtyard. Riley was nowhere in sight.

Isaac slammed his hands on the windowsill. "Son of a bitch!" Riley was in the familiar surroundings of his own law school and he had a significant head start. Isaac would never find him.

He turned from the window and walked back towards the main door. Weaving through the cubicles, he opened his cell phone and keyed in the number he'd memorized many months before. When he reached the twisted metal door, he heard a familiar voice on the line.

"What has happened?"

"Samuel. I'm sorry. Riley escaped," replied Isaac, the disappointment clear in his voice. There was a long pause and Isaac instinctively looked down at the floor, ashamed of his failure. The growing silence made him nervous as his mind swirled around what Samuel might be thinking. When he opened his mouth to plead his case, Samuel finally spoke.

"I know you did your best. How did he escape?"

Relieved, Isaac recounted the story in the dim light of the office. "... and then he ran into a room and locked the door," Isaac concluded. "By the time I got through, he had climbed out of a window." Isaac peered out a gap in the metal door to ensure no one was there before stepping out into the hallway and leaving the building.

"So he saw you?"

"Yes," Isaac replied. And as the image of their first encounter played in Isaac's mind, a thought occurred to him. "There was something about the way he looked at me," Isaac paused as he crossed the street to the parking garage. "He wasn't surprised. It was like he was expecting me."

"How is that possible?" Samuel asked. "Could he have seen your car?"

As Samuel spoke, Isaac entered the garage and saw Riley's BMW. Standing beside it, Isaac had a perfect view of his black Suburban. Samuel was right. "He must've gone into the parking garage before coming on campus."

Samuel let out an audible sigh. "Isaac. We have entered into the final days of the world as we know it. The power to eliminate the freedoms of all is now in the hands of the few. You have trained for this moment – the moment The Prophecy foretold. And now, when we are so close to our goal, we must remember our training and fight to maintain our discipline. We cannot falter. We cannot make mistakes."

The truth of Samuel's words hit Isaac hard. Everything they had accomplished meant nothing unless they completed the mission. "You're right," replied Isaac. "I'll get rid of the car today."

"Good."

"What about Riley?" Isaac asked. "He saw me at the canal. He saw what happened to Alexander and Varden. We can't let him get away."

"Do not worry about Mr. Riley," Samuel said. "He will show himself soon enough. When he does, I will know. And so will you." And then the line went dead.

The bus jerked to a start and Riley grabbed the overhead rail to steady himself.

"Behind the yellow line." Riley was still standing on the platform, staring out the window. "Sir?" the driver snapped.

"Yeah. Sorry," Riley said and stepped behind the bright yellow line painted on the rubberized floor. Riley walked down the aisle past rows of blue plastic seats that were upholstered in fabric that looked like it came directly from the floor of a Las Vegas casino.

There were only a handful of riders on the bus. A couple of elderly ladies were sitting on the front row, holding plastic shopping bags in their laps and talking in voices so low you could barely hear them over the engine noise. About half way down the aisle, Riley passed four teenaged boys dressed in the current hipster fashion of skinny jeans and button down shirts with the long sleeves rolled tight. They were discussing a band they had seen the previous night – each interjecting his opinion over the other.

The last several rows of the bus were completely empty so Riley made his way to the back. He settled into the window seat and watched as the shops and houses surrounding the SMU campus passed slowly through his field of view.

Despite having just run for his life, Riley's mind was surprisingly organized and lucid. First, he needed to get his bearings. He had jumped on the bus without noticing the number or destination, so he had no idea where he was headed. Leaning on the seat next to him, Riley looked down the aisle and saw the digital sign in the front window that read *City Place / Uptown*. Riley's apartment was in Uptown but he quickly dismissed any thoughts of going there. If Isaac could find Riley's office, he could surely find his apartment. Riley needed to find somewhere else to hide and to make some sense out of what had happened.

What he really needed was a phone. He cursed the fact that he'd left his phone locked up in his trunk. A burst of laughter rang out from the teenagers a few rows ahead. Riley looked over to see them huddled around one of the boys, who was apparently playing a video that had caused the eruption of laughter. Then Riley had an idea.

He stood from his seat and walked up to the boys, who were now analyzing the best parts of the video. One of them was in mid-sentence when he saw Riley and suddenly stopped talking. All four of them turned to see Riley holding a fifty-dollar bill up in the air.

"Fifty dollars to whichever one of you is willing to loan me your phone for five minutes." Before he could finish the sentence, the boy farthest away dove over the top of his friends and snatched the money from Riley's hand.

"Shit!" exclaimed one of the boys, disappointed he hadn't acted just a second faster.

"Sorry," said the winner to his friends while he dug in his pocket and removed a new iPhone. "You snooze, you lose." He handed Riley the phone.

"Thanks. I'll be right back here," Riley said, gesturing to the back of the bus. "I won't be long but let me know if we reach your stop." Riley walked to the back of the bus and, after settling into his seat, he reached into his back pocket and pulled out his wallet. He dug inside until he located Agent Coffman's card hiding in a collection of old receipts.

He removed the card and studied it. The left hand side was embossed with the blue and gold seal of the F.B.I., and in the center, it read:

DEPARTMENT OF JUSTICE
FEDERAL BUREAU OF INVESTIGATION
DALLAS FIELD OFFICE

BRINSON COFFMAN
SPECIAL AGENT
DATA INTERCEPT TECHNOLOGY UNIT

Riley read the last line again. He hadn't noticed it before, nor was he sure what the Data Intercept Technology Unit was. It didn't sound like a group that would ordinarily show up at a homicide scene. Then again, given who Christoph Varden was and that his body that had been dumped in the shallow grave, maybe it made sense. Riley decided he had enough mysteries to solve without creating another, so he dialed the number on the card and waited while it rang.

"Coffman," said a terse, baritone voice.

"Agent Coffman?" questioned Riley, wanting to be sure.

"Yes, this is Special Agent Coffman. Who's this?"

"This is Michael Riley."

"Riley?" he asked, clearly surprised to hear Riley's voice. "Is there something you need?"

Riley's blood boiled in an instant. "You're damn right there's something I need! I almost got killed this afternoon!" Riley exclaimed.

"Hold on a minute," Coffman said. "What the hell are you talking about?"

Riley's outburst had caused half the bus to look back at him. He took a deep breath to steady himself and lowered his voice. "I was having lunch with a friend near campus. When we finished, I walked back to my car and saw the black Suburban from the canal sitting in the parking garage. I ran to campus so I could be in a more public place to call you. But Isaac was already in my office building looking for me."

"Wait a second," interrupted Coffman. "You saw this Isaac guy?"

"Saw him?" Riley asked. "He chased me through the building!"

Riley had Coffman's full attention. "Okay, Mr. Riley. Calm down and walk me through the rest of what happened."

Riley spoke through gritted teeth, "Agent Coffman. You've got to tell me what's going on here. I'm being chased by people who want to kill me. The least you can do is tell me why!"

"Why don't we start with you telling me what happened, Mr. Riley, and we'll take it from there. That's the best way to help this investigation and get all of this behind us," said Coffman, leaving little doubt that he was either unable or unwilling to give Riley any information.

It would do no good to push Coffman any further, so Riley detailed the rest of the story as the bus lumbered along Cole Avenue towards downtown. They had just passed Javier's, Riley's favorite Mexican restaurant, when an intense beam of sunlight shone into his eyes. Riley squinted towards the source of the reflection. It was a high-rise office building, wrapped in silvery-blue reflective glass. The sight of the building triggered a memory from the recesses of Riley's mind. He stopped talking mid-sentence.

"Riley," prompted Coffman. "Mr. Riley?" he repeated seconds later.

Riley slowly stood from his seat and stepped to the center aisle. The hazy memory was taking shape.

"Mr. Riley!" Coffman said, his frustration evident.

Emerging from his thought, Riley finally responded, "I'll call you back."

"Call me back? What?" Coffman asked, incredulous.

"I gotta go," said Riley.

"Wait a second…" Riley heard Coffman say as he ended the call. Riley leaned over and pushed the long rubber strip running just beneath the windows and down the length of the bus. Upon contact, a bell sounded and the *Next Stop* sign illuminated at the front. Riley's body swayed forward as the bus immediately began to slow. Bracing himself with the seats on either side of the aisle, Riley reached the group of teenagers.

"Thanks," he said, handing the phone back to its owner.

"Easiest fifty bucks I ever made," said the kid.

When the bus came to a stop, Riley stepped onto the sidewalk. He watched as the bus pulled slowly away from the curb and continued down the street. Then he turned in the opposite direction and began walking back to the silvery high-rise. There was someone in there he had to see.

CHAPTER 11

Sarah walked into the office in the back of the basement lab and closed the door. John was in his chair behind the desk and he motioned for her to take a seat.

"Sarah's here," John said, as Sarah settled into the chair and crossed her legs.

"Sarah," came Samuel's voice from the nearby speakerphone, "John tells me you have made a breakthrough?"

"I have," Sarah said. "I told you I would."

"Of course you did," replied Samuel matter-of-factly. "So tell me: what have you accomplished?"

Sarah tucked a few unruly strands of dark red hair behind her ear and adjusted her stylish glasses. "I've broken the encryption."

"That is excellent news," Samuel said, excitement seeping into his words. "Does the file contain everything we need?"

"It's easily the most complex computer code I've ever seen. So far, I've identified 5 different encryption methods, three compression techniques and more than 10 file formats – and all within the twenty-two megabyte container. It's brilliant. And," Sarah said, unable to stifle her astonishment, "it appears to do exactly what you said it would."

When Samuel first told Sarah of the file and its capabilities, she didn't believe it. *"The Prophecy foretold of an emerging force that would one day destroy our nation,"* Samuel had told her. *"That emerging force has taken its final form. It is a computer file named Ceterus. But do not fear. The Ceterus file is both the cause and the cure of all our problems. Once we have it, you will understand."*

What Samuel described next was, from a programming perspective, so complex that it defied imagination. Sarah couldn't fathom who on Earth had both the genius and the will to create such a masterpiece. After learning of Christoph Varden's murder, everything made sense – everything except The Prophecy.

Months ago, when she received his unexpected call that afternoon on Dangerfield Island, Samuel had referenced The Prophecy as the guiding force behind his operation. At the time, Sarah was driven by the promise of payment and the intellectual challenge of building the technology Samuel described. She had known nothing of Lincoln's Prophecy and couldn't see how a letter written 150 years ago could relate to an advanced computer program developed by the world's leading cyber-security expert. Now, having seen the Ceterus program first-hand, Sarah knew of its unprecedented power. She also knew that the modifications she was working on would deliver that power directly to Samuel. But what was he going to do with it? Somehow, she had to find out.

"So now that you have seen the Ceterus file and understand what it can do, it is time to make our modifications," Samuel asserted.

"That's right. We've had our portion of the code finished for days. Now that we've decrypted Ceterus, all we need to do is build a bridge so the two files can communicate. We're already working on it and should have it finished in a few hours. Then we'll have *almost* everything we need," Sarah said with a hint of skepticism.

John leaned his bulky frame on the desk. "Almost?" he asked, unaware of yet another hurdle they had to cross. "What else do we need?"

Sarah looked directly at John. "To be of any use, we have to install Ceterus behind the most sophisticated security systems ever devised. We're talking about layers of intrusion prevention systems and next-generation firewalls with artificial intelligence. Getting behind that kind of security is more than a little tricky."

Sarah could tell from the blank stare on John's face that he was still confused. "To put it simply, all this work is pointless unless we can somehow find a vulnerability in every layer of the best security known to man." Even to Sarah's highly technical mind, the task seemed completely insurmountable.

John threw his hands up in the air in surrender. "How the hell are we going to do all that? We have no... "

"You both continue to doubt," said Samuel, his calm voice instantly silencing John's protest. "Each obstacle is an opportunity to strengthen your resolve. Soon, you will see that we can go farther than you dreamed possible." Samuel's words hung in the air. "There are vulnerabilities in every system, as there are in every man. You simply must find one and exploit it."

CHAPTER 12

A ndrew Dyll adjusted his tie as he walked along the sterile corridor of the J. Edgar Hoover Building in Washington, D.C. Even as an Assistant Director, he wasn't often invited to the building's seventh floor and being there set his nerves on edge. He entered the waiting area of an executive suite at the end of the hall and was greeted by the elderly receptionist.

"You can go on in, Mr. Dyll. They're expecting you." Andrew looked over to acknowledge the instruction, but the receptionist had already returned to her paperwork.

"Thanks," he said simply, as he walked towards the heavy oak door that was just beyond the receptionist's desk. A blue plastic sign at the center of the door said: LOUIS J. WEBSTER – DIRECTOR. Andrew laughed internally at the absurdity of having a nametag on this particular door. *If you don't know who's office this is before you get here, you wouldn't be here,* he thought.

He reached for the doorknob but stopped short, unsure of the protocol on how to enter the

Director of the F.B.I.'s personal office. One thing was certain, you didn't just barge in like you owned the place – even if you were expected. He gave a light knock to announce his presence before cracking the door open and poking his head inside.

"Ah, Andrew," came the familiar voice of Andrew's boss, Caton Fenz, the Executive Assistant Director of the Operational Technology Division. Andrew stepped into the room as Fenz worked his thick frame from a red leather chair and stood in preparation for formal introductions.

Fenz was an old-line field agent but you couldn't tell from looking at him. After more than a decade of riding a desk, he looked more like an overweight lineman for the Washington Redskins than a trained field agent. He was completely bald but maintained a thick and neatly trimmed beard that was mostly gray. As always, he was wearing a dark blue suit.

Having only been in the Director's office one other time in his career, Andrew scanned the room with interest as he made his way towards Fenz. The spacious corner office was lined with windows facing Pennsylvania Avenue. There was a seating area and a credenza covered with various pictures and awards and, at the end, a silver ice bucket next to an assortment of soft drinks.

"Sir, you remember Andrew Dyll," Fenz said to the Director. "He heads up our Data Intercept Technology Unit." Andrew looked up to see Louis Webster circling his desk with his hand already outstretched.

"Sure I do!" said the Director energetically as Andrew thrust his hand into the Director's. "How the hell are you, Andy?" asked Webster with a vigorous handshake.

"I'm fine, sir," Andrew smiled.

"Have a seat." Webster motioned to a chair as he passed Andrew on his way to the credenza. "Something to drink, Andy?" the Director asked.

"Yes sir. A Coke would be great," Andrew replied. When he turned to take a seat, Andrew noticed another man working at a small table along the back wall. Though he'd only met the man once, Andrew knew it was Edward Ross, the Director's long-time assistant.

"What do you think of this year's team?" asked the Director over the clank of ice cubes hitting the bottom of a glass. There was little question which team Webster was talking about. He was a serious Blue Devil fan and must have remembered that Andrew also graduated from Duke.

"Well, sir, they're awful young this year. I think there's only one player returning for his junior year. But," Andrew paused to take the glass of Coke from the Director. "Thank you, sir. But," he continued, "with Coach K around, there's always a good chance they'll make a run."

"Well, you know what I say," said Webster as he returned to his chair behind the desk. "Give that man a pile of shit and he'll carve you the statute of David."

Light laughter filled the room. "You're right about that, sir," said Andrew, taking a sip of his drink. And as the laughter subsided, Andrew looked admiringly on the Director. He was sixty-seven years old but exuded the enthusiasm and stamina of someone half his age. His youthful energy was complimented by his physical appearance. He had a full head of brown hair and was as thin and fit as the day he joined the Bureau.

"You know Ed, don't you?" Webster asked, acknowledging Edward Ross for the first time. Ross looked up from his work and smiled, then stood and walked towards the other men.

Andrew got up and offered his hand to Ross. "Yes, sir. We've met a few times."

"Hello, Andy," said Ross. "I've been reading your operations reports for so long, I feel like I've been working beside you for years." The handshake that followed was awkward, as Ross extended his left hand, rather than his right. And it was then that Andrew remembered the story behind his appointment as the Director's assistant. Ross got the job after he sustained multiple gunshot wounds during a classified operation that, as legend had it, saved the life of two sitting U.S. Senators and perhaps even the President himself. Though Ross survived, his wounds left him unfit for field duty. The Director said he would *never let such a man leave the Bureau* and immediately took Ross on as his assistant.

"Well, let's get down to it," Webster said after the handshake was complete and Ross returned to his desk. "What's the latest with the Varden mess?"

"Andy's got most of the details," Fenz responded, "but the short of it is: the crime scene is clean. We scoured the Varden estate from top to bottom. The only third-party DNA we found was from…" Fenz trailed off and snapped his fingers as he searched for the name.

"Lupita Suarez," Andrew prompted.

"Right. The maid," continued Fenz. "We went ahead and checked her out but she was in Mexico City visiting her family at the time of the murder. Not that she was ever really a suspect." Fenz picked up his water glass from the Director's desk and took a sip. "Am I missing anything, Andrew?" Fenz asked, crunching on a piece of ice.

"Nothing related to the crime scene. But I just heard from Agent Coffman," Andrew said hesitantly. "There's been a development." Director Webster leaned forward, placing his elbows on the desk as Andrew continued. "Sir, as you may remember, when Varden's body was dumped by that canal in Texas, there was a witness."

"Right," said Webster. "A law professor. What was his name again?"

"Michael Riley."

"That's right. So what's happened with Mr. Riley?"

"The man who dumped the body, the man now known as Isaac, apparently saw Riley's car as he fled the scene."

"Shit," said Fenz.

"Shit is right," chimed the Director. "Go on, Andy."

"Well, sir, he tracked Riley to his law school and apparently chased him through campus." Webster leaned back in his chair and let out a heavy sigh. Andrew continued. "Riley was somehow able to escape and hop a city bus, where he called Coffman to report what happened."

"Where's Riley now?" asked Fenz.

Andrew's mouth went dry and he took a quick drink from his Coke. "We don't know," he said reluctantly.

"Aw, hell." said the Director. "If he was talking to Coffman, how'd we lose him?"

"I asked the same question," Andrew assured him. "Coffman said Riley was telling him what happened, when he suddenly said he'd have to call Coffman back and hung up. No explanation. No indication where he went."

"Have you tracked the bus route?" asked Fenz.

"We have, but he could've gotten off anywhere along the route and there's no way to know where he went from there. He could've walked somewhere close by or he could've caught a cab to the other side of town. We honestly don't know at this point. But we've got guys on it. We'll find him."

"Stay on it, Andy," said Webster. "You know what's at stake here. We've got to keep this thing in a box. The last thing we need is a dead law professor." The Director stood, indicating he'd heard enough.

"Yes, sir," said Andrew as he got to his feet and walked towards the door.

"One more thing, Andy," said Webster.

Andrew stopped short of the door and turned to face the Director. "Yes sir?"

"Do you trust Coffman on this case?"

The question caught Andrew off guard and he paused to think it through. "Um, yes sir," he responded. "He's young but certainly capable."

"Keep an eye on him for me, will you? This case is a hell of a lot to handle for a young agent. Losing Riley, I don't like how this thing is going."

"Will do, sir," Andrew responded.

"I want regular reports on this case. I want to know where we are and where we're going. So if anything happens, or nothing happens, you report it to Ed here." Webster added, gesturing towards his assistant. Ross set his pen down and looked over at the Director, who continued. "No detail is too small. Ross'll make sure I get what I need."

The request struck Andrew as odd. The Director of the F.B.I. rarely took an interest in the daily minutia of a specific case. But who was he to question Louis Webster? "Yes sir. I'll handle the reports myself," said Andrew. And then he opened the door and left the office.

CHAPTER 13

Riley crossed the street and entered the shade of the Live Oak trees in front of the silver high rise. He passed through the glass doors and into the ground floor lobby, which was rather small for a building of its size. The guard barely glanced up from his newspaper as Riley passed the security desk and got on the elevator.

He pressed the button for the fifteenth floor and as the elevator began its slow ascent, Riley looked out the window and down at the Knox/Henderson shopping area. He watched the people below and was stunned at how casually everyone was going about their business. They were strolling along, laughing and discussing their latest purchases. They didn't have a care in the world. In that moment, Riley felt completely disconnected from the world he knew.

The elevator slowed to a stop and an electronic bell chimed, separating Riley from his thoughts. He stepped into the lobby and crossed the polished travertine floor to a set of double glass doors, each of which had the name *Shavin & Zane, L.L.P.* etched in the center.

He opened the door and entered the reception area, where he expected to be greeted by a bouncy young paralegal. No one was there. Riley looked around, as if he could have overlooked someone in the small room.

"Hello?" he said, his voice echoing off the hardwood floors. Instead of a response, he heard a muffled argument coming from the end of a nearby hall. Riley walked slowly towards the argument until he could clearly hear the conversation through an open office door.

"I've already given you a three week extension. Are you really asking me for another two weeks?" came an outraged male voice. Then, after a moment's pause, the same voice continued, "Well, are we ever going to take this case to trial? Or is your legal strategy to just delay this thing until all my clients die of old age?"

Riley peered through the doorway and saw a long, glass-top desk sitting on an oriental rug at the far side of the office. File folders were scattered about the desk and stacked on the floor. Behind the desk, a black leather high-back chair was turned away from the door and facing a set of bookshelves on the back wall. A phone cord stretched from the desk to a receiver that was hidden behind the back of the leather chair.

"I'm just not doing it," came the man's voice from behind the chair. "You had thirty days to respond and I've given you an extra three weeks on top of that. So you've now had fifty-one days to get your response on file. Fifty-one! If you can't get it done in fifty-one days, I can't imagine how another two weeks will make any difference."

There was a pause while the lawyer on the other end made her argument. "Look, Courtney," said the man in response. "The hearing is set for Monday morning at nine a.m. If you're not there, that's all the better for my clients." The chair spun around and a bearded man with gold-rimmed glasses slammed the phone down on its base.

"Son-of-a-bitch!" he muttered to himself. "That woman will be the death of me." The man pushed his glasses up to his forehead and squinted while pinching the bridge of his nose. He leaned back in his chair and rubbed his temples.

"Well, there's no negotiating with you," said Riley.

The statement startled the man, who snapped forward in his chair and looked towards the door. He strained to identify the fuzzy figure across the room. Then, with a flick of a hand, his glasses fell back to the bridge of his nose, bringing the image into focus.

"Oh, just what I need," the man said sarcastically, "a legal critique from Professor Riley."

"That bedside manner of yours could use some polishing," Riley responded with a smile. "How you doing, Eliot?"

"I'm thinking of strangling my opposing counsel. You know any good lawyers that can get my ass out of jail when I do?" Eliot asked.

"Don't look at me, buddy. I know way too much to defend you."

Eliot looked out over the top of his glasses. "I said I wanted a *good* lawyer," he retorted with a hint of a smile. "What brings you over this way?"

Riley looked around the office at the scattered files. "I came to apply for the office clerk position." Riley walked to the desk and sat down in one of the upholstered guest chairs facing Eliot's desk. "It looks like you could use one."

Eliot lifted some papers on his desk, pulled out a security badge and held it up for Riley to see. It had the picture of a cute blonde woman, who looked to be in her late twenties. "Daphne's on maternity leave for eight more weeks," Eliot said, flipping the badge back onto the desk. "This place'll likely be a complete shithole until she gets back. Now, really. What's going on? I don't think you've ever just dropped in on me like this."

Riley thought for a moment, trying to determine the best way to approach the topic. "I've come to ask you about Christoph Varden," Riley said cautiously.

Eliot was visibly surprised. "Varden?" he asked. "How do you know Christoph Varden?"

"It's a long story and it's probably best if you don't know much about it. You do represent him, don't you?" Riley asked, hoping he remembered correctly.

"Well, I wrote his will. Now I represent the estate. It took that jackass family of his about two seconds to file a lawsuit after he died. But I don't understand. What's the Varden estate got to do with you?"

"Look, Eliot. I would never ask you this, but it is really important," Riley said, looking his friend in the eye. "Did Varden have any secret, off-shore bank accounts?" Eliot's face twisted in confusion. "You're handling the estate," Riley continued. "You'd know if Varden was hiding assets somewhere."

Even asking such a question was completely out of character for Riley. Eliot knew something serious was going on. "I'm not supposed to talk about any of this, but to my knowledge, there were no hidden assets. From a financial perspective, Varden's clean."

"What do you mean 'from a financial perspective'?" Riley asked. "Was there something unusual about another part of the estate?"

Eliot leaned back in his chair and let out a long sigh. He threw his glasses on his desk and said, "We're walking a tightrope here, my friend. I know you wouldn't ask if it wasn't important. And I want to help you out." Eliot thought for a moment about what he could say. "I'll tell you this: the will is perfectly normal except for one provision. And that provision has nothing to do with money."

"What's it about?" Riley prompted.

Eliot paused again and chose his words carefully. "It directs me to read something to one of Varden's old business partners."

"To read something?" Riley asked, completely confused.

"Yeah. Varden wrote something and asked me to read it to a friend of his. But what ever it is you're looking for, that provision can't have anything to do with it. I mean, what Varden wrote doesn't even make any sense."

Riley looked down at the floor for a moment, hesitating to ask the next question. He had little choice. "What does it say?" he asked, lifting his gaze.

"Riley, the Judge held an expedited hearing yesterday and issued an order sealing this entire case." This news took Riley by surprise, but Eliot was on a roll and couldn't be stopped. "If I willfully breach a court order, I could get disbarred. Do you know what happens if I get disbarred?" Eliot didn't wait for an answer. "I get a divorce, that's what happens. But do you know what happens *before* I get a divorce?"

"Um, I don't..." Riley started but was cut off.

"Claudia cuts off my balls and stuffs them in a jar!" Claudia was Eliot's hard-charging wife of more than twenty years. "And you know what else? She'll make damned sure the Judge awards her *my* balls as part of the property settlement! So my balls will forever sit in a mason jar on the mantle of Claudia's new Uptown condo where she'll sit with her new young boyfriend and drink a toast to my pickled balls and to the good life they've brought with them. Meanwhile, I'll be toiling away in this fucking dungeon until I drop dead of a heart attack!"

Riley threw his hands up in surrender. He didn't want to cause his friend any trouble with the courts or his wife. "Okay, Eliot. I get it. You can keep your balls. I didn't know about the court order."

"Well, there's no way you could have known," Eliot's blood pressure was returning to normal. "I'd like to help you, Riley. I really would. But my hands are tied here."

Riley thought through his options. Whatever was in the capsule Isaac cut from Varden's hip, it had led Isaac to kill Alexander and probably Varden himself. Then, to tie up the only loose end linking him to the other crimes, Isaac tried to kill Riley. The Varden will, sitting somewhere in Eliot's files, was Riley's only potential lead to figuring out why Isaac wanted him dead. He had to know what it said without getting Eliot into any trouble. Suddenly, an idea came to mind.

Riley pulled his wallet from his back pocket and removed Agent Coffman's card. "There is something you can do to help," Riley said. "You can point me to a phone."

"Sure thing," said Eliot. "You can use the phone in Stefan's office. It's not like he does any work around here. Someone may as well get some use out of it."

"Thanks," Riley said. He closed the wallet and reached back as if returning it to his pocket. But instead, he stuffed the wallet deep down into the cushion of the chair. "I'll let you know before I leave," he said as he stood and then left Eliot's office.

He walked down the hall and into Stefan Zane's office, which, except for the fact it was perfectly clean, was a mirror image of Eliot's. He picked up the phone on Stefan's desk and dialed Coffman's number.

"Coffman," came a sharp answer.

"Agent Coffman? This is Michael Riley."

"Riley? What the hell happened? You just hung up on me in the middle…"

Riley was in no mood for a lecture. "I'd rather talk about it in person," he said, interrupting Coffman.

"Okay. Fine. I'll come get you. Where are you?"

Riley hesitated. He didn't want to involve Eliot any more than he already had. And he felt safer meeting Coffman in a crowded place. As he considered what to do, Riley wandered over to the window and looked down at the street below. He watched as the first patrons began to arrive at the popular bars and restaurants at the corner of McKinney Avenue and Monticello.

"I'll meet you at Acme Food and Beverage on McKinney in three hours," Riley said, knowing the area would be crawling with people by that time of night.

"Three hours? Why can't I meet you now?" Coffman protested, but the line was already dead.

Riley's hand rested on the receiver as he collected his thoughts. Then he walked back down to Eliot's office, where he saw his friend hovering over a document with a yellow highlighter. Riley knocked on the door and Eliot looked up from his work. "Everything okay?" he asked.

"Yeah. Everything's fine," Riley said. "I'm going to get out of your hair."

Eliot stood and walked around his desk. "Yeah. I've to get out of here pretty soon myself. I'll walk you out."

When they got to the reception area, Eliot stepped out in front of Riley and opened the front door. "Sorry I couldn't help you out," he said. When he looked back, he saw that Riley had stopped short of the door.

"I think my wallet fell out in that chair in your office," Riley said, patting his pockets. "I'll just run back and get it."

Without waiting on Eliot's response, Riley turned and walked quickly back to the office. When he got there, he went directly to Eliot's desk and began shuffling through the stacks of paper. He had only moments to complete his search and he had to be careful not to disturb the ordered chaos on the desk. He sifted quickly through the papers, his heart beating faster with each passing second.

"You find it?" Eliot said, his voice echoing down the hall.

Riley lifted a file folder on the desk, knowing he was out of time. He looked under the folder and saw what he was looking for: it was the face of Eliot's blonde paralegal, staring back at him.

"Michael?" asked Eliot, the voice sounding closer than before.

"Yeah. I found it," Riley responded as he grabbed the paralegal's security badge and quickly stuffed it into his back pocket. Then he turned in place and threw his hand down into the cushion of the chair. When he stood up, his heart stopped at the sight of Eliot standing in the doorway.

"You okay?" Eliot asked.

Riley held the wallet up for Eliot to see. "Yep," he said in as casual of a tone as he could manage. "It got jammed into the cushion somehow. I couldn't find the damn thing," he said as he rounded the chair and headed for the door.

"It's probably best that you're teaching, rather than practicing," Eliot said, putting his arm around Riley's shoulder. "You're a complete mess."

CHAPTER 14

Riley arrived at Acme Food & Beverage an hour early. His narrow escape from Isaac had shaken his confidence in the F.B.I. and their ability to keep him safe. Over the past few hours, he had felt much better knowing that no one had any idea where he was. If he was going to come out of hiding, he was determined to ensure there were no surprises. That meant finding a place inside the restaurant where he could see Coffman when he arrived.

Riley watched the restaurant from across the street as groups of friends and co-workers arrived for happy hour. He patiently scanned the parking lot and the surrounding areas, looking for anything that resembled Coffman or the F.B.I. Seeing nothing, Riley jumped in behind a group of patrons and tried to blend in as they crossed the street and entered the restaurant.

With its mixture of metal, leather and reclaimed wood interior, Acme Food and Beverage had a modern, industrial feel. The decor appealed to the young professional crowd that was swarming the bar near the front of the restaurant.

Riley turned sideways to weave his way past the bar and up to the hostess – a busty co-ed wearing a black cocktail dress that showed every curve.

"I'm headed to the back bar," Riley yelled over the noise of a thousand different conversations. The hostess acknowledged Riley with a nod as he walked past her and into the main dining area.

The muddled chatter from the packed dining room reverberated off the metal ceiling tiles and filled the air. Riley made his way through the sea of tables towards the circular fireplace separating the dining area from the second bar at the back of the room. Passing the lounge area in front of the fireplace, he entered the bar and found an opening at the counter.

"What can I get you?" asked a twenty-something bartender with tattoos canvassing both arms.

Riley didn't want a drink but decided a beer would help him blend into the crowd and might calm his nerves. He glanced at the taps along the back of the bar. "I'll have a Blood and Honey," he responded. Moments later, the pint appeared and Riley threw a five dollar bill on the bar before turning to face the dining area.

He sipped his beer and generally did his best to look like a regular patron, rather than one who had witnessed a murder and was hiding out to meet the F.B.I. It was no good. He fidgeted with the cardboard beer coaster as he realized the fireplace between the bar and dining area completely blocked his field of view. Shifting his position, he attempted to survey the restaurant around the bulk of the fireplace. But with each passing minute, he felt increasingly trapped and vulnerable. He soon accepted he had no idea how to set up a secret rendezvous with the F.B.I.

Feeling the need to move, Riley took his beer and stepped outside through an adjacent door. A three-foot wall of stacked railroad ties surrounded the patio, which was furnished with a variety of mismatched metal tables. Riley knew instantly he'd have to find another place to wait. There were only a handful of people outside that evening, which meant Riley was completely exposed. Plus, the patio faced the wrong direction, making it impossible to see the front door where Coffman would arrive.

Riley glanced down at his watch and muttered under his breath. "Shit." He still had a little time but he felt completely incompetent. He looked out across Monticello Avenue searching desperately for a solution. Then he found one.

Riley set his pint down on the nearest table and walked to the back of the patio, where he opened a small gate and stepped out onto the sidewalk. He darted across the street to the Corner Bar – a neighboring dive that was in a constant state of disrepair. As usual, the patio was crowded with SMU students and young professionals jostling for a seat at one of the broken-down picnic tables.

An enormous bouncer sat on a bar stool out front and waived Riley through. Mixing with the crowd, Riley turned around and looked back across the street. From where he was standing, he could clearly see the parking lot, valet stand and, most importantly, the front door of Acme Food & Beverage. A brief smile crept onto Riley's face.

He leaned on the black wrought iron fence and, keeping an eye on the parking lot across the street, Riley's mind began to wander. *What would have happened if Isaac had caught me? Is there any way Varden's will actually contains any answers to this mess?*

"Can I get you anything?" Riley turned and saw an attractive, dark haired waitress holding a server's tray over her shoulder.

"No, thanks. I'm just waiting on someone," Riley said.

"Okay. My name is Kat if you need anything."

"Thanks, Kat." Riley turned back to his position at the fence and caught a glimpse of something across the street. His breath caught in his chest. A man had just cut straight through a group of customers in the parking lot and stepped inside the restaurant. His determined, mechanical gate clearly distinguished him from the rest of the crowd. Riley closed his eyes tight to capture the image. When the details collected, his blood ran cold. The man he had seen was tall and athletically built with an unmistakable shock of closely cropped blonde hair. Isaac had found him again.

Riley's feet felt like they were set in concrete as a wave of panic washed over him. Instinctively, he attempted to rationalize away what he'd seen. But with each attempt, Riley grew increasingly sure the man who wanted him dead was, at this moment, methodically searching Acme Food & Beverage.

A series of rapid-fire questions flashed through Riley's mind. *How could Isaac have known where I'd be? Was he somehow listening in on my call to Coffman?* And then, an even more terrifying thought entered his mind. *Did Coffman tell Isaac where I'd be?* Fear suddenly focused his thoughts. He didn't have time to contemplate all the possibilities. He had to get the hell out of there.

He wove through the crowd to the front of the patio, where he found the giant bouncer sitting on his stool and checking the ID of a suspiciously young looking co-ed. Somehow the girl passed inspection and Riley stepped over to the bouncer.

"I know this is a really strange question," Riley said, getting the bouncer's attention, "but is there any way I could borrow your phone?" The bouncer's reluctance to share his phone was instant and visible. "Please? It's really important," Riley said with a depth of desperation that began to thaw the man's resistance.

The bouncer looked Riley up and down. He would never loan his phone to a typical Corner Bar customer, who would surely run off with it or drop it in a pint of beer. But Riley wasn't the typical customer. He was old. Respectable. And, most importantly, he looked determined to stand there until he got his way.

"Make it quick," he said in a scratchy baritone voice as he handed Riley his phone.

"Thank you," Riley said with deep appreciation. He opened the phone and with his thumbs hovering over the keypad, he hesitated. Who could he call? After seeing Isaac across the street, he sure as hell wasn't calling Coffman. Then he realized there was only one person he could trust.

"Hello?"

The mere sound of her voice brought Riley a sense of calm. "Amie?"

"Michael? Where are you? Are you okay?"

"Not really. Can you come and get me?"

"Of course. Where are you? What's going on?"

"I'm at the Corner Bar. But pick me up at the corner of McKinney and Hester. I'll wait for you there."

"Michael, you're scaring me. What's happened?"

"I'll tell you when you get here. When can you leave?"

"I'm on my way now," Amie responded as she grabbed her bag from the kitchen counter and headed out to her car.

"Thanks. See you soon," Riley responded.

He ended the call and handed it back to the bouncer. "Thanks a lot."

"No problem, man," replied the bouncer as Riley rushed past.

Riley walked quickly down McKinney Avenue. As he left the fluorescent haze of the Corner Bar's patio, he passed into relative darkness. There were few streetlights along this stretch of road, which comforted Riley as he concentrated on putting as much distance as possible between him and the murderer close behind.

A block away from Corner Bar, the area was mostly residential with aged apartments and condominiums running down both sides of

McKinney Avenue. Given the number of homes in the area and the thick crowds just a block away, Riley was surprised at how few people he saw along the street. Just ahead, a lone streetlight marked the intersection of McKinney and Hester.

He knew he had arrived well before Amie and looked for a place to wait. Riley noticed the brown apartment building at the corner had an interior courtyard that opened to the intersection. He cut across the grass and beneath the Live Oak trees that covered the front yard. Reaching the building, Riley stepped behind a staircase that descended from the second floor apartments to the courtyard. He crouched down to make himself as inconspicuous as possible, and he waited.

CHAPTER 15

Amie sat anxiously in her gray Volkswagen Touareg waiting for the traffic light to change. Finally, she turned onto McKinney Avenue and drove north towards Hester. Passing quickly out of the commercial district, the road grew dark and Amie's field of vision was limited to the reach of her headlights.

Her eyes darted from left to right, scanning each shadowy apartment complex with increasing apprehension. She passed one building after another and, seeing no signs of Riley, Amie's nerves began to fray.

Up ahead, she saw a street sign that was partially concealed by a Crape Myrtle and cast in a faint orange glow from the streetlight above. Amie slowed her car to a crawl and leaned forward to read the sign through the top of the windshield.

SLAP!

The sudden sound rang through the cabin. Amie instinctively jerked the wheel and slammed on the brakes. Her heart pounded in her chest. She turned in her seat and her head whipped around to the passenger window. Inches from the glass, she saw the familiar face of Michael Riley. A wave of relief washed over her.

Amie unlocked the door and Riley immediately pulled it open. "Thank God!" he said, jumping into the passenger seat. "We gotta get out of here." Riley slammed the door shut and pointed down Hester Street. "Take a left."

Amie turned the wheel and hit the accelerator. "What happened?"

"I'll tell you in a second. Turn left here," Riley said with another point of his finger. Amie turned and forced herself to hold her questions as Riley navigated them through one turn after another. Minutes later, Amie's patience had run thin and she pulled over beside a neighborhood park.

"What're you doing?" Riley asked, a hint of panic in his voice.

"We've been turning at random for five minutes, Michael. No one knows where we are. Hell, I'm lost and I've been driving. You've got to tell me what's going on!" Amie exclaimed.

Riley twisted in his seat, looking out each window for signs they were followed. The streets were perfectly still. Slowly, he accepted that Amie was right. They were alone. Still, sitting in the car somehow made Riley feel uneasy. "Okay," Riley relented, glancing around one last time. "I'll tell you, but not here. Let's go." Riley opened the door and stepped outside before Amie could object.

Amie circled the front of the car and they walked down a concrete path into the heavily wooded park. Up ahead, the path split and Riley led Amie to a set of stairs that ran down into a deep ravine. When they reached the bottom, they stopped at a park bench and sat down.

Amie faced Riley and waited while he took one last look around. Certain they were alone, Riley said, "Isaac found me again."

"What do you mean *again*?" Amie asked.

Riley realized he hadn't talked to Amie since lunch. So much had happened since then that it felt like a lifetime. Riley looked into Amie's eyes, which were filled with concern. Then he took a deep breath and began his story.

Amie listened to every word as Riley described the chase through SMU campus and his narrow escape on the city bus. When Riley concluded, she asked, "But you said Isaac didn't see you at the canal. How does he even know you exist?"

"I'm not sure. Maybe he saw my truck parked under the bridge when he left," Riley speculated. "He could've pulled my information from the license plate. Once he had my name, a simple Google search would tell him the rest."

Amie nodded in agreement. "I guess so. But you said he found you *again*. How'd he find you after you got off the bus?"

"That's a good question. And I don't like any of the answers," Riley responded. "I wanted to meet Coffman in a crowded place. So I called him and told him to meet me at Acme. I ended up across the street at the Corner Bar so I could see Coffman arrive. So, I'm standing there watching the door and ten minutes before I was set to meet Coffman, Isaac shows up and walks right inside."

"Holy shit," Amie said, her eyes wide with shock.

"I know. He knew exactly where I'd be and when I'd be there," Riley continued.

"Michael, this is crazy!" Amie exclaimed. "Who else did you tell about the meeting at Acme?"

"No one," Riley responded. He waited silently to see if Amie would draw the same conclusions he had, hoping she'd come up with a less terrifying explanation.

Amie's highly logical mind circled around the potential answers. "There are only a couple of reasonable explanations I can think of. And you're right," she added, "neither one is good."

"What're you thinking?" Riley prompted.

"Either Isaac was somehow listening in on the call, or Coffman leaked the information."

"Those were my thoughts exactly."

"I'll tell you," Amie continued, "from a technical standpoint, listening in on the conversation would be very difficult unless you had either direct access to Coffman's phone or some seriously high-tech equipment."

"I was afraid you'd say that," Riley said. "That means it's more likely that Coffman, and who knows how many others in the F.B.I., are up to something."

The two of them sat on the bench for a long moment, silently working through the options. "What do you think we should do?" Amie finally asked.

That very question had been turning in Riley's mind since he left Corner Bar. With everything that had happened, he saw only one viable option. "I've got to find out what's behind all this."

"*We* have to find out," Amie protested. "Michael, you're not doing this by yourself."

Uncertainty shone on Riley's face. The thought of having Amie's help was comforting, but with Isaac out there, Riley knew it would be dangerous. When he looked over, he saw a calm determination in Amie's eyes. She was going to join him whether he liked it or not. The truth was, Amie's sharp mind was an asset he couldn't afford to lose.

"Okay," Riley responded, "*We* need to find out what's behind this." Amie relaxed and leaned back on the bench as Riley continued. "Right now, we simply don't know who's involved in this and why. If we can figure *what* they're after, maybe that'll tell us *who* is after it and who we can trust."

"Makes sense. There's just one problem," Amie said. "Varden could've hidden anything in that capsule. How do we figure out what's in there if we don't even know where to start?"

A mischievous smile spread across Riley's face. He pulled the stolen security badge from his back pocket and held it up for Amie to see.

"Who's Daphne White?"

CHAPTER 16

Sarah entered the small office in the back of the Georgetown basement laboratory and closed the door. John was seated behind the desk and, upon seeing Sarah enter the room, he pushed the speakerphone to the far side of the desk. A dial tone sounded and Sarah carefully dialed the phone number written on the scrap of paper in her hand. The phone rang and then connected.

"Sarah," said Samuel, knowing only one person had the phone number.

"I've finished the modifications to the Ceterus file," she responded.

"And have you tested it?"

"I have. It works perfectly," she reassured him.

"Excellent."

"We have everything we need to proceed," said Sarah with confidence.

"That is good news. I am proud of you. Our entire endeavor has rested on your shoulders and you have carried the burden with exceptional skill. I have some more good news. I have confirmed the existence of a vulnerability that strikes at the heart of the traitors. Now that you've completed your work, we can exploit that vulnerability and bring down the conspiracy that threatens our nation. We will avert the crisis foretold in The Prophesy and a new nation will rise from the ashes."

Samuel's words sent a cold chill over Sarah's body. She knew the immense power of the program she'd help create. She knew that giving it to Samuel was the only way to get the rest of her money. The money, after all, was why she was here. She didn't care about Lincoln's Prophecy or what Samuel thought it meant. But as much as she tried to focus on the money, the fear of what Samuel might do with her creation had taken root in her conscience. She was determined to find out the rest of Samuel's plan before giving him control of Ceterus. And then, the opportunity presented itself.

"John," Samuel said, "please leave the room. I'd like to talk to Sarah alone."

John glared at Sarah in silent protest before pushing his heavy frame from the desk and leaving the office. When the door closed, Samuel continued.

"I want you to bring me the Ceterus file in person."

This was the opportunity Sarah needed. "I'll need the rest of the money you owe me first," she said.

"Of course. I will make the transfer now. Once you've confirmed its arrival, I want you to meet me at the end of the dock at Fletcher's Cove. Do you know the place?"

"I know it," Sarah replied. "I'll see you in an hour," and then she hung up the phone.

Samuel closed the handset of the prepaid cell phone and smiled. He knew Sarah would agree. She was a mercenary. People who would do anything for money were so predictable, and so easy to control. Samuel was thankful he never had that weakness. Money clouded judgment and corrupted principles; it subjected liberty to personal gain, and in doing so, it destroyed nations. Samuel would never allow money to destroy him or his country.

Samuel's plan would save his country. With the exception of the law professor who'd seen Isaac at the canal, everything was falling perfectly into place. And the professor wouldn't be a problem for long. Isaac would take care of Michael Riley, one way or another.

Samuel walked down 17th Street and waited for the light to change at Constitution Avenue. From where he stood, he could see parts of the White House through the foliage surrounding the executive mansion. He wondered what those in the seat of power were doing at that moment and how they would view the world when he was finished reshaping it.

He crossed the street and walked aimlessly through the deserted Constitution Gardens. Along the way, he thought about the next phase of his plan and what he had to do. He looked down at the cell phone still clutched in his hand. His next call would set off a series of events from which there would be no turning back.

As he walked past the polished gabbro panels of the Vietnam Memorial, he stopped for a moment to view his moonlit reflection on the wall. He reached out and traced his finger over the names etched in stone. Each of the men and women immortalized before him had given their lives for something greater than themselves. They had died for their country. Was he willing to do the same? Staring at his reflection in the black stone, Samuel knew he was.

He stepped back from the wall and thousands of names came into view. *There will be some who will never understand*, he told himself. *There will be some who will call me a terrorist, a traitor.* Samuel turned from the memorial and walked into the park. He thought of George Washington, Samuel Adams and Benjamin Franklin. They were all great men who were once called traitors.

Samuel held these thoughts as continued through the park. Up ahead, the path led to a long reflecting pool. He arrived at the edge of the pool and stared into the still waters. A perfect reproduction of the Lincoln Memorial rested on the surface. Through the colonnade, he saw the face of Lincoln himself. Samuel smiled. He had almost forgotten that Lincoln, too, had once been branded as a traitor. And now, he was venerated above all others.

As Samuel stared deep into the water, he knew that, like the great patriots before him, he would be judged by his actions. But the image of Abraham Lincoln was proof that treason was not determined in the moment of action, but through the pages of history.

History would prove that Samuel was right. It would prove that, like Lincoln, he had saved his country from ruin. Samuel turned the cell phone in his hand. It was fitting to make his next phone call under the watchful gaze of the man who had delivered The Prophecy, and, in doing so, had given Samuel the tool he needed to control the minds of men and fulfill his destiny. With a renewed sense of purpose, he opened the phone and placed the call.

CHAPTER 17

This is good. Let's park here," Riley directed. Amie pulled the car over to the side of the street and put it in park. "You sure you want to do this?" The annoyed look on Amie's face said it all. "Okay," he said, throwing his hands up. "I was just making sure."

"So what's the plan?" Amie asked. While driving to the office building, Riley had recounted the general background of Varden's Last Will & Testament and what Riley hoped it would tell them.

"Litigation over the will is ongoing, so there should be a copy in Eliot's active files. It'll probably be in the file room or Eliot's office. But his paralegal is out on maternity leave so the place is a total mess. No telling where it'll be."

"Sounds like fun," Amie said, sarcastically.

"You ready?" Riley asked.

"Ready," Amie responded as she opened her door and got out.

They crossed the street and arrived at the front door of the silver high-rise. Riley removed the stolen security badge from his back pocket and paused to look over at Amie. "Here we go," he said. Amie nodded and Riley held the badge to the magnetic card reader. A green light flashed and a loud click confirmed the release of the heavy magnetic door lock.

Riley pulled the door open and they stepped inside the dimly lit lobby. His eyes immediately darted to the security desk, which was thankfully unoccupied. They crossed the lobby and Riley pushed the button to call for an elevator. Nothing happened. "Shit," he said in a whisper. He anxiously pressed the button with quick repetition. Then Riley felt something brush past him and he spun in place to see what it was.

"Relax," Amie said, holding the security badge up for Riley to see. She had removed it from his back pocket and walked over to the far elevator where she swiped the badge across another magnetic reader. "Try it now."

Riley pushed the button again and the elevator door opened. They stepped inside and Riley pressed the button for the fifteenth floor. The doors closed and the elevator began its slow ascent.

"Nervous?" Amie asked, still looking straight ahead.

"Nah. I do this sort of thing all the time," Riley said, giving Amie a furtive glance. They both let out a quick laugh at the ridiculousness of the situation. Two law abiding and well-respected professors were now breaking into a law office, hoping to find a clue that would tell them why a known killer, and possibly even the F.B.I., wanted Riley dead.

The doors opened and they crossed the fifteenth floor lobby where Amie used the security badge to unlock the glass doors of the Shavin & Zane law firm. A recessed spotlight illuminated the firm's name on the wall above the reception desk and cast a dim glow across the office lobby. Stepping inside, Riley guided the glass door to a silent close before the magnetic locks clicked back into place.

"The file room's just around the corner," Riley said in a whisper, pointing down the hall on the left. "Why don't you start in there?" suggested Riley and he turned towards the hall on the right.

"Wait," she whispered, grabbing Riley's arm. "Where are you going?"

"I'm going to search Eliot's office. There's a chance he's got the file in there to work on it."

"Okay. Let me know if you find anything," Amie said and she walked nervously down the hall where, after turning the corner, she saw an open room on the left that was completely dark. She stepped inside and felt along the wall until she found the light switch. An intense light shot from the florescent bulbs above, filling the room and spilling out into the hallway. Amie quickly shut the door to ensure the light wasn't seen from the outside lobby.

When she turned around, her heart sank. The narrow room was at least thirty feet in length and lined with long filing cabinets that stood six feet tall. Additional boxes and files were stacked haphazardly on the floor and the top of the cabinets. The place was a total disaster. Convincing herself there had to be some sort of logical filing system, Amie stepped forward and studied the labels attached to each of the drawers.

On the other side of the office, Riley groped in the dark until he found the pull chain and switched on Eliot's desk lamp. The desk was layered with the same scattered files Riley had seen earlier that evening. Without moving anything on the desk, Riley began scanning the top layer of folders and papers. He moved slowly from one partially exposed page to the next, searching for the name Christoph Varden and anything that looked like a will. There was nothing there. Realizing he would have to start digging, he reached for a large file at the far corner of the desk.

"I wouldn't do that."

Riley's blood pressure spiked. He snapped upright and was relieved to see Amie standing in the doorway. "Holy shit," he said, clutching his chest. "You could kill someone like that."

"Sorry," she said, holding a large expandable file folder in front of her. "I think I found it."

"Really?" Riley asked. "That was fast." He circled around the desk towards the door.

Amie smiled. "It may've been the only file in the office that was in the right filing cabinet."

Riley took the folder, which was filled with dozens of thick legal documents. He peered inside and when he flipped to the first page, he knew Amie had found exactly what they needed. "This is the lawsuit filed by Varden's relatives," he said excitedly as he removed the document and handed the file folder back to Amie. "A copy of the will should be attached as an exhibit." Riley flipped quickly through the pages. "Here it is!"

Riley looked over at Amie, who had moved around beside him to read the document. "Last Will and Testament of Christoph Varden," she read aloud in a whisper. "Guess that's it," she concluded, but Riley continued flipping pages and scanning the contents.

"We need to make sure this contains the provision Eliot mentioned." Riley traced the words with his finger as he read. He turned the page and his finger stopped. "What the hell?" he asked under his breath. The paragraph he had just read contained the most bizarre instruction he'd ever seen in a will.

"What is it?" Amie asked.

"I have no idea. But it has to be the provision Eliot told me about." Riley read it again but couldn't make any sense of it. "Let's make a copy and get the hell out of here. Did you see a copier anywhere?"

"There's one in the file room," Amie said. Riley followed close behind as Amie led the way down the hallway towards the reception area. At the end of the hall, Amie suddenly stopped and threw her arm out to prevent Riley from taking another step.

"What is it?" Riley asked in a whisper. As the words left his mouth, he looked out into the reception area and knew precisely what it was. A concentrated beam of light shone along the back wall. Its slow and deliberate movement looked like a search light from atop a prison tower.

There was no way to know whether the person holding the flashlight was inside the office or standing in the outer foyer. Riley grabbed Amie's arm and began slowly guiding her backwards and away from the unknown intruder. As they took their first step back, a metallic rattle rang through the air. They froze in place. Then the sound rang out for a second time.

As if she had read Riley's mind, Amie whispered, "Someone's checking if the doors are locked." Then she turned and thrust the Varden file into Riley's arms and stepped silently back towards the reception area. Reaching the end of the hall, she stopped and peered around the corner. A uniformed man in a starched white shirt and dark slacks was walking towards the elevators.

"Looks like a security guard," she said. "He's headed to the elevators."

"Is he going up or down?" Riley asked.

Amie looked at the illuminated button on the wall. "Up," she said. "Why?"

"There are seventeen floors in this building. We've got to get this thing copied and leave the building before he gets back to the lobby. If he's downstairs when we get there, he's bound to ask questions."

"Let's go," Amie said when the elevator doors closed. She led Riley across the reception area to the filing room. They stepped inside and Amie closed the door, casting the room into total darkness before she switched on the light.

"Copier's over there," she said, motioning to the far end of the room.

Riley stepped to the machine and set the file folder on a small worktable. Grabbing a staple remover, he pulled the staple from the document, pushed the will into the automatic feeder and hit the *start* button. Amie anxiously glanced at her watch and wondered how long the security guard would be upstairs. Moments later, the high-speed copier whirred to a stop and Riley placed the originals back in the file folder. He handed the file back to Amie. "Where'd you find this?"

Amie turned to the cabinet and filed the folder back where she'd found it. They left the file room and as Riley reached to switch off the light, Amie turned back to the filing cabinet. "What're you doing?" Riley asked. "The guard will be back any minute!"

Amie removed the Varden file and hurried across the room, where she purposefully misfiled it in a drawer labeled *Aviation*. "Just in case," she said. Riley had no idea what she was talking about but he didn't have time to find out. He turned off the light and they left the room.

Confirming the outer foyer was still empty, they walked quickly across the reception area and left the office. When they got to the elevators, Riley pressed the button and they waited anxiously for the elevator to arrive from the ground floor. The bell chimed and they stepped inside. As the doors were closing, Riley glanced across the elevator bay and saw the indicator light above the adjacent elevator change from seventeen to sixteen.

Riley's pulse quickened. "Shit."

"What?" Amie asked nervously.

"The guard's on his way down. We'll have to run like hell when we get hit the ground floor."

"Shit," Amie said. They rode the rest of the way down in silence, watching the digital display slowly count down. When the display passed two, Amie turned to Riley. "Get ready."

The doors opened and Amie shot out first with Riley close behind. Their footsteps echoed off the tile floor as they sprinted across the lobby. When they reached the glass doors, a bell sounded from the elevator bank. Amie swiped the security badge across the card reader. Riley looked back to see the elevator doors begin to open as the magnetic lock on the front doors released with a heavy click. Amie pushed hard on the door and Riley followed her into the night just as the security guard stepped off the elevator.

The guard crossed the lobby and was nearly to the security desk when he heard the familiar click of the magnetic locks engaging. His head snapped towards the sound. He walked to the door and looked out into the deserted courtyard.

CHAPTER 18

Edward Ross hung up the phone and thought about what he had just learned. As Special Assistant to the Director of the F.B.I., the majority of his job was to sift through the constant streams of information received by the Office of the Director, and pass on only what Director Webster wanted, or needed, to hear. After years in the position, Ross had developed a sixth sense about what information should hit the Director's desk. There was no doubt in his mind that Webster would want to hear about this latest development, regardless of the late hour. So, he opened his phone and dialed the Director's personal number.

"Webster," came the Director's voice.

"Sir, it's Edward Ross. Sorry to bother you at this late hour."

"Hell, Ed. You know I don't sleep," said the Director. "What's got you all hot and bothered this evening?"

"I just received a call from Andy Dyll, sir. It's about Michael Riley; he's the professor who witnessed the Varden…"

"I know who Riley is. What happened?" interrupted the Director.

"Well, sir, he was a no show at the meeting he set up with Coffman."

"Shit. What the hell happened?" asked the Director.

"We're not sure. Coffman showed up and waited for nearly two hours. He called Riley's cell phone, but it went right to voicemail. Either he never intended to show, or something spooked him," Ross speculated.

The Director saw a third option. "Or that Isaac character snatched him right off the streets."

"Yes, sir," Ross agreed. "I suppose that's a possibility. But we do have some good news, of sorts. Remember we were cross-checking Riley with Varden on the off chance there was a link?"

"Yeah," the Director said hopefully.

"Well, there was one. The man's name is Eliot Shavin. He and Riley went to law school together."

"So?" asked Webster.

"Well, sir, Shavin is Varden's estate lawyer."

"I'll be damned."

"But there's more," Ross continued. "When Riley first called Coffman this afternoon, he was riding a city bus that he caught in front of the SMU Law School."

"Yeah, I remember," the Director said.

"There's only one bus route that picks up at that stop. It's the purple line, bus 521. The 521 heads downtown from the SMU stop and, along the way, it runs right in front of Shavin's office."

The Director saw instantly where Ross was headed. "So we think Riley jumped off the bus to go talk to his lawyer friend about Varden."

"Yes, sir. That's the current theory."

"Well it's a good one. Get some men from the field office down there right away," ordered the

Director. "I'll call the Attorney General and get the authority we need from him."

"Yes, sir."

"And make sure Coffman's in the loop on this. It's his case. Let me know what they find."

"Yes, sir. Will do." Ross hung up with the Director and immediately dialed Coffman.

The moonlight reflected off the turgid waters of the Potomac as Sarah merged onto Canal Road. Over the past few years, she had risked her life selling classified information to her Russian contact. The experience had caused a fundamental change in her being. It had somehow rearranged Sarah's DNA and transformed her into someone she hardly recognized. The shy academic she had once been was long gone.

For too many years, she watched in silence as others grew rich off of her ideas and her work. Her frustration grew and, the day she met Kazimir Bulgakov, it finally boiled over. Kazimir understood her anger. He told her she deserved much more, then he showed her how to get it. One evening, she met him at the Eighteenth Street Lounge near Dupont Circle and an exchange was made. When Sarah casually slid a ten gigabyte thumb-drive across the table, Kazimir hung a small duffle bag on the back of her chair and walked out the door.

The stress had been almost unbearable. She waited ten minutes before moving an inch. Three shots of whiskey had no effect. When she finally stood, she nearly blacked out as she took the bag and walked to her car. There, in the darkened parking lot, she opened the bag and saw the money. She couldn't believe it. It was so easy and, most importantly, no one got hurt. In that instant, she became someone else.

Over time, Sarah's transformation empowered her to control her emotions and channel them to her advantage. They focused her thoughts and heightened her instincts. Tonight, as she turned onto the moonlit road leading down toward the water, Sarah's mind was razor sharp.

The road ended in a small parking lot beside the banks of the Chesapeake & Ohio Canal. The Canal ran 184 miles along the shores of the Potomac River from Georgetown to Cumberland, Maryland. Officially, the park at the Canal's entrance was closed at 7 pm. Sarah was not surprised to see the parking lot was completely deserted as she pulled her car beneath an oak tree and shut off the engine. Her hand hung on the ignition as she looked out the windshield and surveyed a small bridge that crossed the Canal to an island on the other side. A forest of old-growth trees cast a heavy shadow across the island and shrouded it in darkness. On the far side of the island, Sarah knew the trees gave way to a small inlet known as Fletcher's Cove.

She reached into her pocket and found the micro-SD memory card that contained the most powerful spy program ever devised. Palming the memory card, Sarah opened her door and stepped out into the night. The air was cool and the faint sounds of the river filtered through the trees. She walked quietly along the banks until she reached the wooden bridge. Stepping onto the bridge, she grabbed the handrail and, with an imperceptible slight of hand, she stuck the memory card to the underside of the rail. There was no way to know what Samuel had planned tonight, but separating herself from the Ceterus program gave Sarah some added leverage that she might need.

Through the trees, she saw the Boathouse at Fletcher's Cove and the outline of a long wooden dock stretching out into the water. Sarah's senses were tuned to the slightest movement as she quietly made her way through the trees to a gravel bike path. When the dock came into full view, she stepped into the shadow of a nearby tree.

Her eyes ran out over the water to the end of the dock. No one was there. She'd expected that. Though she couldn't see him, Sarah knew Samuel was watching her every move. There was no point in waiting. Samuel knew his tradecraft, and that meant he wouldn't show himself until Sarah was trapped in the middle of the cove.

Moonlight reflected off the dock's sun-bleached boards, making it glow in the darkened water. The sounds of the Potomac filled the air and washed over the cove as Sarah walked slowly along the narrow wooden path. At the end of the dock, she turned and gasped at the sight of an unknown man standing only feet away.

"I've startled you," came Samuel's familiar voice. "I am sorry."

"It's fine," Sarah said with forced calm. She strained to identify any distinctive features but the brim of Samuel's hat cast his face in shadow.

Samuel got right to the point. "I have asked you here for two reasons. As you know, the Government can intercept electronic data transmissions at will. So, I thought it best to obtain Ceterus from you in person. Do you have it?"

Sarah stared deep into Samuel's shadowed face. "It's close by."

Samuel smiled and nodded his understanding. "I see. Well, then. That brings us to the second reason I've asked to see you tonight." Samuel paused as he chose his words carefully. The sounds of the river swirled in the air. "I'd like you to finish what you've started."

Sarah didn't know what that meant. She shrugged, "I've already finished."

"Yes," Samuel agreed. "You have finished what you were hired to do. Now I would like you to finish the rest." A silence fell between them. Sarah wanted to hear more. She wanted to know what Samuel had planned but she couldn't appear over-eager. Samuel sensed her resistance. "I would pay you, of course," he added.

Sarah stood silent in feigned contemplation. "What's the job?" she asked.

Samuel had his response ready. The story he told was one of blackmail and intimidation. He would use Ceterus to expose weak points in the Government and bend it to his will. As Samuel described Sarah's role, she laughed inwardly. Samuel didn't have the technical expertise to understand she had already done everything he was asking of her. It was all contained in the micro-SD card hidden on the bridge over the Canal. She could take his money and not lift another finger.

"No one gets hurt, right?" Sarah asked.

"No," Samuel replied. "At least, not physically. Some amount of emotional pain is inevitable."

Sarah could live with that. "When do I get my first payment?"

Samuel smiled. Of all the people he'd recruited, Sarah was, by far, the most intelligent. Ironically, her weakness had proven the easiest to exploit. Sarah was coin-operated and Samuel had access to an unlimited supply of money. "You will have it within an hour," he assured her. "Now, where is Ceterus?"

"Follow me," Sarah said as she stepped past Samuel and led the way down the dock.

Amie hit the button on her keychain to unlock the doors and the tail lights flashed. Riley and Amie ran to the car and jumped in. They instinctively slouched down, trying to hide behind the front seats. "You think he saw us?" Riley asked, hoping they had turned the corner before the security guard reached the front doors.

Amie's eyes shot from one mirror to the next to see if anyone was running after them. "I think we're Okay," she said, trying to catch her breath. She turned to Riley for confirmation.

Riley looked over his shoulder and out the back window. "Looks that way," he said turning back in his seat. He looked down at the will, which was still clutched in his hand. "Keep a look out for a second," he instructed Amie as he unfolded the document and began reading. He briefly scanned each page, working his way to the back of the document where he had seen the strange provision Eliot had mentioned. "Here it is," he finally said.

"What does it say?" Amie asked, looking over at the document and hoping her first act of breaking and entering wasn't for nothing.

Riley read the paragraph in silence. Shaking his head, he said, "It doesn't make any sense. Listen to this:

This provision is to remain confidential. If my death is found to have been caused by unnatural means, I ask my lawyer, Eliot Shavin, to contact Shea Baggett, my most trusted friend and business partner, and deliver the following message: Walker and Halley show the way to where the cause and effect reside. The feet of giants cannot crush the truth they try to hide.

Riley stopped reading and Amie turned in her seat. "Is that it?"

"That's it," said Riley with a shrug.

"Seriously? What the hell's that? Some kind of riddle?"

Riley was still focused on the will. "I guess so. Look at what he says. *'If my death is found to have been caused by unnatural means'.* That can't be a coincidence. The guy was murdered in his own house."

"Yeah. That's really strange. You wouldn't write something like that unless you suspected someone had a reason to kill you, right?" said Amie.

Riley silently read the paragraph again. Reaching the end, he shook his head. "Varden was into something and he must've known it was dangerous. But this doesn't give us much to go on," Riley concluded.

"There's got to be something there," Amie said more confidently than she felt. "Your friend Eliot's supposed to read this to Shea Baggett?"

Riley looked back at the paragraph to double check. "Yeah. Who's Shea Baggett?"

"He's a computer scientist who pioneered the technology needed to send secure messages over the Internet. The kind of thing that made on-line retail possible."

Riley turned in his seat to face Amie. "Okay. But why'd Varden pick him?"

"Varden's company, MicroCon, bought Baggett's company about twenty years ago. Baggett stayed on as Chief Scientist with MicroCon. He and Varden were close friends and collaborators ever since. I guess Varden thought Baggett would be able to make some sense of that crazy message."

Riley looked back at the will. "Walker and Halley show the way to where the cause and effect reside. The feet of giants cannot crush the truth they try to hide." They sat in silence, thinking. Slowly, Riley began to shake his head again. "Doesn't make any sense to me. What do you make of it?"

"Not much," Amie admitted. "I have no idea who Walker and Halley are. And this feet of giants thing," Amie paused, "I just don't know."

Riley had a thought. "The way the will was drafted, this has to have something to do with why Varden was killed. Right?"

"Shit," Amie said, reaching for the ignition.

"What's going on?" Riley asked, looking over his shoulder out the back window. Three dark blue, unmarked sedans had just skidded to a stop in front of the office building. Half a dozen men in dark suits poured out of the vehicles and were headed to the front door. Several of them carried large bags of equipment. There was no doubt who it was. The F.B.I. had somehow tracked them to Eliot's office. "Shit," Riley said.

"Get the iPad out of my bag," Amie directed.

"How the hell did they find us?" Riley asked, knowing full well that Amie had no idea.

"Who knows? Just grab my iPad," she repeated, watching the F.B.I.'s every move in the rearview mirror. The security guard they had narrowly escaped had just opened the door and the agents were filing into the building when Riley turned back in his seat with the iPad in hand. With the last of the agents inside, Amie started the car, shifted it into drive, and pulled slowly away from the curb.

"Where are we going?" Riley asked.

"We're going to see Shea Baggett. And you're going to use that," Amie said, pointing to the iPad, "to find him. But first, we have a stop to make."

Joseph grabbed the duffle bag from the bedroom of his extended stay hotel. It had been packed for days in anticipation of the call he'd just received. He walked back through the living room to the front door. Given what was ahead, he wasn't sure he'd ever return to this place. He turned for one last look around, and when he saw the stained and broken down furniture that filled the cramped living room, he was happy to finally leave. *Good riddance*, he thought.

He opened the door and stepped out onto the sidewalk. The night was cool and the full moon lit the way as Joseph crossed the parking lot and walked to the nearby intersection. Looking down the street for a taxi, he could just make out the white glow of the U.S. Capitol building on the horizon. Moments later, a cab turned the corner and he hailed it to a stop.

He opened the door and slid inside. "Regan National," he said. Without any response, the driver sped off towards the airport.

Joseph rested his head on the back of the seat and closed his eyes to combat the motion sickness that he often felt in the back seat of a cab. As the car bounced over the city streets, he thought about his recent conversation with Samuel.

"The program is complete. It is time to begin the next phase."

"When should I leave?" Joseph asked.

"As soon as possible. Are you ready?"

"I've been ready for days," Joseph reassured him.

"You know how crucial it is that these next steps are executed exactly as we have planned. This is what you have been training for. But this time, it's real."

"I understand," said Joseph. Samuel had detected the faint hesitation in Joseph's voice.

"I know the task ahead of you is unpleasant. I wish there was some other way to achieve our goal. But this is the only way. If everyone does what they are supposed to do, then no one will be hurt. Take comfort in knowing this must happen to achieve a greater good." Samuel paused for a moment, then he added, *"Joseph, I know the weight of your duty is heavy. But you must now carry us or we will falter*

and we will fail. I trust you above all others, which is why I've given you this task. Everything depends on you. I know you will lead the way."

As he listened to these words, Joseph felt a transformation within. He was truly important. He was trusted. He was a leader. It was a feeling of pride and confidence like none he had ever felt. *"I'll do whatever it takes,"* he told Samuel.

"I know you will."

The cab bounced over a pothole in the road. Joseph opened his eyes and glanced down at his watch. He had just enough time to make his flight to Chicago.

CHAPTER 19

The security guard peered out the glass doors at the six men in dark suits who'd just arrived at the building. *Who the hell are these guys,* he thought. Before he could ask, the man at the front of the pack reached into his jacket pocket and pulled out a leather case. He snapped the case open to reveal an identification card and a gold shield, which shimmered under the overhead lighting. Seeing *F.B.I.* printed in bold blue letters at the top of the identification card, the security guard quickly swiped his badge to release the magnetic locks.

The guard took several steps back as the agents filed inside. The one with the badge stepped forward. "I'm Special Agent in Charge, Brinson Coffman with the F.B.I." The guard nodded his head in acknowledgment, but didn't say anything. Coffman looked at the nametag on the guard's uniform. "Sharp, is it?" Coffman asked.

"Yes, sir. Ryan Sharp."

"Mr. Sharp, we're tracking a man we believe has been in this building tonight. Have you seen anyone come in here over the past few hours?"

"No, sir," said Sharp nervously. "It's been really quiet all night," he added, trying to be helpful.

"You been at your desk all night?"

"Sure have," Sharp said. "Except when I go on my rounds. I check each floor a couple times a night."

Coffman looked up and scanned the perimeter of the ceiling. "These work?" he asked, pointing to the numerous security cameras.

"Yessir. They work," Sharp said.

"We're going to need to check your security tapes for the last few hours," Coffman said, and the entire group began walking to the security desk. "What floor is Eliot Shavin's office on?"

"He's with the Shavin and Zane law firm. They're up on fifteen."

"Your security badge gives you access to the entire building?" Coffman asked.

"It does," said Sharp, reluctantly. "But I don't think I can..."

Coffman cut him off. "Mr. Sharp. You know what obstruction of justice is?" Sharp nodded his head rapidly. "You need to cooperate with us, Mr. Sharp. We're tracking someone that we need to find as a matter of national security. The longer we stand here, the farther away he gets. You understand me?"

Sharp thrust his badge towards Coffman. "Yessir."

Coffman grabbed the badge. "Fifteen, you say?" he asked.

"Yessir," Sharp replied.

"Okay. Agent Brandt, Agent Woods – you two stay here with Mr. Sharp and review the security tapes. Let me know what you find. The rest of us will head up to fifteen and take a look around."

"The monitors are right back here," Sharp said, pointing to a room behind the security desk.

Coffman watched until Sharp and the agents disappeared into the security room. "Okay," he said, turning to the other agents. "Let's go." He led the men through the lobby, where he swiped the key card and they got on the elevator.

The team arrived on the fifteenth floor and went directly to the glass doors of Shavin & Zane. Coffman unlocked the doors and his men pushed inside. As the door slid to a close, the men stood in the reception area and awaited Coffman's instruction.

"Okay," Coffman said, "We think Riley was here. We think he was looking for information on Christoph Varden. We know that Eliot Shavin represents the Varden estate in some current litigation. The information we need is somewhere in the Varden files. We just have to find it." The men nodded their understanding.

"Shorney, you and Eric start in the file room." The two men didn't wait for further instruction. Agent Shorney grabbed the heavy black canvas bag by his feet and they set off to find the file room. "John, you and I will split up and search the rest of this place. I'll take this half of the office," Coffman said, pointing down the right hallway, "you take that side. Let me know what you find."

With that, the men headed off in opposite directions.

Coffman decided to start at the far end of the hall and work his way back. He reached the office at the end of the corridor and turned on the lights. "Ah, shit," he said aloud. The place looked like a bomb had gone off. Coffman had little choice but to wade in and get to work.

Minutes later, the small walkie-talkie crackled to life. "Agent Coffman?"

Coffman pulled the receiver from his belt. "Coffman. What do you got?"

"You should come down to the security room. We've got something you'll want to see."

"On my way," Coffman said, leaving Eliot's office and taking the elevator down to the first floor. When he arrived at the door of the security room, he saw the two agents and the security guard huddled around a television monitor. "What do you got?" Coffman asked, and the men instantly parted to give him a clear view of the monitor.

"We just queued the tape up again. Take a look," said Agent Brandt.

Coffman leaned into the desk and saw a black and white image of the glass doors at the front of the lobby. Sharp pushed a button and the tape began to play. Coffman watched with little reaction as he saw the glass doors open and a man walk inside. Coffman instantly identified the man as Michael Riley. "Wait a second," Coffman said, suddenly confused. "Stop the tape."

Sharp hit the button and the frame froze on a dark haired woman who was following behind Riley as he crossed the lobby. Coffman studied the grainy image on the screen. Clearly, the camera system in the office building hadn't been updated for years. "Who the hell is *that*?" Coffman asked, pointing at the image.

"That's why we called you down here," Brandt said. "We have no idea who that is."

"Sonofabitch," Coffman muttered. "Riley's talking to someone," he said he stared at the screen trying to make out as much detail of the woman as possible. *We've got to shut this guy up,* he thought. The radio on Coffman's hip came to life.

"Agent Coffman?"

Frustrated at the interruption, Coffman stood and ripped the radio from his belt. "Coffman," he said, tersely.

"We could use you up here, sir."

Coffman looked directly at agents Brandt and Woods. "Find out who that woman is," he ordered, pointing to the screen on his way out the door. He took the elevator back up to the fifteenth floor.

Agent Shorney was by the copy machine and saw Coffman arrive. "Over here," he said.

As Coffman walked towards the back of the room, he looked over at the other agent, who was meticulously flipping through files in the cabinets along the wall. "You find anything, Eric?"

The agent stopped for a moment and looked up at Coffman. "Nothing yet," he sighed. "The Varden file isn't where it's supposed to be. I'm having to start from the beginning and go through each drawer one at a time."

"Figures," Coffman said, glancing around at the disorderly state of the filing room. "Keep after it," he ordered. Then he turned to Agent Shorney, who had set up his laptop on the worktable beside the copier. "What's this?" he asked, looking at the laptop screen.

"It's a log of the copies made on this machine," Shorney said. He pointed to each column of information as he described it. "It shows the date, time, page count and number of copies of every document processed on this machine. It also shows whether it was copied, scanned or emailed."

"So?" Coffman said, prompting Shorney to get to the point.

"Look here." Shorney pointed to the last entry on the screen.

"Sonofabitch," Coffman said. "So Riley comes in here and makes a single copy of a twenty-five page document."

"That's what it looks like," Shorney agreed.

"Any way to know what he copied?" Coffman asked.

"There is. Most copiers have an internal hard drive that captures images of every document copied. Since this is the last document copied, I'm sure an image is still on the drive. I can pull it but it'll take a little time. And we'll have to get the encryption key from the manufacturer to unlock the drive."

Coffman thought for a moment. Even if they found the hard copy of Varden's legal file in the office, there would be no way to tell what parts of it Riley and his new friend had copied. To narrow their search down to the twenty-five pages Riley copied, they had to have the image from the drive. "Do it," he said, and then he turned and left the room.

CHAPTER 20

Wait here," Amie said, throwing the car in park in front of the convenience store. "I'll be right back." She got out of the car and Riley watched as Amie disappeared into the back of the store. Minutes later, she walked out carrying a plastic bag. She got in the car and handed it to Riley. "Here," she said, "open that."

"What is it?" Riley asked, reaching into the bag. He pulled out a bulky plastic package, which held a cheap, pre-paid cell phone. Riley was confused. He turned and saw Amie digging in her shoulder bag, where she retrieved her own phone. Then she opened the driver's door and casually dropped the phone out on the parking lot. "What're you doing?" Riley asked.

"That building we were just in had security cameras everywhere," she said, putting the car in reverse. She turned the wheel and eased the car back until the front tire hit the phone with an audible crunch. Amie pulled out of the parking lot and back onto the road leading to Baggett's house.

"Okay. But what's the phone for?" Riley asked, still confused.

"If they have my picture, they'll have my name soon enough. Then they'll get my cell phone, which they can use to pinpoint our location through GPS. We had to get rid of my phone and I thought we should have a burner." Riley smiled as he was reminded how lucky he was to have Amie on his side. He opened the package, tucked the new number in his pocket, and slid the new phone into Amie's bag.

Riley turned his attention back to the iPad and providing Amie directions to Baggett's house. "I think that's it," he said as they crept down Fairfax Avenue.

Amie slowed the car to a stop and turned off her headlights. Riley leaned over to look out the driver's side window at the two story, gray brick house on the other side of the street. "That's it?" Amie asked.

She was surprised at the size of the home. It was certainly nicer than an average middle-class house, but Shea Baggett was a top executive of a major technology company. For someone of that stature, the house was rather modest. It made her wonder if Baggett owned this house but actually lived somewhere else.

Riley noticed a bronze number plate next to the front door and compared it to the address he'd found through the Dallas County Tax Assessor's website. "4615 Fairfax. That's gotta be it," he said.

"Let's go find out," Amie said as she opened the door and got out. They followed the red brick walkway that wound through the yard to the front door. Standing on the porch, Amie looked at Riley who gave her a nod before she knocked firmly. The deep bark of a large dog reverberated through the door. The incessant barking continued for a full minute until it was silenced by a voice just beyond the door.

Moments later, the deadbolt slid from its place and the door opened a few inches until it was stopped by a metal chain. "Can I help you?" asked a male voice through the crack in the door.

Even through the partially opened door, Amie recognized the round face and thick black beard. "Mr. Baggett? I'm sorry to show up like this so late in the evening. I'm Doctor Amie Hawkins. I'm a computer science professor at SMU. We met a few months ago at the HP Summit on Innovation."

Baggett stared at Amie for a long moment and then finally made the connection. "Ms. Hawkins. Yes. I remember. We discussed your paper on the use of botnets in multi-stage attacks." Baggett said, peering over at Riley.

Amie took the hint. "This is Professor Michael Riley. He teaches constitutional law at SMU. We hate to bother you, but it's important that we talk to you and it can't wait until the morning."

Baggett looked back and forth at the two, studying them closely. After a long moment, he slowly closed the door and the metallic rattle of the chain sounded through the solid oak panels. Baggett opened the door and stood in the threshold to block the entryway. He was wearing a full set of pajamas and a robe, which compelled Riley to speak. "I'm sorry we've gotten you out of bed, Mr. Baggett. As Professor Hawkins mentioned, this is really important."

"I've read your papers on privacy and technology," Baggett said, ignoring Riley's apology. "I can't say I agree with all your conclusions."

Riley didn't have time for an academic debate. "Sir, we've come here to talk about another matter," he responded. Baggett waited to hear what could possibly be important enough to bring two professors to his door in the middle of the night. "May we come inside?" Riley pressed.

Baggett hesitated for a moment longer before shrugging his shoulders and stepping aside to let them in. "This way," Baggett said, and led the pair into a formal living room adjacent to the entryway.

The hardwood floors creaked beneath their feet as they entered the room. Baggett switched on a table lamp that lit the surrounding area with a soft yellow glow. "Have a seat," he said, motioning to the vintage couch centered on the back wall. Amie and Riley circled the glass coffee table and sat down. "Now," Baggett said as he fell into a dark leather chair, "what's this all about?"

The dim circle of light from the table lamp stopped short of Baggett's chair and Amie struggled to make out his facial features in the shadows. "It's about Christoph Varden," she said. They had expected Baggett to be surprised, but his reaction was muted.

"I figured Chris was somehow behind this," Baggett said with a sigh. "Just about every strange thing to happen to me over the past twenty years had something to do with him."

"It's about Varden's will," explained Riley, anxious to get to the point. "Did you know he left you a message in his will?"

"Doesn't surprise me," answered Baggett. "He wasn't one to break a promise."

Baggett's answer raised Riley's hope. Maybe this guy did know something that could help. "So he told you about his will?" Amie asked.

"In a manner of speaking. And I made a promise to him in return, which is why I allowed you into my house." Baggett looked over at Amie and then pushed off the arms of his chair to stand up. "I think this calls for a drink." He walked to a marble table by the window and poured a tall scotch from a crystal decanter. "Drink?" he asked, still pouring his own glass.

Amie was already shaking her head when Riley said, "No, thank you." They struggled to contain a flood of questions as they patiently watched Baggett take a quick sip from the glass and then replace it with another splash from the decanter.

He seemed to be preparing himself for what he had to say.

"I was at Chris's house about a year ago," Baggett started as he crossed the room. "We were sitting in the library having a drink and discussing various matters as we always did." Baggett lowered himself back into his chair and paused for a long time as he stared out the front window. The image of that moment with Varden appeared vividly in his mind. "At some point," Baggett continued, "Chris stopped talking. But when I looked over and him, his eyes were glazed over. At first, he looked sad. When he finally looked back, I realized he wasn't sad. He was scared." Baggett stared out of the window in silence.

"What was he scared of?" Amie asked softly. Her question dissolved the picture in Baggett's mind, and he shifted his gaze from the window.

"I have no idea," he said sadly. "He said a lot of things that night – most of which I still don't understand. He said he was working on something. He said it was the biggest thing he'd ever done. But I could tell he was somehow conflicted about it. He asked me vague questions about what it meant to be a patriot."

"What kind of questions?" Riley asked.

Baggett's gaze had returned to the window. "I remember him asking me: 'How far can a patriot go before he becomes a traitor?'" Amie and Riley were staring at Baggett, transfixed. "I'd known Chris for over twenty years," Baggett continued. "and I'd never seen him like that before. He was terrified. He was truly terrified. At the time, I couldn't tell if he was scared for his life or scared that somehow he had crossed the line between being a patriot and a traitor. But now, I guess I know the answer." Baggett's eyes began to glisten at the thought of his friend's brutal murder.

Riley gave Baggett a moment before speaking again. "Did he say anything else about what had him so scared?" Riley asked.

"No," Baggett said, blinking hard to clear his eyes. "He just said that one day he might need me to do something for him. I asked what it was, but he wouldn't say. He just said I'd have to read about it in his will. He made me promise to help if the time ever came. It seemed like an innocent promise at the time. I thought he was just being paranoid – though Chris wasn't really prone to such things. And now, he's dead and you're here knocking on my door in the middle of the night asking about the will."

Riley shifted in his seat and pulled out the copy of the will from his back pocket. "Do you mind if I read it to you?" he asked.

Baggett took a long sip from his glass. He held it up in front of his mouth while he savored the earthy burn of the twenty-five year old scotch. When he was finished, he rested the glass on the arm of the chair and closed his eyes. "What is it that Christoph Varden wanted me to hear?"

Riley unfolded the will and turned to the provision in the back. In a slow and deliberate tone, he read the passage.

If my death is found to have been caused by unnatural means, I ask my lawyer, Eliot Shavin, to contact Shea Baggett, my most trusted friend and business partner, and deliver the following message: Walker and Halley show the way to where the cause and effect reside. The feet of giants cannot crush the truth they try to hide.

Silence hung in the air. Baggett furrowed his brow, replaying each word in his mind and trying desperately to decipher the message. Then, Riley saw an almost imperceptible flash of understanding cross Baggett's face. Baggett opened his eyes and fixed his gaze on Amie and Riley.

"Chris made me promise that I would help him," he began. "But whatever that message means, it was enough to get him killed. I want to keep my promise, but I have no idea what Chris was involved with. I don't think he wanted me to die to keep my promise."

"Mr. Baggett, you don't need to put yourself in danger. You can keep your promise by telling us what you know," Amie said. "There are men out there, powerful men, who are willing to do anything to get whatever it was Christoph was working on. They've already killed for it. Whatever Christoph created, he wouldn't want it in the hands of these men." Amie paused as the words sank in.

"We're in this already, Mr. Baggett," Riley added. "There's nothing we can do about that. But you can help us, and help Christoph, by telling us what this message means. Then you'll have kept your promise and stayed out of any trouble."

"I don't know what it means," Baggett said.

Amie's heart sank, but Riley had seen Baggett's earlier expression and knew he was holding something back. "Mr. Baggett," he said, "Christoph Varden was a brilliant man. I don't believe he'd leave a coded message in his will specifically for you if he wasn't certain you'd be able to decipher its meaning."

Baggett took another sip from his glass and stared directly into Riley's eyes. "I only know what one word of that message means, Mr. Riley. But I don't think it will help you," Baggett said.

"What word?" asked Riley.

"Walker. I know who Walker is."

Amie leaned forward, resting her elbows on her knees. "Who is he?" she prompted.

"Harold Walker. He's a brilliant young artist that Chris discovered several years ago. Met him at an art show at the Goss Gallery. Chris liked Walker's work and took an interest in him. He was a young kid, just getting started; working several jobs to make ends meet, he didn't have much time to devote to his artwork. Chris changed that. He bought Hal a studio off Greenville Avenue and gave him a stipend so he could focus on his work. Chris pretty much supported him ever since."

"So what does it mean to you that Christoph pointed to Harold Walker in this message?" Riley asked.

Baggett took another sip and returned the glass to the arm of his chair. "He commissioned a lot of art from Hal – sculptures, carvings, photographs. Damn near anything Hal would be willing to create. But knowing Chris, I think you'll want to look at the paintings. One painting in particular," he said, much more confident now that he had thought through it. "You ask what it means to me that Hal Walker is included in that message, Mr. Riley? It means you won't understand what he was trying to say unless you're standing in Christoph Varden's library."

Amie and Riley sat in silence, hoping for more of an explanation. They didn't get one. "And now," said Baggett, "I think it's time for you to go. There's nothing more I can tell you." Baggett stood and set his now-empty glass on the coffee table.

"Thank you for your time, Mr. Baggett. We appreciate it. You've been a big help," Riley said as he and Amie walked towards the front door.

"Oh, Ms. Hawkins?" Baggett said as Riley opened the front door. Amie turned to look back into the living room. "You're going to need this." Baggett had just torn off a piece of paper and was folding it as he walked to the front door. He handed her the paper, which felt heavy in her hand. "Good luck," he said as Amie and Riley stepped out on the front porch. They looked back into the house at Baggett. "Good luck," he repeated softly and then he slowly closed the door.

Amie and Riley looked at one another and then down at the piece of paper in Amie's hand. She unfolded it and something glinted in the porch light. They looked at the metal object – each knowing instinctively what it was. It was the key to Christoph Varden's house.

CHAPTER 21

Riley and Amie sat in the car across from Baggett's house. The conversation had been helpful, but Riley was disappointed they hadn't learned something more tangible. "I guess it was a victory just getting Baggett to talk to us," he observed.

"I guess," Amie reluctantly agreed. "Though I'm not too sure how much good it did."

"Me either," Riley said. "He just pointed us to Varden's house to find out what the hell's going on. I doubt the F.B.I.'s inviting folks for a tour these days."

"Well, at least we learned one thing," Amie said, optimistically.

Riley turned in his seat. "What's that?"

"Whatever Varden was working on, I think we all agree it got him killed."

"That's true," Riley agreed.

Amie continued her line of thought. "Baggett said it was the biggest project he'd ever done. If that's true, Varden wasn't hiding secret bank accounts or passwords in that capsule. He was hiding computer code. It's gotta be something no one's ever done before. Something with far reaching consequences." Amie marveled at the possibilities. "I mean, Varden already changed the entire world of computing. Hard to imagine what's bigger than that."

Riley thought through Amie's logic. That Varden had hidden computer code in the capsule made a lot of sense. But computer code for what? They needed more information and Riley strained to pull as much from the Baggett conversation as possible. "What do you make of Varden's references to patriotism? What did he mean when he asked Baggett *'How far can a patriot go before he becomes a traitor?'*"

Amie had been focusing on the fact that Varden had gone to such great lengths to build, and then hide, what must be ground breaking technology. She had completely forgotten about the references to patriotism. "I don't know what to make of that," she admitted.

"I wonder if Varden or his company do any work for the government," Riley thought aloud.

"I know they did. All of the major security vendors are players in the government space, including MicroCon. And I know the government has turned to Varden in the past to help design the next-generation security built exclusively for government operations."

"So there might be a government tie and there might not," Riley concluded in frustration. "No way to know."

"There is one way," Amie said as she opened her hand to reveal the folded paper wrapped around the key to Varden's house.

Riley saw the key and then noticed something was written on the paper. "What's that?" he asked.

Amie looked down and there, sticking partially out from beneath the key, was a handwritten note. Amie moved the key to reveal the full text. "It's just a bunch of numbers," she said. "405282. What's that's supposed to mean?"

"I suppose there's only one way to find out," Riley said. Amie looked up and Riley flashed a mischievous grin. "I think I'm going to need your iPad again."

"Coffman, this is Eric." At the sound of his name, Agent Brinson Coffman returned the document he'd been reading to Eliot's desk and grabbed the radio from his belt.

"Coffman. Go."

"We found the file."

"On my way." Coffman clipped the radio to his belt and walked down to the file room, where he found Agent Eric Bauer continuing his search of the file cabinets. "You found it?" Coffman asked, announcing his presence.

"Yeah. I think so, but I'm still looking for more," Bauer said. "I put it over there." He pointed to a folder on top of a cabinet by the door.

Coffman picked up the thick file and read the label on the front tab. "Varden, et. al. v. Estate of Christoph Varden," he read aloud. He looked up at Bauer. "Where'd you find this?"

"Here," he said, pointing to the long drawer he was still searching through. "But all the other files in here are cases about small plane crashes. The drawer is labeled 'Aviation'," Bauer pointed out.

"What's the Varden file doing over there?" Coffman asked, but just as he was finishing the question, he had a hunch. "You think Riley misfiled this on purpose to slow us down?"

"Could be," Bauer shrugged. "Or it could be that he was in a hurry to get out of here and just threw it in a random drawer."

Coffman knew there was no way to find out, but he didn't like the idea of Riley and his unknown friend intentionally misleading them. That could make things more difficult going forward.

Coffman looked to the end of the room and saw Agent Shorney working on the copy machine. "You got anything, Jason?" he asked.

Shorney looked over his shoulder. "Should have the encryption key any minute. We had to find the serial number first so the manufacturer could match it to the right key. They're emailing it to me."

"Okay." Turning back to Bauer, he said, "Let's split this file up and see what we can find." He pulled out half of the contents, and handed them to Bauer.

They spent the next several minutes in silence until Bauer reached the back of the first document and let out a long whistle. "You know how much the Varden estate is worth?" Coffman looked up from his stack of papers. "One point four billion. That's billion with a capital B," Bauer said.

"I guess that's one point four billion reasons for the family to fight," said Coffman, turning back to his reading.

"I wish I had that many reasons to fight with my family," Bauer said.

"Got it!" Shorney said from across the room.

Coffman set his document on top of the filing cabinet and walked over to the copy machine, where he found Agent Shorney typing furiously on the laptop. "You got the key?" Coffman asked, having no idea how to decipher the information on Shorney's screen.

"Better. They sent the encryption key and I've got the hard drive from the copier open here," he said, pointing to the screen. "So, all we have to do is scroll down to the bottom and take a look at the last document printed, which is right here." Shorney stopped the pointer at the bottom of a list of files. With a quick double click of the mouse, a document appeared on the screen.

"Can you print that?" Coffman asked hurriedly. Shorney clicked a few buttons and the copy machine came to life. Seconds later, Coffman pulled the document from the tray and read the top of the first page. "Last Will and Testament of Christoph Varden." Then he turned back to Shorney. "Make a couple more copies. I need all three of us looking through this." Shorney printed the copies and all three agents silently poured through the contents.

Minutes later, Shorney broke the silence. "Turn to page twenty-three." Coffman and Bauer turned quickly to the page. "Look at the second to last paragraph," Shorney instructed.

Coffman had barely finished reading the paragraph before he pulled he radio from his belt. "Brandt!" he yelled into the microphone.

"Yessir," came the instant reply.

"We need a quick background on a man named Shea Baggett. Make sure to include his address."

"I'm on it," replied Agent Brandt.

Coffman turned his men. "We're going to pay Mr. Baggett a visit."

CHAPTER 22

That's it. Up on the right," Riley said, pointing through the front windshield and double-checking their position on the iPad. Amie turned the lights off and stopped the car beside the black granite driveway.

An ornate, wrought iron gate blocked the entrance and towered over the limestone wall surrounding the estate. Riley looked out the passenger window and studied the imposing structure. "Glad they didn't make it too easy on us," he murmured. His eyes traced the iron structure from the top of the arch down to the hinges, where they stopped on a dark recess in the wall just to the left of the gate. The landscape lighting filtered down from above, providing just enough light to guess at the structure hidden in the shadows. "Is that another gate?" Riley asked.

"Looks like it," Amie agreed.

Riley thrust his hand out. "Let me see that key." Amie reached into the cup holder between the seats and retrieved the key, which was still wrapped in the piece of paper. She handed it to

Riley and he got out of the car. As he closed the door, he turned to see if anyone was around, instantly feeling as suspicious as he looked. Thankfully, the street was deserted.

Riley walked quickly up the drive and over to the small iron gate. He tested the knob but, as expected, it was locked. He unwrapped the key and stuffed the paper in his pocket. Riley's frayed nerves caused the key to rattle around the lock before it hit its mark and slid into the mechanism. Taking a deep breath, he turned the key and the gate swung open.

Riley flashed a triumphant smile at Amie, who immediately pulled forward and parked the car in the shadows on the side of the road. She got out and quietly closed the door before hurrying over to the gate. She passed Riley and stepped inside the walled estate. Riley followed and slowly closed the gate.

They stood in silence with their backs against the wall and surveyed the estate. The black driveway ran directly in front of them and stopped at the wooden doors of the six car garage. To the left, an ornate fountain at the front of the estate was lit by an array of flood lamps accenting the formal gardens. To the right, the back of the mansion was completely dark.

"Let's go around back," Amie suggested, preferring to stay clear of the flood lights out front.

"Okay," Riley agreed in a whisper and they dashed across the driveway. They crossed the side yard to the garage and around the corner to a small courtyard behind the house. With the exception of an occasional gust of wind rattling the trees, the night air was perfectly still and quiet.

"Look," Riley said, pointing across the courtyard.

Even from a distance, Amie could see the yellow police tape surrounding a covered terrace. "That must be it," she whispered. "I read that Varden was murdered in his library. If they've got that area marked off, that's got to be it, right?"

Riley nodded. "Makes sense. Let's go see," he said, taking a quick look around before darting across the courtyard. A heavy floral scent hung in the air as they passed the dense rose bushes surrounding the terrace. Arriving at the oak beams supporting the terrace pergola, their path was blocked by multiple rows of bright yellow tape imprinted with bold type: CRIME SCENE DO NOT CROSS.

Riley studied the tape for a moment. Ripping it down would leave an obvious sign someone had disturbed the crime scene. He was considering other options when he felt something move at his feet. He looked down to see Amie on her hands and knees, crawling under the barrier. She stood on the other side and looked back at Riley through the mesh of the police tape. "Come on," she said. Riley was under the tape and standing next to her in seconds.

They stepped over to the French doors that opened onto the terrace. Riley cupped his hands around his face and peered through the paned glass. "It's really dark," he said. "But there's a desk here and it looks like a bunch of bookshelves."

"Is it the library?" Amie asked, wanting more certainty.

"I guess so. Looks like it." Riley looked back at Amie. "We'll have to go inside," he shrugged. Hearing no objections from Amie, Riley reached into his pocket and got the key. He knelt down to get a better view of the door handle while he lined up the key with the lock. The key slid easily inside. Riley stood up, placed his hand on the handle and turned the key. With a gentle push, he silently cracked the door open.

A high-pitched, repetitive beep shattered the stillness of the night. "Holy shit!" Amie exclaimed, instinctively recognizing the sound. "The alarm's on!"

Riley's heart beat wildly against his chest as the incessant noise spilled out of the darkness. Panicked, he spun in place looking helplessly for something to silence the alarm. Amie couldn't wait. Her survival instincts took over. "We've gotta get out of here," she said and grabbed Riley's arm. She turned to run but realized Riley wasn't moving. He was just standing in place, staring at the source of the alarm on the far side of the room. "Michael!" Amie said over the alarm's high-pitched trill.

But Riley's mind was somewhere else. Why would Shea Baggett set us up, he wondered. It doesn't make any sense.

"Michael!" came Amie's voice again. Riley blinked at the sound of his name and began to move. To Amie's astonishment, he didn't turn to make his escape. Instead, Riley pushed the door open and walked directly inside.

"What're you doing?" she asked.

Riley didn't answer. In seconds, he had vanished within the darkened interior of Varden's library, leaving Amie shocked and alone on the terrace. Riley ran across the room to the source of the menacing sound. Digging in his pocket, he retrieved the scrap of paper Baggett had used to wrap the key. He held the paper up to the faint light of the alarm's keypad, sweat beading heavily on his face. Carefully, Riley keyed in the number Baggett had written on the piece of paper: 4-0-5-2-8-2. Entering the last digit, a flurry of rapid beeps sounded before the keypad fell silent and the night grew still again. Riley drew a heavy breath and exhaled to slow his driving pulse.

He stood in the doorway next to the keypad and looked across a narrow hallway and into the interior of the main house. He could see the formal living room and, through the front windows, a multi-tiered fountain that was topped with a heavy bronze statue and surrounded by formal gardens.

"How'd you know that would work?" Amie asked. Riley turned and could just make out her shadow moving towards the desk on the far side of the library. Seconds later, Amie located a silver lamp at the corner of the desk and a muted yellow light filtered through the room.

"I didn't," Riley admitted. "I just guessed."

Amie leaned on the desk to catch her breath. "Good guess," she said. "I damn near had a heart attack. Why the hell didn't Baggett just tell us there was an alarm?"

Riley reached for the French door, which was still open. "Who knows," he said as he pushed the door to a quiet close. He walked over to the desk and, for the first time, Riley and Amie took a moment to look around the room. With a large central sitting area and two stories of floor-to-ceiling bookshelves, the room felt enormous. But it wasn't the size of the room that was so discouraging.

"That's an awful lot of paintings," Amie said, taking a quick inventory. "Must be a few of dozen of them down here alone."

Riley remained optimistic. "Yeah. But remember, *'Walker and Halley show the way'*," he said, quoting the Will from memory. "We're looking for a Harold Walker painting that includes a picture of someone named Halley. Surely Walker didn't paint all of these," he said, hopefully. He took a quick look around the room and saw the spiral staircase in the back corner. "I'll start upstairs. You want to take a look down here?"

"Okay."

Riley headed upstairs and Amie got straight to work. She started by the door and slowly worked her way along the wall, carefully examining each painting in turn. She had hoped that most of the paintings were created by artists other than Walker but her hopes disappeared as she made her way down the length of the room. "Walker painted all of these," she called up to Riley.

"Same thing up here," Riley called down from above. "Most of the frames have the title of the painting at the bottom. There has to be a painting of someone named Halley in here somewhere. We just have to keep looking."

Riley watched from above as Amie got back to work. Then he turned to resume his own search.

He looked at one painting after another. Their subjects varied wildly: there were seascapes, landscapes, still lifes and portraits all interspersed together. Virtually all of them were Walker's. "Did Varden buy every painting this guy ever made?" Riley wondered aloud as he finished his search of the first wall.

When he turned the corner, something overhead caught his eye. The enormous mural spanned the length of the room and covered the ceiling with a swirling scene of dark versus light. Riley scanned the entire image, but his eye was immediately drawn to the bright orb streaking across the middle of the sky. His mind turned as he struggled to make out the details of the object in the dim light of the desk lamp below. Could it be?

He eagerly shifted his gaze to the top of the staircase, where he spotted a light switch. Quickly, he stepped over and flipped the switch, flooding the room with light.

"What're you doing?" Amie asked urgently from below. Riley didn't hear her. His entire focus was on the object painted at the center of the ceiling. It was a giant ball of white light with a series of long tails streaming far behind. In that instant, Riley knew what the object had to be. It was Halley's Comet.

Walker and Halley show the way, he said to himself. But how? Then, it hit him. He grabbed the railing and ran down the spiral staircase to the ground floor. Standing at the base of the stairs, he looked up at the ceiling and was mesmerized by the intensity of the scene above. The dark blues and black of the night sky spread from the far end of the room. At the opposite end, the yellows and pinks of the morning sun burst towards the middle of the ceiling where they clashed with the night sky in a violent explosion of color. There, at the center, Halley's Comet sped into battle like a missile from the night.

Amie walked to Riley's side. "What is it?" she asked eagerly, looking up at the ceiling and then back at Riley.

"Halley's Comet," he said.

Amie's eyes shifted back to the ceiling. When she saw the speeding comet, she knew he was right. "Good Lord," she said. "Halley's Comet. We should've thought of that."

Riley pulled the will from his back pocket and unfolded it. He had the passage memorized but wanted to make sure he got it right. "Walker and Halley show the way to where the cause and effect reside," he read aloud. Then he looked up at the ceiling.

"Halley shows the way," he said softly as he studied the trajectory of the comet. His eyes followed the invisible path drawn from the center of the dust tail through the nucleus of the comet. It pointed towards the far side of the study. When he traced the path across the room, his heart sank. The comet pointed to the left of the door leading into the study. *It's just a wall*, Riley thought in disbelief. *There's nothing there but more paintings.*

Frustrated, Riley turned towards Amie and was surprised to see a broad smile on her face. "What?" he asked. Amie reached for Riley's arm and pulled him towards her. She looked up at the ceiling and positioned Riley directly under the nucleus of the comet. Following her gaze, Riley looked up at the ceiling. "What is it?" he asked again when Amie had set him in place.

"Look," she said, pointing across the room. When Riley looked in the direction of Amie's outstretched finger, he understood why she was smiling. The line of the comet didn't point to the wall, it pointed through the door at the other end of the library. And standing directly beneath the comet, the angle of doorways between the study and the adjacent hall left only a small gap that allowed Riley to see across the living area and out the front windows to the formal garden. Through the narrow gap in the doors, only one object was visible in the distance: a multi-tiered marble fountain topped with a bronze statue of two men.

Riley looked back at Amie. "Holy shit."

"Come on," Amie replied, grabbing Riley's hand and stepping towards the door.

CHAPTER 23

Sonofabitch!" Coffman exclaimed, storming down the brick walkway of Shea Baggett's Highland Park home. Reaching the black sedan at the end of the path, he threw open the passenger door and hopped inside. He turned the ignition and the onboard computer system came to life. "Someone give me Varden's address," he snapped at the other three F.B.I. agents, who were now standing on the sidewalk awaiting instruction.

Shorney removed a notepad from his coat pocket and flipped through the pages. "1880 Crestlake."

Coffman entered the information into the computer's GPS program. As the computer calculated the route, Coffman turned back to his men to confirm what they'd learned from their conversation with Baggett. "We know Riley came here to ask about the will. We know he was with a woman that Baggett claims he didn't know. We know Baggett told them the provision had something to do with Varden's library. And we know they left here almost an hour ago."

"I think Baggett knows who the woman is," Shorney said.

"So do I," Coffman agreed. "But we don't have time to pull it out of him. We've got her picture from the surveillance cameras. It's not the best picture, but it's good enough. We'll find her." Coffman glanced at the GPS, which displayed the shortest route to Varden's estate. "Varden's place is about twenty minutes from here."

"That's too long," Shorney observed. "Riley could be long gone by then. DPD can be there in five. Want me to call it in?"

Coffman's blood boiled in an instant. "Have you lost your fucking mind?" he fumed. "We can't use locals. Locals will ask questions. Locals will fuck this whole thing up! This is a Federal case. We will not call Dallas Police. You understand?"

All three men nodded their understanding. "Yes, sir," Agent Brandt affirmed.

"What about Baggett?" Shorney asked.

Coffman glanced back at the house and made a quick decision. "Leave him," he ordered. "Let's go."

The men sprang into action. Seconds later, the two black sedans sped off into the night.

Joseph woke when the overhead speaker crackled to life. "The captain has illuminated the fasten seatbelt sign, indicating we have begun our descent into Chicago's O'Hare International Airport."

Joseph lifted the window shade to see the waters of Lake Michigan below and the bright lights of Chicago just ahead. As he stared down at the city lights, Joseph became lost in his own thoughts. So far, his role in Samuel's plan had been peripheral. For the most part, he'd pick up messages or items from dead drops around the city and either took them to another dead drop or to the lab in Georgetown. But things were different now.

The task before him was like nothing Joseph had ever done. *People always talk big,* Joseph thought. He'd been around such people most of his life. Joseph's father and brother had always talked about fighting back, but they never had the courage. Joseph was determined to be different.

The next twenty-four hours would change his life and, perhaps, the world. He would soon pass the point of no return. The mission ahead was both dangerous and gut wrenching. But it had to be done. *All is lost unless you succeed,* Samuel had told him.

"It's now time that we ask you to turn off all portable electronic devices and return your seatbacks and tray tables to their full and upright position." Joseph pressed the button on the side of the armrest and his seat returned to the uncomfortable ninety-degree position. He glanced down at his watch. It was late. He'd have to find a hotel near the target and wait until morning.

The plane shook as it descended through a pocket of warm air and Joseph's stomach churned. He closed his eyes and waited for the plane to land.

CHAPTER 24

Riley's eyes were still on the comet streaking across the ceiling when Amie grabbed his hand and led him across the library. "Hold on," Riley said when they reached the doorway. He flipped the light switch beside the door and cast the library back into darkness.

They stood in the threshold for a moment and, as their eyes adjusted, they noticed a shimmering white light filtering into the library. Tracing the light across the floor and out the front windows, they once again saw the fountain in the distance.

"Come on," Amie said, stepping cautiously into the hallway and crossing into the formal living room. The high ceilings and hard surfaces throughout the room amplified their every movement as they made their way to the front of the house. The front door was made of thick wrought iron that overlaid a double paned sheet of glass. Amie unlocked the heavy deadbolt and, with some effort, opened the door to let in the cool night air. They stepped outside and followed the granite walkway down to the formal gardens.

Amie led the way through the sculpted hedges towards the center of the garden. The sound of crashing water grew louder with each step until it reached a crescendo at the base of the fountain. A cool mist filled the air as the water cascaded down the white marble structure. "What's the will say again?" Amie asked.

This time, Riley recited it from memory. "Walker and Halley show the way to where the cause and effect reside. The feet of giants cannot crush the truth they try to hide." Riley looked up at the back of the bronze figures standing over the rushing waters. The figures didn't look like giants. "Cause and effect...feet of giants," Riley repeated as he circled the base of the fountain.

Arriving at the other side of the fountain, Riley looked back up at the statue. Two life-sized men were cast in bronze in the middle of a heated debate. On the left, a tall man in a lab coat stood with a clipboard tucked under one arm and his other arm outstretched. He was lecturing and pointing down to a second man who was sitting calmly, wearing a three-piece suit and a knowing smile.

"Thomas Weller and Jonas Salk," said Amie.

Riley looked over to see Amie standing beside him. "Who?" he asked.

Amie pointed to a bronze plaque at the base of the figures. "Thomas Weller and Jonas Salk," she repeated with a smile. "That's clever, considering whose fountain this is."

"I've heard of Jonas Salk. He developed the polio vaccine. But who's Thomas Weller?" Riley asked.

"Weller was the first person to grow the polio virus in a lab. Without Weller, Salk couldn't have developed his famous vaccine."

Riley looked up at the faces of the bronzed men. "Virus and anti-virus. Cause and effect," he said as a smile crept onto his face. "That's clever. What these guys did for medicine is what Varden did for computer security."

"Exactly. And there's no doubt they're *giants* in their field," Amie observed.

"The feet of giants cannot crush the truth they try to hide," Riley recited the provision from the will again. He looked at the men's feet, just above the base of the statue. A gust of wind dusted Amie and Riley with the cold spray from the fountain. "Flip you for it," Riley said, half-heartedly.

Amie looked up at the bronze men towering overhead and the water crashing around on all sides. "Not a chance," Amie chuckled.

Riley glanced down at the pool surrounding the central structure of the fountain and let out a heavy sigh. He sat on the stone ledge and pulled off his loafers before swinging his legs around and slowly dropping them into the water. A wave of goose bumps covered Riley's body as his feet touched the surface of the water. The water line was just above Riley's knees when his feet found the bottom of the pool.

His feet firmly planted, Riley considered his options. The fountain was constructed of three basins stacked on top of one another like a tiered wedding cake. Above the highest basin, water rushed from beneath the statue and cascaded down the concentric levels until it splashed into the pool below.

The feet of giants, Riley said to himself as he looked up at the statue. Weller and Salk's feet stood at least fifteen feet above. Riley shook his head. *How the hell'd I get myself into this?* Then he stood and waded slowly into the fountain.

Cold water ran down the front of Riley's shirt and pants as his chest met the lip of the lower basin. Placing both hands on top of the stone, Riley climbed up to the top of the ledge and sat with his legs dangling over the side. Cool water rushed all around him and over the edge of the basin to the pool below. Without hesitation, he spun in place and attacked the fountain's upper tiers.

In seconds, Riley was standing in the top pool. His clothes were completely soaked. He looked up at the bronze faces and down to their feet. *The feet of giants*, he repeated. Pushing forward, Riley waded to the center of the fountain and immediately began his search. He grabbed the bronzed wingtip shoes of the Salk statue and began lifting and pulling at them with all his strength. The statue didn't move. He turned to the feet of the Weller statue but the solid metal figure refused to give way.

"Sonofabitch!" Riley yelled in frustration. *Think, dammit! The feet of giants...the feet of giants,* he repeated silently as he studied the placement of the bronze shoes. It was then that he noticed each man had one foot extended out in front of the other. The tips of the men's shoes almost touched. Together, they formed a type of crude arrow that pointed to the center of the pedestal and the bronze plaque below.

Desperate to find something, Riley grabbed the edges of the plaque with both hands. Anticipating resistance from the thick metal panel, he coiled his body and pulled hard. It instantly gave way and sent Riley stumbling backwards with the bronze plaque held high in his hands. The water splashed around him as he struggled to regain his balance. Still reeling, his foot hit the curved wall of the basin, causing him to lean dangerously close to the edge. Instinctively, he twisted his body and threw his hands out to catch himself. The plaque flew through the air, clattered over the edge and splashed down to the pool far below.

Riley was on all fours in the top basin when he heard Amie's voice over the sound of rushing water. "You okay?"

"No," Riley responded, soaking wet and feeling stupid. Slowly, he got to his feet and turned back to the statue. His eyes darted to where the plaque had been, but instead of seeing the solid white marble of the statue's pedestal, he saw a small rectangular cavity. Riley stared at the hole in disbelief. *Sonofabitch.* Anxious to finally know what this was all about, he waded to the pedestal and thrust his hand into the narrow opening.

Moving his hand over the interior surfaces of the cavity, Riley felt only cold, damp stone. With some trepidation, he pushed his hand deeper inside. His arm was now buried deep into the pedestal and Riley began to wonder if they had made a terrible mistake. Then, something moved almost imperceptibly beneath his fingers. He ran his fingers back and felt it again. He searched for the edge of the object, which was thin and flexible. Finding the corner, Riley grabbed it and began pulling it from the hole.

When the object emerged, Riley turned it in his hands. It was a black rubber bag about six inches long. The top of the bag had been rolled over several times and was sealed shut with a plastic buckle. It was a waterproof bag, designed to keep its contents completely dry. To avoid opening the bag around all the water, he pressed on its exterior to determine whether anything was inside. It seemed completely empty until he reached the bottom, where he felt something hard. And in that moment, Riley knew he'd found what Christoph Varden had tried so desperately to hide.

Needing both hands to climb down, Riley held the bag with his teeth and began his slow, watery descent. Arriving at the lower pool, he turned and Amie saw the black bag for the first time. "You found it?" she asked excitedly.

Riley pulled the bag from his mouth and waded over to the edge of the pool. "I think so. I found something," he said, stepping over the marble ledge and onto dry land. Riley handed the bag to Amie. "Take a look."

Amie opened the buckle and unrolled the top of the bag. She slipped her hand inside and grasped the object at the bottom. Pulling it out, Amie held it in her outstretched hand for Riley to see.

"It's a thumb drive," he said, disappointed. "That doesn't tell us anything."

"No," Amie agreed. "But what's on it might."

With Varden's Will finally deciphered and the thumb drive in hand, Riley was anxious to leave. He slipped his wet feet back into his loafers. "Let's get out of here."

"Great idea," Amie said, needing no convincing. She led the way out of the garden and around the mansion to the back gate, where they slipped silently out of the property. The engine of Amie's SUV came to life and echoed off the limestone wall as the car sped down the darkened road. They were turning out of the neighborhood when Amie looked in her rearview mirror and saw flashing blue lights in the distance.

CHAPTER 25

Agent Shorney pointed out the front window of the speeding car. "There it is," he said, reading the street sign ahead. Coffman slowed to make the turn onto Varden's street. He'd been to the estate many times during the initial murder investigation and had become familiar with the neighborhood's layout.

"There," Coffman said, pointing towards the enormous limestone blocks of the wall surrounding Varden's mansion. Seeing the black granite driveway ahead, Coffman hit the brakes, casting the surrounding estate walls in a dim red glow. He rolled down the window and pulled to a stop in the drive. "What's the number?"

Shorney removed a small notepad from his inside jacket pocket. Flipping to the last page, he found the six-digit code, "157917." Coffman reached out the driver's window and punched the numbers on the metal keypad beside the driveway. Hitting the last number, the heavy iron gates slowly opened.

Waiting, Coffman's mind raced around the possible consequences of Varden's Will. "I hope Varden didn't do anything stupid," he said.

"I hope Riley's smart enough not to get involved," Shorney added. Coffman knew there was little chance Riley would turn back now. He'd broken into his friend's law office and followed Varden's will to Shea Baggett. Riley seemed determined to continue down this very dangerous path.

The gates finally opened and Coffman eased the car up the drive. He parked by the garage and grabbed a flashlight from the center console. "Let's go," he said. Shorney was already reaching for the door handle.

They got out of the car to find Agents Bauer and Brandt walking up the driveway from the car behind. Coffman wasted no time. "You two head around front. We'll go around the back." Bauer and Brandt sprang into action and disappeared around the front of the mansion. "Come on," Coffman said, leading the way around back.

The back of the house was completely dark. The agents moved quietly past a small gurgling fountain in the center of the courtyard and arrived at the terrace, where Coffman slowed and held a hand up. Shorney stopped instantly and looked for any movement in the courtyard behind while Coffman inspected the yellow police tape that blocked the terrace entrance.

"Doesn't look like anyone's tampered with the tape," he said. "Maybe Riley didn't come here after all," Coffman hoped. He pulled out a small knife and sliced through the tape. Returning the knife to his pocket, he quietly stepped onto the terrace.

Approaching the French doors, Coffman could see the interior of the library was completely dark. He pressed his back against the white stone wall beside the door and slowly turned his head to get a better look inside. Unable to see through the darkness, he reached across the door and tested the silver handle. With little effort, the handle gave way and the door clicked open. *Shit.* He knew the F.B.I. had locked the door upon closing the crime scene. Someone had recently unlocked it and Coffman knew it had to be Riley.

He drew his Glock 22 from the holster and turned back to see that Agent Shorney had done the same. "Let's go," he said, opening the door with a heavy push. The agents charged into the room. The light from Coffman's flashlight slashed through the darkness. Coffman swept the room, his gun trained on the center of the flashlight's beam.

Keeping an eye on the interior of the library, Shorney felt along the wall and found a light switch. Flipping the switch, the room filled with light. The agents moved quickly, searching behind the desk, chairs and couch with coordinated movements. Coffman dropped the flashlight on the couch and gripped his gun with both hands before crossing the room and pushing open the bathroom door with his foot.

"Clear," he said, his voice echoing off the hard tile surfaces.

"Clear," Shorney repeated as he finished his visual scan of the upper balcony.

Coffman stepped back into the study and surveyed the cavernous two-story room. The dark leathers and wood, combined with the floor-to-ceiling bookshelves created a warm and inviting feel. Various works of art were displayed throughout the room and covered the tables and the library walls. The sheer size of the room drew Coffman's eyes upward to the second floor balcony and on towards the ceiling. His gaze froze upon the painting that spanned the entire length of the room.

It was like nothing Coffman had ever seen and his reaction was immediate. Somehow he knew the extraordinary painting held the answer to Varden's riddle. "Check the next room," he directed Shorney, who turned and left the library. Looking up at the ceiling, Coffman stepped to the middle of the room. He squinted up at the tempest of color at the center of the painting. *Walker and Halley show the way.* As he trained his mind on the possible connection, his radio crackled to life.

"Coffman," came Brandt's voice from the speaker.

Frustrated at the interruption, Coffman pulled the radio from his belt. "What?"

"You should come out front," Brandt said. "We may have found something."

Coffman glanced up at the ceiling and then back down to the radio. "On my way," he said and headed to the front of the house. Entering the formal living area, he looked out the front windows to see Agent Brandt walking up to the house from the garden. They met on the front porch, "What do you got?" demanded Coffman.

"We did a quick sweep of the gardens," Brandt began, leading Coffman down the granite path towards the large marble fountain. "We'd cleared the far side and were working our way back towards the house when we saw something odd."

Coffman had no patience for riddles. "Well? What was it?" he demanded as they reached the far side of the fountain.

Brandt stopped and pointed down into the lower pool. "We saw that," he said.

Brandt pointed to a bronze plaque lying on the floor of the fountain. Through the ripples in the water, Coffman could just make out the names etched in bronze relief: *T. WELLER & J. SALK.* Coffman was about to say *"So?"* when Brandt spoke again. "And then we saw that." This time, Brandt pointed to the top of the fountain, where a dark cavity sat at the base of the statue.

A green stain from the bronze figures ran down from above and outlined the opening in a perfect rectangle. As Coffman's eyes went from the stained opening to the plaque and back again, he made the connection. The plaque that was now discarded in the bottom pool was once covering the hole above. Coffman quickly made another connection.

"Wait here," he ordered and then he ran back to the house. He stormed through the front door and went straight to the center of the library. Standing directly beneath the comet painted on the ceiling, he turned back towards the front of the house. He traced the comet's invisible path, which passed through the narrow gap in the doorway, out the front windows, and into the gardens. When he saw where the path led, a knot tightened in his stomach. It led directly to the fountain and to Varden's secret compartment. Halley's Comet had shown the way.

Coffman snapped the radio from his belt. "Brandt. Get up there and see what's in that hole."

"Sir?" Brandt responded, clearly hoping he had misheard the order.

"Get up there and look inside that hole!" Coffman repeated.

"Yes, sir," Brandt said hesitantly.

By the time Coffman made it back outside, Brandt was climbing out of the lower pool, soaking wet. "Well?" Coffman asked.

"It's empty," Brandt responded, trying to catch his breath.

Coffman dropped his head in disbelief and stared at the plaque lying on the bottom of the fountain. He knew Varden's secret was out and that Riley now possessed a copy of the one thing that was certain to get him killed.

Reluctantly, Coffman pulled out his cell phone and called his superiors.

CHAPTER 26

Tucked into a wooded area just east of downtown Dallas sat the quiet neighborhood of Greenland Hills, though few called it by that name. Because all the streets began with the letter "M," the neighborhood was known simply as *The M Streets*. Developed in the early 1920's, The M Streets were made up of just under a thousand Tudor-style homes. The high-pitched roofs, pronounced gables, and stained glass windows gave the neighborhood a quaint and cohesive feel.

When she first came to Dallas, Amie fell in love with the small stone house on McCommas Boulevard at the northern end of The M Streets. The day that SMU called to offer her a teaching position, she bought it. Tonight, that house would provide a much needed sanctuary.

Amie and Riley needed a quiet place with a computer where they could open the flash drive in private. "I would say we could go to my apartment," Riley had said, "but I don't think it's safe."

Amie agreed. "Let's go to my place. I should have everything we need to access the drive." Deciding it was their best option, they drove across town.

Driving down lower Greenville Avenue near The M Streets, Riley stared silently out the passenger window. In an area known for its bustling nightlife, the streets were deserted and strangely peaceful at this late hour. "It's funny," Riley thought out loud, breaking the silence that had settled into the car.

"What's that?" Amie asked.

"How quickly life can change." Riley said, almost dreamily. "I was just out for a morning jog. Same place I've jogged for years. And then," Riley snapped his fingers, "utter chaos."

Amie chuckled. "Tell me about it. I was just sitting down with a cup of tea when you called." Riley turned and Amie could sense he was about to apologize. "But I'm glad you did," she said with a smile.

Riley suppressed his apology and smiled back. "Me too," he said.

Amie slowed the car and turned onto her street. "When this is over," she said, "you're going to owe me a significant bottle of wine."

Riley considered it playfully. "I suppose that's a reasonable price for breaking and entering. I hope your cell mate doesn't drink it all." The two of them exchanged a look and laughed as they rounded the block and turned into the alleyway behind Amie's house. She pressed the garage door opener on her visor and they pulled into the detached garage, which, due to the collection of boxes and spare computer parts stacked along the walls, barely had room for the car.

They squeezed out of the car and Amie closed the garage before they crossed the back yard and climbed the stone stairs to the back door. They entered through the kitchen and Amie threw her keys on the counter as she stepped inside. She looked back at Riley and, seeing him in the light of the kitchen, noticed his wet clothes were sticking to his body.

"You look miserable," she said. "You want me to throw those clothes in the dryer?"

"Please," he said, glancing around. "You got anything for me to change into?"

"There's a robe hanging on the back of the bathroom door. It may be a little small but it's the only thing I have that may fit."

"Thanks," Riley said, walking to the bathroom. While Riley changed, Amie made a pot of tea and was setting the tray down in the living room when she heard the bathroom door open.

"In here," she called. Riley emerged wearing a thick terry cloth robe and holding his wet clothes out in a bundle. "Oh," Amie said, walking towards him. "I'll take those. You get some tea. I have some coffee cake there as well."

"Thanks," Riley said, as Amie took his clothes and walked past him towards the dryer. By the time she got back, Riley had poured two cups of tea and was working on a piece of cake.

"Now," she said, grabbing a cup of tea and sitting down at her desk, "let's see what all this mess is about." She held up the flash drive and inserted it into the front of the computer. Riley shifted his position on the couch to see the monitor.

"What do we got?" Riley asked excitedly. Amie was still clicking on the keyboard.

With the final press of a button, she stared intently at the screen. "I'm not sure, actually. There are three files. Two of them are encrypted. But this one," she clicked on a file, which instantly launched the word processing application. "This one's not," she said, curiously.

Riley edged closer to the screen. As the program finished opening, he expected to see a copy of the document. Instead he saw, a small dialog box in the center of the screen.

"Figures," Amie said to herself.

"What's wrong?" Riley asked.

"It's password protected." Riley's head dropped with disappointment. "Not to worry," Amie continued lightly. "This is easy to break. There are tons of ways to crack open a document." Amie pecked at the keyboard.

"Great," Riley sighed and leaned back into the couch. "How long will that take?"

"If we were in my lab at the school, we'd break it in no time. But I don't have the same tools or computing power here. We'll have to let it run for awhile." Amie clicked on the keyboard for a few minutes and one program after another began to appear on the screen. With the programs up and running, Amie stood and took another sip of tea. "There's not much more we can do until this finishes up," she said, motioning to the screen. "I think I'm going to turn in for the night." The two of them looked at one another and an unfamiliar tension filled the room.

"You have a blanket I can use?" Riley asked, fidgeting and sizing up the couch.

"Don't be silly, Michael," Amie said with a smile. "You can sleep in the bed. I think it'll be okay." Riley gave her a grateful smile and then slowly stood to follow Amie back to the bedroom where they fell instantly asleep.

CHAPTER 27

Joseph crouched in the juniper bushes between the historic houses, and he watched. The neighborhood was so quiet he could hardly believe it was only fifteen miles from the bustling city of Chicago and its 2.7 million residents. *Quiet is good,* Joseph thought. It would help ensure no one knew he was ever there.

He looked through the evergreen branches and studied the structure across the street. It was a two-story, brick and limestone house, exactly as Samuel had described. Four sets of windows with black shutters were spaced evenly across both floors. In the center of the ground floor sat the red front door he had been watching for more than an hour.

Joseph glanced at his watch. *He's running late,* he said to himself. Minutes later, the door began to open and Joseph's muscles flexed in anticipation.

The door opened slowly and Joseph could just make out the murmur of a conversation within. A thin and balding man emerged from the house and stepped out onto the front walkway. He was dressed casually in jeans and a light sweater. Joseph watched as the man closed the door, slung a green backpack onto his shoulder and headed towards the street.

Joseph's eyes cut back to the house when the door opened again and a three-year-old girl wearing a pink princess dress and a tiara ran out into the front yard. "Come and get me, Daddy! Come and get me!" she laughed as she ran circles in the yard. Her father, who had just reached the street, turned and flashed an enormous smile at the sight of his daughter. He set his bag on the curb and hunched over. Shaping his hands into a pair of claws, he crept across the yard.

"I'm going to get you and eat you for breakfast, little Anju!" he said with a snarl as he clamped his imaginary claws.

"No! No! Don't eat me!" she screamed with laughter, running in ever-faster circles. The man was getting close when the door opened for a third time.

"Anju!" the mother snapped. Anju stopped in her tracks and looked over at her mother. Just then, the man grabbed her and began tickling her stomach.

"I've got you! And I'm so hungry, I may just eat you right now!" He bent down and pressed his mouth to her stomach.

"Sheetal!" yelled the mother again. "You're going to miss your train," she said with forced harshness, but couldn't help but smile.

"Okay, okay," Sheetal said, straightening Anju's dress. "I'll have to eat you after work." He kissed Anju on the forehead and she ran back to the house. Sheetal looked up at his wife, who was staring at him with playful disbelief. "Sorry," he said, throwing his hands up in surrender. "I'm going."

He stood and as he crossed the yard, his wife called out to him. "I love you."

Sheetal picked up his bag and turned back to see her standing in the doorway. "I love you to, Hil." He turned towards the train station and the red door shut again.

Joseph smiled. The scene he had just witnessed confirmed beyond a doubt that they had picked the right man. He looked down at his watch. Sheetal's train for downtown Chicago was scheduled to leave in ten minutes. If he missed his train and came back to the house, all would be lost. So Joseph watched and waited. Twenty minutes later, he knew Sheetal was speeding towards his downtown office. It was time.

Joseph unzipped the duffle bag at his feet. He pulled out a black jacket, put it on and zipped it to the top of the collar. Reaching into the jacket pockets, he removed a pair of black gloves and slipped them on. He patted the inside jacket pocket to confirm his final article of clothing was still there. Looking into the bag, he took an inventory of the remaining items. He had everything he needed.

Joseph grabbed the bag and waded through the bushes. Arriving on the other side, he took one last look around. The quaint neighborhood street was calm and quiet. Joseph turned his attention to the red door and walked directly towards the house, his thoughts consumed with the task at hand. He stepped up onto the covered front porch, where he quietly set the black duffle bag down by his feet.

Unzipping his jacket, Joseph pulled a black ski mask from the inside pocket and rolled it down over his head and face. The eye and mouth holes of the mask were encircled with a jagged red stitching that caught in Joseph's peripheral vision as the mask fell into place. He reached towards the doorbell, but stopped short upon seeing his gloved hand shaking in front of him. It wasn't fear or second thoughts that caused him to tremble – the time for second thoughts had long since past. It was the sudden burst of adrenaline coursing through his veins. He took several deep breaths to steady his hand before picking up the duffle bag and pressing the doorbell.

Inside, Anju was just settling into her highchair for breakfast when the doorbell rang. Hillary locked the highchair's table into place before rounding the corner and crossing the living room to the front door. She turned the doorknob and the door flew open with a violent kick. Hillary's heart pounded with fear and she stumbled backwards from the force of the blow. Staggering, her foot caught on the corner of the rug and she fell hard to the floor.

Before she could open her eyes, she felt the heaviness of someone straddling her and pinning her hands and shoulders to the floor. When she saw the black ski mask, she let out a gut-wrenching scream that was quickly muffled by the cold, leather-gloved hand of her assailant. She kicked and fought to break free, her muted screams intensifying as the hopelessness of her struggle grew. She twisted her head violently from side to side, trying to release the full force of her screams from beneath the man's hand.

"Shut up," said Joseph over the muted screams. "Shut your fucking mouth!" he ordered, but the woman kicked and screamed louder against the sound of Joseph's voice. Knowing she had to be silenced, Joseph reached behind his back and grabbed the heavy handle of his hunting knife. Drawing the knife from its sheath, he swung it around and held its pointed tip an inch from the woman's eye.

"You'll shut your mouth or I'll carve your fucking eye out," he said, circling the blade slowly over her eyelid. Hilary's eyes widened and her body froze with fear as a tear rolled down the side of her face. "That's right," Joseph said approvingly. "Now, I'm going to take my hand off of your mouth. If you say one word, I won't start with *your* eye," he said, shaking his head slowly from side to side. "I'll start with hers." He pointed the knife towards the kitchen. Hilary's eyes welled with tears and she began to cry. "Do you understand?" he asked.

Her eyes pinched shut, Hillary nodded her understanding and sobbed through the gloved hand that was still held tight against her mouth. "Good," said Joseph, slowly lifting his hand from her face. He placed the cold tip of the knife to the woman's throat. "Now," he said, "You're going to get Anju and we're going to take a drive."

CHAPTER 28

Michael Riley awoke with a chill. He'd kicked his blanket to the floor during the night and found himself lying on the bed in a robe that, in its twisted state, exposed far more than it covered. He grabbed the bottom flap and pulled it over his leg. Blinking hard to clear his head, he swung his legs to the floor and tightened the robe around him. Amie was still sound asleep, so Riley stepped quietly from the bedroom and closed the door.

Curious if the computer had cracked the password, he went to the desk and clicked the mouse. The screen came to life with a picture of a sprawling vineyard. A second later, a text box appeared requiring a username and password. *Figures.* He'd have to wait until Amie woke up. Riley headed to the kitchen to make some coffee but stopped short when he saw his reflection in the hallway mirror. The borrowed robe was at least two sizes too small and Riley chuckled at how ridiculous he looked. He decided he'd better change and found the laundry room.

He pulled on his jeans and button down shirt and slipped on his loafers. Slightly more presentable, he was searching the kitchen for the coffee filters when he heard a dog barking outside. Dogs were common in this neighborhood but the intensity of the bark put Riley on edge. He stood in the kitchen, transfixed as the ferocious bark grew to a fevered pitch. Suddenly, there was a sharp yelp and the dog went silent.

Riley's skin grew warm as his body went on high alert. Something felt terribly wrong. He stepped to the kitchen window and lifted a slat in the mini-blinds. Scanning the back yard and the perimeter of the fence, everything appeared to be in place. Riley breathed a sigh of relief. His imagination was getting the better of him.

He took one last look around and caught something moving out of the corner of his eye. His pulse quickened. A tall shadow appeared from the alley, moving slowly along the fence line towards the garage. Further down the fence, a missing board allowed a narrow view into the alley. Riley focused on the gap and waited while the dark figure continued its path. When it crossed the break in the fence, the image flashed by in a second – the athletic build, the cropped blonde hair. Riley's muscles tensed. There was no mistake.

Riley ran to the bedroom and threw open the door. Instinctively, he looked to the bedroom window, but the heavy curtains blocked his view.

"Amie," he said anxiously as he approached the bedside. She was still asleep beneath a thick down comforter. Riley reached for her leg. "Amie! Wake up!" he said, giving her leg an urgent shake. Amie's eyes popped open and she sat up in bed.

"What's wrong?" she asked, hearing the panic in Riley's voice.

"He's found us," Riley responded in a loud whisper. Amie was wearing little more than a thin tank top. "You better get dressed," he said. Amie threw the covers aside and swung her bare legs to the floor.

"Who?" she pressed, hardly wanting to hear the truth. She grabbed a pair of jeans from the chair beside her bed. "Who's found us?"

Riley stepped over to the window and moved the curtains to peek into the back yard, but the angle of the garage blocked his view. "Isaac," he said, turning from the window. "Isaac's found us."

Amie's expression twisted in fear. "Isaac? How's that possible? How could he find us here?"

"I've got a guess. But we've got to get out of here. We need that document off your computer. What's your username and password?"

Amie stepped into her jeans. "ahawkins, Macy2003 with a capital M" she said.

Riley ran down the hall to the living room. The picture of the vineyard was still up on the screen when he arrived and pushed the desk chair to the side. Attacking the keyboard, Riley typed in the username and password. "Come on," he quietly urged as the password was accepted and the vineyard vanished. He had expected to see the document open at the center of the screen but instead, he saw several layers of text windows with lines of indecipherable computer code.

"Sonofabitch!" Riley scanned the screen, trying to make some sense of it all. His eyes darted from one window to the next, but it was no use. Beads of sweat formed on his forehead as panic set in. He reached for the mouse to start clicking boxes at random when he felt a soft hand cover his own.

"Let me do this," said Amie firmly.

Riley stepped away from the desk. "I'll watch the back." He ran to the kitchen and returned to the window. His eyes swept to the small gate near the garage and the metal latch that held it closed. Moments passed. There was no shadow, no movement. But then, a glint of sunlight flashed off the handle and a sliver of light appeared down the length of the gate as it slowly opened.

Riley's heart pounded against his chest. He yelled over his shoulder, "He's coming in the gate! Hurry!"

Amie worked frantically at the keyboard. Scanning the lines of computer code, she finally saw the password: Echelon. She moused over the password and quickly copied the text. Turning to the desktop, she pasted the password into the Varden document.

Riley watched through the blinds as Isaac stepped quietly into the yard and closed the gate. "He's coming!" Riley said again, dropping the blind to ensure Isaac didn't see him through the window. He hurried back to the living room where Amie was just opening the document.

"It's a letter!" she said excitedly. She'd started to scan the contents when Riley grabbed the mouse from her hand and sent the letter to the printer.

"We don't have time," he said. "We've got to get out of here!" The printer whined and pulled a piece of paper from the tray below. They stood by the front door, waiting anxiously for the page to print. The letter was emerging from the top of the printer when the sound of breaking glass pierced the air.

Amie spun towards the sound, the warmth of adrenaline spreading over her body. "Holy shit!" she said, looking back at the printer.

Riley placed his hand over the page, ready to grab it the instant it was ready. "Come on!" Riley yelled, but the printer kept its slow pace, indifferent to the urgent situation. Then, another crash shot from the back of the house. The sounds of splintered wood and shattered glass were unmistakable. Isaac had kicked in the kitchen door. He was in the house.

Riley looked at Amie and down at the printer, which continued its mechanical whir. Slowly, the last line of text printed to the page and the paper fell into the tray. Riley grabbed the letter and threw open the front door. They dashed outside and had reached the edge of the front porch when Amie suddenly stopped.

"Shit," she said, then turned and ran back into the house.

Riley couldn't believe it. *What the hell is she doing?* He stood on the porch, paralyzed. Just as he turned to go after her, Amie reappeared at the door.

"Let's go," she said holding up the black flash drive she'd just retrieved from the computer. She ran past Riley and into the front yard. Riley was right behind her as she cut across the grass.

Isaac burst into the kitchen with a heavy kick of his combat boot. Drawing his black H&K pistol, he peered down the sightline as he stepped over the shards of glass and wood that now covered the floor. He searched the kitchen and bedroom in seconds. Seeing no one, he turned down the hall to search the front of the house. His finger tensed on the trigger and he swung into the living room. The room was empty and the front door wide open.

Isaac ran to the door and stepped outside. He looked to the neighbor's house, then across the road, searching for any signs of movement. His eyes swept the horizon and down the street. Then he saw them. Half way down the block Riley and Amie were running for their lives.

Isaac threw his gun in the holster beneath his jacket and sprinted after them. Within seconds, he was hurtling down the street towards his prey. His well-conditioned body had reached its full stride when Riley looked back and saw Isaac gaining ground. Riley and Amie doubled their efforts but it was no use. The longer the foot race continued, the more certain Isaac was to catch them.

They reached the intersection at Greenville Avenue with Isaac close behind. Riley looked down the street at the dozens of bars and restaurants. "This way," he said, grabbing Amie's hand and running across the street. Riley glanced quickly into each bar as they raced past, looking for anything that was open. Just ahead, he saw the red and white marquis of the Granada Theater. And there, just past the theater, he saw what he was looking for.

Snuffers was a locally-owned restaurant with a loyal breakfast crowd. Reaching the green front door, Riley and Amie stepped inside. The door closed and Amie looked through the window to see Isaac was only seconds away. "He's right behind us," she warned Riley.

"We can't outrun him. We're safer in here," Riley said, looking around the crowded room for a place to sit. There were two seats open at the far end of the bar. "Over here," he said. Doing their best to look like ordinary customers, they walked the length of the bar and sat down.

Riley looked back at the front door in time to see Isaac step inside. Isaac immediately scanned the restaurant. The dining room was packed with customers and he took his time completing the search before shifting his gaze down the length of the bar. When he saw Riley, Isaac's eyes narrowed and a smile appeared across his squared face. "Shit," said Riley, staring back at Isaac.

"Does he see us?" asked Amie, who'd been hiding her face since they sat down.

"He's looking right at me," said Riley, hardly moving his lips. Isaac was capable of anything and

Riley couldn't anticipate his next move. *He might just pull out his gun and start shooting,* Riley thought, watching for any sudden movements.

Just then, a man at the far end of the L-shaped bar took a last sip of coffee, stood up and walked past Isaac for the door. Isaac glanced at the chair and then back at Riley. The question spinning in Isaac's mind was obvious: *Should I sit and wait or just kill them right here in this crowded restaurant?* After a long moment, Isaac made his decision. Keeping his eyes locked on Riley, he stepped to the bar and sat down.

"What's he doing?" Amie asked, refusing to look.

"He's sitting at the other end of the bar, watching us."

"Great," replied Amie nervously.

Riley saw an opportunity. If Isaac was willing to sit there and wait, then they had some time to come up with a plan. He turned and looked around the restaurant. It was basically a rectangle with the bar on one side and the dining area on the other. The restrooms were in the back at the end of a short hallway. To the right of the hallway, a metal swinging door led into the kitchen. Riley turned back to the bar and an idea began to take shape.

He leaned close to Amie. "I think we need to split up."

Disapproval flashed across Amie's face. "What? Are you kidding me?"

"If we force him to choose between the two of us, he'll pick me."

"I'm not just leaving you here," Amie interrupted. "Besides, how can you be so sure?"

"I'm the one who saw him kill Alexander at the canal." Amie's expression changed from disapproval to concern. "And if you get out," Riley assured her, "then I can get out."

Amie thought for a moment. Splitting up would force Isaac's hand and, perhaps, provide the opportunity they needed. "What're you thinking?" she asked.

Riley glanced down the bar. Isaac was still seated at the other end, staring intently at his every move. Leaning closer to Amie, Riley explained his plan. When he was finished, he leaned back and tried to read Amie's expression. She was sitting with her eyes closed, playing through Riley's plan again in her mind. It was dangerous, but given the situation, it was probably the best they could do. Finally, she opened her eyes. "Okay."

"Alright," Riley responded. "Remember, don't worry about me. Just keep moving." Amie nodded reluctantly. "You ready?" Riley asked.

"No," she said, knowing she'd never be ready. Placing her hand on the bar, Amie turned slightly in her chair, creating a clear path to move. "Okay." She took a deep breath and waited for Riley's signal.

Riley looked back down the length of the bar and felt his pulse quicken as he met Isaac's unflinching stare. A flood of questions ran through his mind but it wasn't time for second guessing. It was time to get out of there. His eyes trained on Isaac, Riley reached over and touched Amie's hand. "Go!"

CHAPTER 29

Amie jumped up and walked towards the back of the restaurant. Seeing Amie on the move, Isaac gripped the bar and his body tensed in anticipation of the chase. But he hesitated when he saw Riley hadn't moved. He had to choose who to follow. Frustration fell heavily on Isaac's face as he wrestled with the decision. Knowing Riley was the one he needed most, Isaac's muscles slowly uncoiled and he settled back into his chair. His complete focus returned to the man who had witnessed his crimes.

Riley was both scared and relieved to see that he was right – he was Isaac's target. Had Isaac chased after Amie, Riley was fully prepared to take his chances by tackling the man in the middle of the restaurant. Thankfully, that didn't happen. Riley took a nervous look at his watch. Their timing would have to be perfect.

The plan had been for Amie to walk as casually as possible, but sensing the danger around her, Amie broke into a run as she reached the restrooms at the back of the restaurant. Before entering the hallway, she took a sharp right and pushed through the metal door and into the kitchen. A dozen workers in white uniforms were hard at work behind stainless steel appliances.

"Hey!" yelled a man from behind a warming station. "You can't be back here!"

Amie didn't break stride as she made her way to the back of the kitchen. She wove through the kitchen staff, who jumped out of the way like a parting sea. Reaching the back wall, she saw the heavy metal door that led to the alleyway behind the restaurant. She pushed hard on the silver handle that ran across its center. The door flew open and crashed against the side of the brick wall as Amie sprinted out of the building. She had only minutes to save Riley's life.

She ran down the sunlit alley behind the neighboring theater. Taking a hard right at the corner of the building, Amie jumped down the stairs leading to a passageway between the high brick walls of the theater and the adjacent bar. Her footsteps were still echoing off the walls when she reached the end of the passage and sprinted towards her house.

Her front door was wide open when she cleared the front steps. She ran straight through the living room and grabbed her bag from the leather chair on her way to the kitchen. Amie snatched her keys off the counter and ran out the splintered back door. Reaching the garage in seconds, she jumped in her car and pressed the button on her visor. The garage door slowly opened and Amie jammed the key into the ignition. The engine roared to life. The door was still opening when she threw the car into reverse and slammed on the accelerator.

The tires squealed in place before they gained traction and shot the car backwards. Suddenly, the car's roof rack collided hard with the garage door but Amie kept her foot on the gas. The crash of scraping metal echoed down the alley. Finally clear of the garage, Amie spun the wheel and slammed on the brakes before throwing the car into Drive and speeding off down the narrow alleyway.

Back at the restaurant, Riley glanced at the clock hanging over the bar. Every fiber of his body told him to run, but he had to give Amie time. *Two minutes,* he told himself, making a mental note of the exact time. *I'll give her two more minutes.* Riley's knee bounced nervously as he watched the second hand's deliberate tick. At the end of the bar, Isaac waited with immutable patience.

It was time. Riley turned in his chair to see into the main dining area. The restaurant staff was buzzing around the room refilling coffee mugs, seating guests and bussing tables. The kitchen door swung open and a tattooed waiter emerged holding a tray over his shoulder that was overloaded with plates and drinks. The waiter struggled to balance the load as he walked carefully down the aisle between the bar and the dining area. This was Riley's chance.

The waiter was only feet away and Riley tensed in anticipation. When the waiter passed his chair, Riley jumped off the barstool and ran towards the back of the restaurant. The clatter of dropped utensils and sounds of general commotion grew as, one-by-one, the patrons saw Riley making his escape. Then, as he threw open the kitchen door, Riley heard the crash of dishes and glass that he'd expected.

He looked over his shoulder and caught a glimpse of the tattooed waiter lying on his back in a pile of shattered ceramic dishes and food. Isaac had collided with the waiter and tripped over the debris as he forced his way past. The image vanished when the kitchen door closed behind him. Riley shot between the silver appliances, passing stunned kitchen workers along the way. When he reached the back wall, he heard Isaac bursting into the kitchen. Riley sprinted to the back door and slammed his body into the metal bar, releasing the latch and sending the door flying.

Isaac was bowling through the kitchen staff when Riley stepped outside. He looked down the alley and saw a familiar gray Volkswagen skidding to a halt a just few feet away. Amie had made it just in time. Riley ran to the car. Amie reached across the passenger seat and grabbed the handle. When the door opened, her frantic voice pierced the cool morning air. "He's right behind you!"

Riley grabbed the top of the doorframe and when he swung around to get in, he saw Isaac hurdling towards them. Isaac had reached the hood of the car when Riley jumped inside and slammed the door. Amie floored the accelerator and the car lurched forward. The side mirror clipped Isaac's torso with a loud thump and sent him tumbling to the ground.

"Mother fucker!" exclaimed Riley. He looked over his shoulder to see Isaac clutching his side and staring coldly at the speeding car.

"You okay?" asked Amie, glancing at Riley for any signs of injury.

"He's trying to kill me!" Riley yelled.

"Michael! Are you okay?" Amie repeated.

Hearing her for the first time, Riley turned back in his seat and took stock of his body. "Yeah. I think so."

They reached the end of the alley and took a hard right onto McCommas Boulevard. Amie accelerated through the red light at Greenville Avenue and sped down the quiet residential street. As their distance from Isaac grew, Riley's body slowly relaxed.

"Where are we going?" he asked.

"Far away from here," Amie said with no destination in mind. "Somewhere safe where we can read that stupid letter and find out what this is all about."

CHAPTER 30

Sarah was unsettled when she left the office in the back of the Georgetown laboratory. The abduction of Sheetal Aiyer's wife and daughter had gone as planned. While that meant the operation was still on track, the abduction raised far more questions than answers. By the time she reached her desk, Sarah's analytical mind was working carefully through the questions one by one.

She logged back into her computer and entered the complex password to open her encrypted email account. There was only one message, which appeared at the top of the screen. Sarah looked to make sure no one was around and then clicked on the email. The decryption process finished in seconds. When she read the text, the air instantly left the room. Sarah's heart pounded hard against her chest. The message was just two words long, but it answered all her questions. She knew exactly what she needed to do. Sarah deleted the message, logged out of her computer, and gathered her things.

"Where are you going?"

Sarah was startled and turned to see John standing only feet away. *Had he seen the message?*

"Out," Sarah said, instantly regaining her composure.

"Out where?"

Sarah didn't have time for this. She had to think quickly. "It's none of your business where I go," she snapped. "I don't answer to you and, I'm sorry to say, Samuel doesn't tell you everything."

"So you're doing something for Samuel?"

"Yes. If he calls, tell him I got his message and I'll report back in three hours." John watched in silence as Sarah opened the metal security door at the front of the basement and walked out of the laboratory.

She climbed the short flight of stairs and emerged at street level. For security reasons, she never parked near the laboratory. Today, she'd left the 1989 Ford Escort near Montrose Park. The car was well below what she deserved but it served a more important purpose. She'd bought it two months ago for $800 cash. The title was never changed to her name, so if anyone ever grew suspicious or ran the plates, they'd find the car was still registered in Boonsboro, Maryland to a forty-three year old gas station attendant named Dustin Mauck. If questioned, he would report that he sold the car to a blonde woman named Rachel Wade. And there, the trail would hit a dead end.

Sarah got in the car and put it in Drive. She turned onto P Street and glanced at her watch as she crossed over Rock Creek Park. It had been fifteen minutes since she'd received the email. *Two hours and forty-five minutes*, she reminded herself. Pulling onto 21st Street, she found an open parking place and shut off the engine.

Eventually, the car would be impounded and likely sold at auction without questions, but there was no reason to take unnecessary risks. Sarah glanced around the car and, after confirming she was leaving nothing behind, she pulled out a handkerchief and wiped down the interior. Satisfied, she got out of the car and casually wiped the driver's door handle before tucking the handkerchief back in her pocket.

Across the street, the brick and metal façade of the Hotel Palomar towered overhead. The covered portico was bustling: bellmen loaded luggage onto carts, guests filled the walkways and darted between an endless procession of cars and taxis that pulled slowly through the circular drive. Sarah crossed the street and hopped inside an empty cab.

"16th and M," she ordered.

The driver didn't react to the urgency of her command and took his time starting the meter and pulling away from the curb. Her destination was only a mile away, but walking would have taken her twice as long and she couldn't waste a minute of her time.

"Eight dollars and a penny," said the driver as the cab came to a stop.

Sarah handed him a ten-dollar bill and got out of the car. Standing on the busy street corner, Sarah performed an exercise she'd done a thousand times. She closed her eyes, took a deep breath and mentally changed her identity from Sarah back to the renowned scientist, Jordan Sloane.

When she opened her eyes, the white colonnade of Washington D.C.'s prestigious University Club drew Jordan's gaze. Founded in

1904 as a gathering place for the highly educated and highly ambitious, the University Club remained exceedingly particular about its membership. But no club catering to academics could turn down a Millennium Prize winner. Just twenty-four hours after submitting her application, Jordan Sloane received a personal phone call from the Club's President welcoming her to the privileges of membership.

Jordan didn't care about the camaraderie of fellow academics. She never went to the Club's sports lounge or the exercise studio. She didn't get massages or swim in the pool. Jordan paid the exorbitant membership fees for one reason: the privacy and security of the women's lounge.

"Welcome back Ms. Sloane," said the receptionist.

"Thanks," Jordan said in a tone that didn't invite further conversation.

She swept through the foyer and down an ornately decorated hallway to the far end of the building. At the end of the hall, she entered the women's lounge and quietly closed the door. The sitting room was furnished with rich upholstered armchairs and a white leather couch. A door on the opposite side of the room led to the dressing area and showers. Jordan stood silently against the door and listened. Hearing nothing, she called towards the dressing area. "Hello?" There was no response.

She walked quietly into the dressing room, which was filled rows of oak lockers on either side of the central aisle. Jordan walked along the center aisle, glancing down each row of lockers. "Hello?" she said cautiously. When she reached the final row, she knew she was alone. She walked quickly back down the aisle and directly to locker 125.

Keep calm and keep moving, she told herself. Jordan concentrated on the lock and dialed in the combination. The door swung open to reveal a duffle bag and a small lockbox. She sat down on the bench that ran the length of the lockers and set the items in her lap. She placed the lockbox on the bench beside her and unzipped the bag. As expected, there were two sets of clothes and, beneath the clothes, a bottle of brown hair dye.

She zipped the bag and grabbed the lockbox. The fingerprint scanner embedded in the lid flashed and the lock clicked open. Inside was a small bundle of cash, three passports and a pistol.

Jordan stared at the gun and the revelations of the past hour swirled in her mind.

Samuel had lied to her. He said no one would get hurt and then he abducted that poor family and subjected them to unbearable things. What else had he lied about? There was no way to know. While deeply disturbing, it wasn't the abduction that caused Jordan to tremble in fear – it was the two words contained in the encrypted email: *Get Out.* When dealing in state secrets, there was little time for pleasantries. Kazimir Bulgakov always did get right to the point. The message meant the moment she had always feared had arrived. It meant she had been discovered and that Jordan Sloane was finally dead.

She flipped through the passports in the lockbox – Ireland, Switzerland, Belgium. The bright red cover of the Swiss passport caught her attention. She opened it and gazed at the picture. The woman staring back at her looked completely different – everything except the eyes. The eyes were hers. She glanced at the name: Alessia Bichsel.

The events that led her to this moment clouded her mind. One after another, images of the secrets she'd sold, the lies she'd told, Kazimir, Samuel, and the events to come crashed over her. They stood as an impenetrable barrier between who she was and who she would become. She had to break through. Slowly, she closed her eyes and concentrated on her breathing. With each focused breath, the images of her past faded into the distance. When her mind was completely clear, she whispered softly, "I am Alessia Bichsel. I am Alessia Bichsel."

She closed the passport and thought of her small cottage on the shores of Lake Lucerne in Greppen, Switzerland. She imagined herself standing on the balcony overlooking the lake. The morning sun warmed her skin as she watched the sail boats drift by. Alessia Bichsel would be safe there – at least for a little while. Other passports and identities were hidden beneath the floorboards of the cottage's guestroom closet. Lake Lucerne would not be her final destination, but it was a good place to start.

Alessia glanced at her watch. Her flight departed in two hours. She could already smell the fresh mountain air.

Sheetal Aiyer sat at his workstation at MicroCon's downtown Chicago offices and gazed at the framed picture of his wife and daughter. An alert from his computer drew his attention to a series of monitors displaying results from the day's first round of tests. Each day, con artists, thieves and thrill seekers create more than 200,000 unique programs designed to attack or disrupt the world's computer systems. To secure its customers against the ever-changing threat, MicroCon employees worked around the clock to identify the malicious programs and keep their anti-virus software up to date. As new threats were identified, MicroCon updated its software, which was automatically pushed to computer systems around the world. But before sending the update to the customer, it had to be thoroughly tested in the MicroCon lab.

The lab itself was a cold, windowless room. Inside, rows of servers, test equipment and a full staff of network engineers kept the system running twenty-four hours a day. While Sheetal managed the lab, he spent most of his time in the relative comfort of his small, sixth-floor office where a bank of monitors provided real-time access to lab below. He was analyzing the results of a new virus signature test when the phone rang.

Keeping his eyes on the monitor, he reached over and picked up the receiver. "Sheetal."

"Mr. Aiyer?" came the unknown male voice.

Sheetal looked away from his monitor and tried to place the caller's voice. "Yes, this is Sheetal Aiyer. Who's this?"

"Check your email, Mr. Aiyer," said the voice. Just then, the familiar two-tone alert of an incoming email sounded.

Confused, Sheetal grabbed his mouse and clicked a button to pull up his email program. "Who is this?" he asked again.

"Did you get the email?" the caller asked, ignoring the question. Sheetal looked at the top of his inbox and saw a new email with an indecipherable address. "Open the email, Mr. Aiyer," said the voice a moment later. Sheetal hesitated. A basic rule in computer security is to never open strange emails. "Mr. Aiyer," said the man more forcefully, "Hillary and Anju want you to open the email."

"What did you say?" he asked, certain he'd misheard the man.

"Your wife and your daughter want you to open that email."

"What?" Sheetal asked, his voice shaking.

"Open the email," commanded the caller. Sheetal was terrified at the coldness of the man's voice. Slowly, he moved the pointer over the email and clicked the button on his mouse. "Is it open?" asked the voice.

"Yes," said Sheetal. "Who is this? Is my family okay?" he asked with ever-deepening fear.

"Whether your family's okay is up to you," said the man. "What do you see in the email."

Sheetal looked back at his computer screen. "It's a link to a website."

"Click the link."

With the mention of his family, the security concerns of clicking on an unknown link didn't enter Sheetal's mind. He hovered the mouse over the link and pressed the button. A new browser window opened. When the webpage loaded, the screen went completely black. "What's happened?" Sheetal asked.

"Did you click the link?"

"Yes. My screen went black."

"Keep watching." The caller entered a remote command to a distant server and sent a secure video streaming across the Internet.

Seconds later, Sheetal's blank screen came to life in a blur of black and white. He watched as the picture slowly took shape. When it came into focus, the image before him was terrifying.

"Oh God! What've you done?" he yelled. Transfixed by the horrifying video feed, he felt as if the life had been ripped from his body. His wife and daughter sat on a bare concrete floor surrounded by metal walls. They were bound and gagged, their backs tied to one another. There was no audio, but seeing their trembling bodies and crying eyes, Sheetal knew his wife and daughter were terrified. His eyes filled with tears. "Where are they?" Sheetal cried. "What do you want? Oh God! What have you done?" Sheetal began to sob hysterically. "Let them go! What do you want from me? I'll do anything. Just tell me what you want. Please just let them go!"

The caller waited patiently for Sheetal's pleas to subside. When he finally fell silent, the caller sent another remote command and Sheetal's monitor went black. The video had served its purpose and he now needed Sheetal's full attention. "Calm down," said the voice in a quiet, steady tone.

"Let them go! Please just let them go!" Sheetal cried.

"The best thing you can do for your family is shut up and listen." The caller waited for the sobs to die down. "Are you listening?"

Sheetal wiped his eyes with his hands and tried to breathe. "I'm listening," he said. "What do you want?"

"I want you to change the world, Mr. Aiyer. But first, some rules. If you tell anyone about this, your family dies. If you make a phone call, your family dies. If you send an email or a text message, your family dies." The caller paused to allow the instructions to sink in. "You understand the rules?"

"Yes," Sheetal said with his eyes shut tight. He had to pull himself together and concentrate on the man's instructions.

"Good. Now. It's time for you to go home. From the time we hang up, you'll have one minute to leave your building. If you're not out front in one minute, you know what'll happen, don't you?"

"Yes," replied Sheetal, his voice shaking.

"Tell me."

Sheetal swallowed hard. "My family dies." Saying the words tightened his stomach and he felt like he was going to be sick.

"Good. Then we understand one another. When we hang up, you'll go downstairs and walk – do not run – to the corner of Chicago and Franklin. Catch the Brown Line towards downtown. At Fullerton Station, you'll transfer to the Purple Line. When you arrive in Evanston, go directly home. Speak to no one. Do you understand?"

"I understand."

"Excellent. You have one minute," said the caller, then the line went dead.

Sheetal dropped the phone, grabbed his wallet, keys, and cell phone from the desk and left his office. The elevator doors were opening as he approached and his colleague, Jillian, was stepping off the elevator. "Are you okay?" she asked, seeing that Sheetal was visibly upset.

"I'm fine," he said as he frantically pushed the elevator button and the doors closed. Seconds later, he walked out of the building and turned towards the Franklin Street station.

Joseph closed his laptop and stared out the window of the Starbucks Coffee shop. He had a clear view of the stairs leading up to the Franklin Street train station. His conversation had gone as planned. Sheetal Aiyer would do exactly as he was told. Joseph glanced down at his watch. He'd walked the path between the MicroCon office and the train station several times that morning and knew that Sheetal should be arriving any second. As if on cue, Sheetal rounded the corner and headed up to the station.

Joseph threw the laptop into his shoulder bag and walked out onto the street. Keeping a safe distance, he followed Sheetal up the stairs to the station. On the elevated platform, he blended into the crowd and watched Sheetal's every move. Sheetal kept to himself and didn't speak to anyone. Minutes later the high-pitched screech of metal sounded the train's arrival. The silver doors opened and Joseph watched from the crowd as Sheetal stepped to the edge of the platform and got on the train. Joseph drifted onto the car with the last of the passengers.

Sheetal found a seat by the window and closed his eyes, trying to hold back the tears. He didn't move until the train pulled into Fullerton Station, where, as instructed, he changed trains for the Purple Line. Thirty minutes later Sheetal arrived back at the same station where he'd caught the morning train. Joseph watched from the back of the car as Sheetal got off the train and walked quickly from the platform. When he had disappeared down the stairwell, Joseph pulled out his phone and made a call.

"Yes," answered Samuel.

"He just left the station. He'll be home in five minutes."

"Excellent. Good work, Joseph. We will speak soon."

Sheetal reached the bottom of the stairs and began to run – his mind blank with shock. He ran through the familiar tree-lined neighborhood as fast as his body could take him. Turning onto his street, he cut across the neighboring yards to his house and burst through the red front door.

"Hillary!" he yelled as he ran inside. "Anju!" His head spun desperately from left to right, looking for any signs of his family. "Hillary!" he yelled again. Then he saw it. The note was written in red crayon on a piece of Anju's yellow construction paper: *Go to the living room. Sit in the blue chair.* Sheetal grabbed the note off the entryway table and read it again. Gripping the paper tight in his hand, he turned and stepped slowly towards the living room.

When he rounded the corner, he saw a flood of light filling the living room. All the furniture had been removed except for his blue leather wingback chair, which now sat in the center of the room. A dozen, halogen construction lights circled the chair, bathing it in heat and light.

"What the fuck is going on?" he screamed. "What do you want from me?" he shouted into the empty room. There was no response. Sheetal looked down at the note still clutched in his hand. With nothing left to do, he walked into the intense light and heat of the halogen bulbs, sat down in the chair and began to cry.

"Mr. Aiyer."

Sheetal looked up at the sudden sound of the voice but was blinded by the lights. "Who are you?" he asked, his voice shaking with emotion.

"There is something under your chair, Mr. Aiyer. Reach down and get it," instructed the man.

Sheetal reached under the chair where his hand crossed a soft piece of material. He grabbed the object and held it up in the light. It was a black ski mask. He turned it in the light to see the eyeholes had been crudely patched over with pieces of torn denim sewn in place with a dark red yarn.

"Put the mask on."

"What do you want from me?" Sheetal pleaded hopelessly as he slowly pulled the mask over his head.

"I will tell you what I want," said the voice from behind the lights. "But first, I must tell you who I am. My name is Samuel."

CHAPTER 31

Turn here," Riley said, pointing to the left. Amie turned the wheel hard and hit the accelerator. Riley looked out the back window and kept watch as the car raced down the neighborhood street. "I don't think anyone's following us," he said cautiously.

"We're safe?" Amie asked.

"I think so. No way Isaac could have followed us," said Riley and the car immediately began to slow. Riley turned to face the front. "Where should we go?" he asked.

"Glencoe Park is just ahead," she said. "We can talk there."

Approaching the park, they drove slowly around the perimeter and peered between the trees to confirm the park was empty. Amie stopped on the side of the road and killed the engine. "Okay," she said, turning sideways in the seat to face Riley. "It's time for some answers. Where's that letter?"

Riley reached into his back pocket and pulled out the letter. Staring at the roughly folded paper, he had no idea what it would say. It really didn't matter. Over the past days, his life had been turned completely upside down. He'd witnessed a murder, been chased through campus by a killer, and had multiple near-death experiences. Whatever Christoph Varden had to say, it had to shed some light on what the hell was going on.

He unfolded the letter and used the dashboard to press the deep wrinkles from the page. Amie placed a reassuring hand on Riley's shoulder as he lifted the letter and read it aloud.

My Dearest Friend,

If you're reading this, it's because I've been carrying a secret. Now, with my death, I fear that secret is in the hands of those who would use it to destroy all that we hold sacred. I must now rely on you to understand what I've done and trust that you will do as your conscience dictates. I love my country. I am a patriot. This is my confession.

For more than a decade, this country has waged a war to destroy global terrorist organizations. While the terrorists are wounded, they are not beaten. To maintain their operational status, these fragmented groups leverage most powerful communications tool ever devised: the Internet. Terrorists cannot operate without email, instant messaging and social media.

And so, the Internet has become a new front line in the war on terror. Every day the terrorists become increasingly sophisticated. They continue to develop new evasion and counter-intelligence techniques that have created virtual blind spots on the Internet where they can meet and plan their next attack. These blind spots have severely impacted our ability to identify, track and defeat terrorist activities. To defend itself against future attacks, the United States had to act.

Last year, members of the F.B.I's Data Intercept Technology Unit asked me to be lead scientist and developer for the Ceterus Program. The Program had one goal: create a technology that would eliminate the blind spots. The technology would ensure the United States maintained its strategic advantage in the digital war on terror. The F.B.I. was convinced I was the only one who could achieve this goal. I was uncertain it could be done, but my love of country left me no choice but to try.

After many months of development, I completed my work and the Ceterus Program entered an operational phase. The power of what we had done was immediately apparent. Within weeks, Ceterus had identified and prevented of a significant terrorist plot on U.S. soil. The Ceterus Program was initially a success, but then it changed. The F.B.I. demanded a rapid expansion of the Program. I knew then that Ceterus must have oversight or it could overtake us and destroy what it was meant to protect. This is the task that I now give to you.

The result of my work is stored on the flash drive where you found this letter. On it, you will find a copy of the Ceterus File, which is already in use by the F.B.I. But I have left you something else – something the F.B.I. doesn't have: the Ceterus Key. Should the F.B.I. abuse the power entrusted to them, you must use the Ceterus Key to undo what they've done. I leave it, and its future, in your hands. Load the small file onto your machine; it will lead you where you need to go.

Your loyal friend,

Christoph Varden

When he got to the end of the letter, Riley dropped his hands to his lap and stared out the front window of the car. "Holy shit," he said softly. "Varden created some sort of computer program for the government that taps into the Internet?"

"Not the government," Amie corrected, "the F.B.I.'s Data Intercept Technology Unit."

"What's that?" asked Riley.

"The DITU is the F.B.I.'s clandestine electronic intelligence gathering organization. They're based in Quantico, Virginia and specialize in the covert collection of digital data inside the United States. It's the F.B.I.'s version of the National Security Agency."

"A domestic NSA?"

"That's right. The existence of the DITU has only recently come to light. I learned about it because computer security experts have been going crazy trying to figure out how far the DITU has gone to penetrate their systems."

Suddenly, a memory triggered in Riley's mind. "Wait a second," he said, reaching into his back pocket and pulling out his wallet.

"What is it?" Amie asked, sensing his excitement.

Riley opened his wallet and removed Agent Coffman's card. "Look," he said, handing it to Amie.

Department Of Justice
Federal Bureau Of Investigation
Dallas Field Office

Brinson Coffman
Special Agent
Data Intercept Technology Unit

"Holy shit!" Amie exclaimed. "Coffman's part of the DITU? Why didn't you tell me that?"

"I didn't know what it was," Riley explained. "Things are starting to make a lot more sense." Riley looked out the front window for a moment to collect his thoughts. Looking back at Amie, he said, "So, here's what we know: Varden was working on a top secret program to help the DITU with domestic intelligence gathering."

"Looks that way," said Amie.

"And someone outside the F.B.I. found out about Varden's program and had him killed to get a copy of it. They searched Varden's house and didn't find it. Somehow, they figured out he had implanted a copy of it under his skin, so they dug him out of his grave and stole it."

Amie was nodding her head in agreement. "Sounds right to me, except for one thing: we don't know that the person who killed Varden is outside the F.B.I."

Riley's skin grew cold at the thought but he knew Amie was right. Isaac could be working for anyone – including the F.B.I. There was no way to know for sure. "True," he said, and then something else occurred to him. "The fact that Varden was working on a secret spy program for the DITU explains a lot about Coffman's behavior at the canal, don't you think?"

"How so?" Amie prompted.

"Well, it explains why the F.B.I. showed up instead of the local police, right? They must've already taken over the case because of Varden's work on Ceterus." Amie nodded her agreement. "Second," Riley continued, "it explains why Coffman was so eager to direct our conversation away from Varden. I mean, any discussion about Varden could potentially expose something about Ceterus, right?"

Amie thought for a moment to process Riley's logic. "That could explain it," she said. "It's also highly likely that, as a member of DITU, Coffman already knew exactly why Isaac had killed Varden. There was no need to ask many questions."

"Right," Riley agreed.

They sat in silence to digest everything they'd learned. Riley was deep in thought when Amie spoke. "What does Ceterus mean? It sounds Latin."

"It is. It means *the rest* or *the other*," Riley said. "Strange name for an electronic spy program. Does that mean anything to you?"

"Not really. Could mean anything," Amie said, shrugging her shoulders. "The only way to find out is to open this drive and see." Amie held up Varden's flash drive for Riley to see.

"How are we supposed to do that?" Riley asked. "It's encrypted, isn't it?"

"I have something in my lab that'll take care of that."

"Your lab?" Riley asked with a slight laugh. "We can't go to your lab. Isaac showed up at your house this morning. They know who you are. I think they can find your lab at SMU."

Amie's shoulders dropped. There was no doubt Isaac knew she was an SMU professor and he'd almost certainly know about her lab. She let out a sigh and searched for another solution. It didn't take long. "Bradford's lab!" she said excitedly.

"Who?" Riley asked.

"Robin Bradford. He's a colleague of mine. He's got a separate lab on the other side of campus. We've been working on some joint projects, so I have access to his lab." Riley was clearly not convinced and Amie pressed on. "Michael, to open this drive, we need specialized equipment. We can't just go to some Internet cafe. Robin's lab has everything we need."

Going to campus was a risk. The last time Riley was there, Isaac had been waiting. There was no reason to believe he wouldn't be waiting there again. But if accessing the drive required special software they'd have to take their chances that Isaac didn't know about Bradford's lab. Riley nodded. "Okay," he said. "Let's do it."

"Good," Amie said, starting the car and pulling away from the curb.

CHAPTER 32

"My name is Samuel," said the man from behind the circle of blinding halogen lights. The patches of thick cloth sewn onto the black ski mask left Sheetal Aiyer unable to see the man who had kidnapped his family and now held him hostage in his own home.

"What do you want?" Sheetal asked, his voice quivering uncontrollably. "Where's my family? What've you done to them?" In a momentary show of defiance, Sheetal pushed himself up from the leather chair.

"If you want to see your family again, you will sit down!" Samuel commanded with authority.

Sheetal collapsed back into the chair and pleaded with his captor. "What do you want?"

"I want you to listen," said Samuel. Sheetal nodded and his head fell down to his chest. The only way to get his family back was to do exactly as the faceless man said. "Good," said Samuel. He began walking a slow circle around the room.

"On a cold December night in 1773," Samuel began, "a group of Boston patriots, acting in defiance of British tyranny, disguised themselves as Mohawk Indians and marched to Boston Harbor where they boarded British merchant ships and dumped 342 chests of tea over the rails and down into the water." Samuel had circled around the chair and paused directly in front of Sheetal. "Do you know what act of defiance I'm referring to, Mr. Aiyer?"

Tears ran down Sheetal's face and were absorbed by the black ski mask. He struggled to stay focused on the faceless voice. "The Boston Tea Party," he stammered through his tears.

"That's right, Mr. Aiyer – the Boston Tea Party," said Samuel with an approving smile as he resumed his slow path around the room. "This single act of defiance triggered a chain reaction that eventually led the American people to rise up against their oppressors and regain their freedoms."

Sheetal was desperately searching for a connection between his family and anything Samuel was saying. Nothing made sense. "Why are you telling me this?" Sheetal pleaded.

Samuel leaned over the chair to speak directly into Sheetal's ear. "Because today, Mr. Aiyer, today we will perform a single act of defiance." The words hung in the air and a wave of fear flooded Sheetal's mind. He wanted to scream.

Samuel stood and continued circling the chair. "Do you know the name of the man who led that group of patriots to throw off the chains of government?" A moment later, Sheetal lifted his masked head and while no words were spoken, Samuel knew Sheetal had made the connection. "That's right, Mr. Aiyer. He too was named Samuel. It was Samuel Adams and his Sons of Liberty who lit the fuse that destroyed tyranny in this land. We will do the same."

"Why are you doing this?" Sheetal asked.

"I'm doing this because on November 26, 1864, another patriot and guardian, Abraham Lincoln, warned us this day would come. It was through Lincoln's Prophecy we learned of a rising power that, if left unchecked, would one day destroy this great nation."

"I don't understand," said Sheetal. "What Prophecy?"

That Sheetal had never heard of Lincoln's Prophecy came as no surprise. "The Prophecy that predicted corruption in the highest halls of power – the Prophecy that foretold of the government's playing on our prejudices and fears to take what is not theirs. Lincoln prophesied the American people, in this moment of truth, would cower to their fears and trade their freedom for the illusion of safety. It is this Prophecy that has brought me directly to you."

"Why me?" Sheetal asked. "I don't know anything about a Prophecy."

"How long have you worked for MicroCon, Mr. Aiyer?" Samuel asked.

Sheetal was confused by the sudden change of topic and took a moment to answer. "Fifteen years," he finally said.

"And MicroCon is the largest digital security company in the world."

"Yes."

"Tell me, Mr. Aiyer – how many of the Fortune 1,000 companies are MicroCon customers?"

"I don't know."

"All of them," said Samuel. "Every one of the Fortune 1,000 have at least one MicroCon product installed in their networks. Banks, hospitals, telecommunications, retail stores – they all have MicroCon to protect them from the outside world."

Sheetal sat in silence. He had no idea what Samuel wanted him to say. "What do you do for MicroCon?" Samuel asked, though he already knew the answer.

"I'm a Senior Quality Engineer. I supervise the testing of our software updates. I make sure they're safe to run on our customers' systems before we release them to the public."

"When you release a new update to your software, you simply upload it to the customer's system automatically, don't you?" pressed Samuel.

"Yes. Security software has to be updated several times a day to catch the latest viruses."

"When you upload the new software to your customers, is there anything that would prevent the file from loading?" Samuel asked.

"No," Sheetal responded, trying desperately to see where this was going.

"And you are the last person at MicroCon to approve the safety of the update?"

"Yes."

"So whatever file you release, you can ensure your customers' security systems accept it and load the file behind the firewall?"

Sheetal now understood what Samuel wanted him to do. The consequences of inserting an unknown file into the top 1,000 companies in America could be catastrophic. Once inserted behind the firewall, the person controlling the software could do anything they wanted. It all depended on what the inserted file was designed to do. Sheetal's mind scrambled for a way out – a way to stop this before it started. Then, the black and white image of his family in that dark, metal room flashed before his eyes. There was no way out. He would do anything Samuel wanted.

"Yes," Sheetal said softly. "I can push a file into our customer's systems."

"Mr. Aiyer, you asked me why I have chosen you. And now you know." Samuel reached into his pocket and pulled out a small, black flash drive. He held it up and gazed at it for a long moment, amazed at how such a small device had so much power. "Hold out your hand," Samuel commanded.

Slowly, Sheetal extended his hand and held it open. Samuel stepped towards him and gently placed the drive in Sheetal's palm. "In a moment, I will leave," Samuel said. "You will return to work and insert the contents of this drive into the next security release. I will be monitoring the release, Mr. Aiyer. If I do not see that file appear within the next two hours, well" Samuel smiled, "you know what will happen." Sheetal nodded his understanding. "No, Mr. Aiyer. I will need to hear you say it."

Sheetal's sobs came uncontrollably. "You will kill them," he said through the tears. Seconds later, he heard his front door close. "Hello?" he cried. There was no answer. Slowly, Sheetal reached up and removed the black ski mask. He stared down at the flash drive in his hand. He didn't care what the contents of the drive would do. He only cared about his family.

CHAPTER 33

Amie and Riley pulled into the student parking garage at the edge of the SMU campus and parked the car. "Probably best to avoid the faculty lots," Amie said as she reached into the back seat and grabbed her shoulder bag.

"Good idea," Riley agreed, knowing there was a good chance either Isaac or the F.B.I. was watching the campus and waiting for them to appear.

They got out of the car and walked to the door at the end of the garage. When they reached the threshold, Riley suddenly stopped and threw his arm out. "Wait," he said. Amie stopped in her tracks. Riley peered out of the door and around the corner. He scanned the all buildings and cars in view, looking for anything unusual - though he had no idea what that would be. "Okay. Let's go."

They walked briskly down the tree-lined sidewalks to the center of campus, passing an occasional student along the way. "Where are we headed?" Riley asked.

"Boaz Hall. Robin is borrowing some lab space from the business school. If anyone's looking for us, they'll probably be at the law school or my lab. I doubt they'd stake out the business school. We should be relatively safe." Amie pointed up ahead to a narrow sidewalk that ran along the school's Olympic sized swimming pool. "Let's cut through here."

They emerged from a group of trees at the end of the sidewalk and crossed the street towards a long, four-story brick building designed in the same Georgian Revival style that was prevalent throughout the SMU campus. Columns on either side of the building's large white door supported a triangular pediment, where the name BOAZ HALL appeared in gold block lettering. Amie led the way through the door and down the grey-carpeted hallway to a door at the far end the building.

She produced her faculty ID badge from her shoulder bag and swiped it across the card reader to the right of the door. The magnetic lock clicked and Riley followed Amie into the lab, which was smaller than he'd expected. Rows of servers filled most of the twenty by twenty room but a small area had been carved out at the front of the lab for three computer terminals.

Amie went straight to the nearest terminal and sat down in a green swivel chair. "Grab a chair," she said, retrieving the Varden flash drive from her bag. Amie was already typing commands on the keyboard when Riley pulled up a chair and sat down.

"How long will it take to break the encryption?" Riley asked.

"Not long. It's really low level stuff and we've been working on decryption algorithms here for a long time." Amie typed a series of commands that trained the full computing power of the lab to decrypting the Varden file.

"So what do you think we'll find?" Riley asked when Amie had finished typing.

"I don't know. Given DITU's history, I bet it'll be something we've never seen before. Keep in mind, the two key problems in electronic surveillance are getting access to the data and converting it into meaningful intelligence. For the most part, the government has focused on getting data from corporations because that's where it's easiest to collect."

"How much data are we talking about?"

"A lot. It's estimated that government spy agencies collect enough data every three hours to fill the Library of Congress. But like I said, the volume of data is only half the story. It's the overlapping of multiple data points to create useful intelligence that's really interesting."

"What do you mean?"

Amie thought for a moment. "Let's say the government collects your personal contact list. That obviously gives them a lot of information about who you know, but it provides no information about how well you know them. You need another data point to tell you that – like email and texts. With that, you can determine how strong the link is between you and someone on your contact list by how often you talk to them. Add a third data point, like GPS from your cell phone. Now, based on your previous GPS patterns, they can build a predictive grid of where you'll be at a given time in the future and who you'll likely be meeting."

"That's incredible," Riley said. "Can they really do that?"

"They can. Google recently did an experiment using GPS data collected from individual cell phones. They were able to predict where someone will be at any given time over the next year with 80% accuracy. And that's just using one type of data point. Think what the Government could do with all the data they've got."

"Sounds like Big Brother from Orwell's 1984."

"It is. That's the power of big data. It's exactly the type of technology the F.B.I. and NSA are building to track suspected terrorists. And the data they collect from corporations is essential to their success."

"They've got the law on their side, too," Riley commented. Amie turned in her chair, prompting Riley to explain. "Two laws, really: The Patriot Act and the creatively named Protect America Act. That's how mega-companies like Google, Microsoft and Facebook are able to share the data and avoid any sticky privacy issues. Most Americans don't know a thing about it."

"Or they believe it's justified to capture the bad guys," Amie offered. "The government and corporations have every reason to play on our fears."

"Why do you say that?" Riley asked.

"The stakes are high. The government wants to stop another 9-11 and the corporations make millions selling data feeds and helping the government sort through it all."

"So the government gets stronger while corporations get richer."

"Exactly," Amie agreed just as an electronic bell sounded from the computer terminal. She swiveled her chair to face the screen. "See? Cracked it in no time," she said, pecking on the keyboard with a satisfied smile.

Riley dug into his back pocket and pulled out the Varden letter. "The result of my work is stored on the flash drive where you found this letter," he read aloud. "Load the small file onto your machine; it will lead you where you need to go."

"Got it," Amie replied, making a few last keystrokes. "Okay. Here goes." Amie executed the program, which immediately opened the MicroCon anti-virus software loaded on the computer and began a system scan. Minutes later, a window appeared with a simple message: *File Identified.*

"What's that mean?" Riley asked.

"Looks like the Varden file we loaded commanded the MicroCon anti-virus program to locate another file that was already on the system." Just then, a second window appeared with lines of text and computer code. "Oh my God," Amie said in a whisper, grabbing Riley's arm. "What's this?" asked Amie in disbelief.

Riley leaned in to get a better view of the screen. "What is it?"

Amie studied the screen for several long minutes. "Good Lord," she said. "It's a surveillance program – a very sophisticated surveillance program. And its been planted on *this* machine." Silence fell in the room as Amie continued to study the code with an academic focus. "This has to be it," she finally said.

"It, what?"

"This is what Varden built for the F.B.I. This has to be Ceterus. I can't believe there's an F.B.I. spy program on a computer buried in an obscure SMU lab. How'd it get here?"

"Varden was working for the surveillance branch of the F.B.I.," Riley said. "My guess is the F.B.I. put it there."

Amie continued to scroll through the lines of text. The more she read, the more she struggled to believe what she was seeing. "Oh my God," she said again.

Riley waited impatiently as Amie continued to study the text. Finally, his patience wore thin. "Amie. What's going on? What is this thing?"

Amie tore her eyes from the screen and looked at Riley. "It's the most comprehensive intelligence-gathering program I've ever seen. This thing allows the F.B.I. to collect any data it wants from an infected machine."

"What type of data?" Riley pressed.

"It can access any files stored on the system – anything from a presentation for work or a spreadsheet with your household budget. I've seen that kind of surveillance program before. But Ceterus goes way beyond that," Amie said with academic excitement. "This thing has direct control over the computer's microphone, camera and Bluetooth functions."

"Wait," Riley said, "are you telling me the F.B.I. can hit a button somewhere that will turn on the microphone and camera for this computer?"

Amie was nodding her head. "Exactly."

"That would be like having an F.B.I. agent sitting right here in the room with us," Riley said in complete disbelief.

"Yes. Except for one thing."

"What's that?"

"You would have no idea the F.B.I. was in the room at all," Amie said.

Riley threw himself back in his chair and breathed a heavy sigh. "Holy shit," he said. The full scope of the program's capabilities came into sharp focus and triggered a thought in Riley's mind. "Ceterus," he said slowly.

"What?" asked Amie. "What about it?"

"We know the F.B.I. already has access to data that flows through corporations, right?"

"Right," Amie said, curious what Riley was getting at.

"So if the F.B.I. was able to plant this program onto everyone's machine, they'd have both the corporate and the personal information. They'd have *the rest.*"

"Ceterus," Amie said, now remembering that Riley had said Ceterus meant the rest. Amie covered her mouth. "Good God."

"But here's a question: Isn't anti-virus software supposed to detect this kind of thing? Why didn't your anti-virus program detect Ceterus?" Riley asked.

"It did, but only after we loaded the file Varden gave us. That's part of Varden's genius. He's disguised Ceterus to look like part of the MicroCon security software. So the anti-virus software thinks Ceterus is safe to run. Remember what Varden said – he built Ceterus for the F.B.I., but he built the Ceterus Key in secret so he could expose the F.B.I. if they abused their power. We just loaded the Key, and that's the only way we found

Ceterus. Without the Key, this thing is undetectable."

"So we're holding the only key to control a massive, and highly illegal, F.B.I. spy program and expose it to the world."

"It sure looks that way."

A long silence settled into the room. "Holy shit," Riley said, looking off into the distance.

"What?"

"Isaac," Riley said, still in a daze.

"What?" Amie demanded. "What about Isaac?"

Riley thought back to the canal and to Varden's naked and mutilated body. "The capsule," Riley said.

Oh my God, Amie thought, now realizing where Riley was going.

"Varden put a copy of Ceterus in that capsule," Riley concluded.

Amie grabbed Riley's arm. "And now Isaac's got a copy."

"Yes. But what does that mean? What could he do with it?"

"Anything he wants. You could modify this thing to do literally anything you want." Amie couldn't believe what she was saying. "If you wanted to, you could take complete control over every machine with the program installed."

"Jesus," Riley exclaimed. "How do we find out how many computers are infected?"

Amie thought about it. If the F.B.I. had planted the Varden program on an obscure computer at SMU, they'd probably infected millions of machines. To find out for sure, they would have to leave campus. "We need access to a public network. Something outside the SMU systems."

"Well that's easy enough," Riley said, standing up and grabbing Amie's shoulder bag. "I've got just the place."

CHAPTER 34

Sheetal Aiyer walked into his office at the MicroCon research facility and shut the door. He closed his eyes and leaned against the door for a long moment – his mind a swirl of fear and hatred for a man whose face he'd never seen. Then he opened his eyes and got to work.

He sat down at his desk and thrust his hands onto the keyboard. With a few quick commands, he logged into the MicroCon Labs web portal where the update Samuel was waiting for appeared at the top of the screen. Sheetal checked the test results from engineering and confirmed the entire team had cleared the file for release. They just needed his final approval.

Sheetal reached into his pocket and pulled out the black thumb drive. His hand was shaking when he reached to insert the drive into his computer. He had dedicated his entire life to protecting people against the very act he was about to commit. If he did this, everything he had ever worked for would be lost. But what choice did he have?

He steadied his hand and loaded the flash drive onto his computer. A second later, a window appeared displaying its contents. As expected, there was only one file. Sheetal clicked on the file and a question appeared at the center of the screen: Upload file? He moved the mouse and hovered over the question.

What am I about to do? he asked himself. *You're saving your family,* came the unqualified answer. On the commute back to his office, Sheetal had spent his time trying to find a way out – a way to save his family and prevent what was almost certainly a terrorist attack. Samuel had given him two hours to upload the contents of the flash drive. Sheetal had only been allowed a brief glimpse of his family tied up in a metal room with concrete floors. There was no way the authorities could find his family before the deadline. The room could be anywhere. Where would the police begin their search? There simply wasn't enough to go on.

As his finger hovered over the button, Sheetal knew no matter what he did, his life would change forever. His eyes wandered from the monitor and found the picture of his wife and daughter at the edge of his desk. Whatever changes were about to come, he knew he couldn't face them without his family. His fate was sealed. Slowly, Sheetal closed his eyes and pressed the button.

CHAPTER 35

Riley pulled to a stop on Young Street and parked at a meter. "Come on," he said and hopped out of the car.

They followed the sidewalk to the corner at Ervay Street and were waiting for the signal to change when Amie asked, "Where, exactly, are we going?"

"You said you needed a public network to see how far Ceterus had spread." Riley swept his hand out at the building in front of them. "Hard to get more public than this."

Amie looked out to see the J. Erik Jonsson Central Library. The eight-story building had a concrete, multi-faceted façade surrounded by a series of dark tinted windows. It was the crown jewel of the Dallas Public Library system, housing nearly five million volumes.

"Perfect," said Amie with an approving smile.

They crossed the street and entered the open courtyard in front of the library. Located at the city center and directly across from Dallas City Hall, the Central Library's courtyard was a crossroads for Dallas pedestrian traffic. It was teeming with a mixture of businessmen, government employees, and homeless people, who often spent the day in and around the Library.

Riley and Amie wove through the crowd to the library's main entrance. Inside, the atrium was lit by a series of art deco fixtures that surrounded an enormous welcome desk. Riley led Amie around the desk and through a set of metal detectors to an elevator bank.

"There are some computers tucked away up on the sixth floor," Riley said as the doors opened and the elevator made a strained ascent.

They stepped out into the sixth floor lobby. The burnt orange carpet reminded Riley of his days at the University of Texas as they walked past a librarian shelving a cartload of books and headed to the back corner of the floor.

"That'll work, won't it?" Riley asked, pointing to a lone desk with a computer terminal.

Amie looked around to confirm they were alone. "Works for me."

Amie sat down and, with the click of the mouse, the ancient computer terminal came to life. She searched her bag and retrieved the black flash drive. Riley looked around nervously while Amie inserted the drive into the machine and began pecking at the keyboard. With the stroke of a few buttons she executed the file. Just as it had done at SMU, the file launched the computer's anti-virus program, which began scanning the machine. Moments later, the results appeared on the screen: File Found.

"Good Lord," Amie said in a whisper. She turned to Riley, "It's everywhere. They've planted Ceterus everywhere."

Riley was still staring at the screen. Unlike what happened at the SMU lab, the anti-virus program was still scanning the computer. Suddenly, a second file appeared on the list. "What's that," Riley said, pointing at the screen. "I thought Ceterus was only one file."

"It is," Amie said, turning quickly back to the monitor. "That's not right," she said, bewildered.

"What is it?"

"I don't know but it isn't Ceterus," Amie said, her mind searching for an explanation. "Or, at least, it isn't the same version we saw at the lab."

"What do you mean, *not the same version*?" Riley asked.

"I mean it looks like someone has taken the original Ceterus file and modified it in some way. It's some sort of variation. Whoever did it has re-infected the machines with the new virus."

"What?" Riley was reeling.

Amie pushed back from the desk and shook her head. "This is bad, Michael. We know the F.B.I. planted Ceterus. But who else has the technical ability to infect so many computers with the second file? And what the hell does this second file do?"

"I don't know what it does," Riley admitted, "but I think we know who planted it."

Amie stared out the window. She didn't want to acknowledge her conclusion. "Isaac," she said, blankly.

"Or whoever he works for," Riley agreed. "What could they do with a file like this?" Riley asked.

Amie's deepening concern was evident in her expression. "Anything, really. Once they're inside the computers, they could change the payload and ask the virus to do whatever they like – anything from data collection to shutting the machines down completely."

"Why use Ceterus? Why not build something on your own?"

"Because," Amie explained, "Ceterus is more complex than something you could build in your garage. It would take years to develop if you started from scratch. Varden designed levels of encryption, compression and file masking that haven't been seen before. It's got everything you need to hide something in a network." Amie looked up at Riley, who had a glazed look on his face. "Michael?"

"Sonofabitch," he whispered, emerging from his thoughts. "Dennis Levine."

Amie was completely confused. "Who?"

"Dennis Levine," Riley said, moving closer to the desk. "Alexander. The man Isaac killed at the canal. His real name is Dennis Levine. May I?" he asked, motioning to the keyboard. Amie pushed her chair away from the desk and Riley grabbed the mouse to pull up a browser.

"Michael, what's going on? What've you figured out?"

"I don't know yet. Maybe nothing," he said as he pecked at the keyboard. "The Dallas Morning News did a story the morning after Alexander was killed. The article said the guy's real name was Dennis Levine." Riley scanned the search results and clicked on the short news article.

"So?"

"So that's not all it said about him." Riley moved away from the screen so Amie could see. "Take a look," he said excitedly.

Amie turned to the monitor and began to read. But when she finished the article, she still had no idea what Riley was talking about. "I don't get it," she said urgently.

Riley read from the article. "The F.B.I. identified the man as twenty-seven year old Dennis Lavine, who grew up in Colmesneil, Texas, forty-one miles southeast of Lufkin. Lavine worked as a ranch hand in Colmesneil and was a member of the East Texas Militia, which attracts members from all over East Texas."

"Okay," Amie responded, still missing the connection. "He was in the East Texas Militia."

"What if all these guys are all part of some ultra-conservative militia group? Think about it. They're highly organized, highly motivated and well financed. Maybe this militia thing is what ties them all together."

"Maybe," Amie said without much conviction.

"Look up the East Texas Militia and see what they're all about," Riley suggested. Amie reached for the keyboard and typed in the search terms. When the results appeared, Riley pointed at the top one. "Try that one." Amie clicked the link and the East Texas Militia's website appeared.

At the top of the page was what appeared to be a letter written by Abraham Lincoln in 1864. Amie read the letter and asked, "That mean anything to you?"

Riley shook his head. "Nope."

They scanned the rest of the site, seeing nothing of interest until they saw a short paragraph that read: *Tyranny, whether foreign or domestic, cannot go unchecked. We, the Sons of Liberty, believe that all men should live without government interference. We have seen tyranny in our own land and are duty bound to resist.* The word "resist" was highlighted in blue, indicating a hyperlinked text. "What's that?" Riley asked, pointing to the link.

Amie moved the mouse and hovered over the link.

CHAPTER 36

Amie clicked the link and a new window opened. A moment later, the image of a darkened room lined with rows of computer servers came into view. A clock was positioned at the bottom right of the screen that read: *1 hour, 58 minutes*. Riley and Amie exchanged glances but before they had a chance to comment, a voice from off camera began to speak in a slow and precise cadence.

"My name is Samuel. One hundred and fifty years ago, Abraham Lincoln warned us of a gathering storm that would one day wash away our rights as free men and women. Lincoln's Prophecy warned us that corporations have been enthroned and an era of corruption in high places will follow, and the money power of the country will endeavor to prolong its reign by working upon the prejudices of the people until all wealth is aggregated in a few hands and the Republic is destroyed."

Amie and Riley looked at one another with trepidation. Then, a dark silhouette entered the picture and sat down in the center of the frame.

The lights of the server stacks blinked in the background as the man continued.

"I am here to tell you," Samuel continued in his precise cadence, "that Lincoln's Prophesy is true. Corporations been enthroned through the power of information. Information about you and me – who we are, what we think and where we go. All of this is information is stored by corporations. As Lincoln predicted, control over this information has led to corruption in high places as corporations and the government conspire to share this power.

"So why do we let them? Because, as Lincoln prophesied, the government has played upon our prejudices and our fears. In this post-9/11 world, our government has convinced us we are under constant attack – that terrorists are everywhere. Our government has played on this fear so well that we have grown to believe the collection and tracking of our every thought is for our own good. And to comfort us, they tell us that those who have nothing to hide have nothing to fear."

The man paused for a long moment before continuing. "Our world is interconnected. Airports, banks, hospitals, railway systems – all are connected and all are compromised. The conspirators have access to it all through a program named Ceterus.

"Ceterus is the disease, but it is also the cure. We, The Sons of Liberty, shall use it to wipe the slate clean. By the time the clock on this video expires, you will know the power they have and what they have taken from us. If the leaders of our country do not confess their crimes, the clock will reset. We will begin again and again. Every twelve hours will bring a new demonstration until the truth has been revealed."

The video went black. Only the clock remained on the screen, which now read: *1 hour, 56 minutes.* Riley and Amie sat for a long moment in stunned silence. "Holy shit," Amie finally said. "He mentioned Ceterus by name."

"That's not all," Riley said, navigating the browser back to the militia's webpage, where he quickly scanned the text. "My God," he said.

"What?" Amie asked.

"The group references the Sons of Liberty here."

"So what does that tell us?" Amie asked.

"A lot," Riley responded. "The Sons of Liberty were formed during the American Revolution. There were groups all over America but the most famous was in Boston, where the Sons were led by a man named Samuel Adams. But there are other, less famous members." Riley turned to face Amie. "Men like Isaac Sears and Alexander McDougall."

Amie shook her head in disbelief. "My God," she said. "Samuel, Isaac and Alexander."

"Exactly," Riley said. "Historians credit Samuel Adams with leading the Boston Tea Party, which most British citizens at the time considered an act of terrorism. Today, of course, we see this as an iconic act of patriotism." The thought triggered a conclusion in Riley's mind. "I'll bet that's what these guys think they're doing now," he said, vaguely as the conclusion took hold.

"What?" Amie prompted.

"They think whatever they're planning will one day be seen as patriotic. That's why they've taken the names of famous revolutionaries. They're acting to uncover and reverse a government crime they believe has destroyed our freedoms." Riley and Amie exchanged glances.

"Ceterus," Amie said.

"Exactly. And that's why Isaac and this Samuel character were after Varden's copy of Ceterus. They wanted to steal it and use it against the government and its corporate conspirators."

"Makes sense," Amie agreed. Then she recalled something else. "The video mentioned wiping the slate clean."

"Yeah. Any idea what he meant?"

Amie was terrified she knew exactly what Samuel meant. "I think they're in a position to do exactly what they said – wipe the slate clean." Riley waited for an explanation. "The video focused on government and corporate collection of data and our interconnected world," Amie continued. "My guess is they've modified Ceterus to break these connections. The question is: What connections? Where are they going to attack?"

"He's already told us," Riley said, excitedly. "He gave us a list of targets: airports, banks, hospitals, railway systems."

Amie shrugged helplessly. "There are thousands of airports and banks. How would we ever know which ones he's talking about?" Amie shook her head. "This is huge, Michael. And it's way too big for us to handle on our own. We need help."

"Who? Coffman?" he asked. "You've got to be kidding. Every time we call him, Isaac shows up to kill us."

Amie knew Riley was right, but calling the F.B.I. wasn't the best option – it was the only option. "I don't think we have a choice," she said. "Samuel's in a position to launch the largest cyber attack in history. With the touch of a button, he could drop a nuclear bomb on the global network. Everything, from air traffic control to your bank account, is at risk. And, according to the video, we've got less than 2 hours to do something!"

Riley felt trapped. The last two times he'd reached out to Coffman, Isaac had known exactly when and where Riley would be. He didn't want to call Coffman again. But something had to be done and time was running out. Since it was the F.B.I.'s program that had been hijacked, the F.B.I. would instantly understand what Samuel had done. And they were probably the only ones who could act in time to stop the attack. Amie was right – there was no choice.

But Riley wasn't going to take any chances this time. They had to meet Coffman in a public place with plenty of space where they could see Isaac coming. It needed to be a place they knew better than either Isaac or Coffman. Slowly, the rough sketch of a plan fell into place. "Okay," Riley finally said. "Let's call Coffman. I've got an idea."

CHAPTER 37

Riley slid into the passenger seat of Amie's SUV and dug for his wallet. By the time Amie settled in on the driver's side, Riley had retrieved Coffman's card. He stared at it for a long moment before looking over at Amie.

"Okay," Riley said. "Let's do it."

Amie pulled the pre-paid cell phone from her bag and handed it to Riley.

"Coffman," came a familiar voice after the third ring.

"Agent Coffman? This is Michael Riley."

"Riley? Where the hell've you been? We've been looking all over for you."

"I know. I think it's time we meet."

"You're damn right it's time we meet," Coffman said sharply. "I'm at the Federal building downtown. You need to come in."

"I'm not coming in," Riley said forcefully. "You're going to meet *me*."

Coffman's blood began to boil. *Who the hell does this guy think he is?* "You're a law professor, Riley. Ever heard of a crime called interference with a government investigation? Because that's what you're doing here. Now you and your friend need to..."

"We know about Ceterus," Riley interrupted with a matter-of-fact tone that silenced Coffman in an instant. "We know who built it and what it does," Riley continued.

"How in the hell did you..."

"More importantly," Riley interrupted again, "We know someone's hijacked it, modified it, and is preparing to launch an unprecedented cyber attack. *And*," Riley said forcefully when Coffman tried to interject, "We've got an idea about who these people are. But if you want to talk about it, you'll have to do it my way."

The mention of Ceterus had chilled Coffman to his core. Even within the F.B.I., Ceterus was a deep secret. Only members of the F.B.I.'s clandestine Data Intercept Technology Unit had any idea the program existed. If Riley knew about it, Coffman shuttered to think what else he might know. To find out, Coffman decided to play Riley's game. He couldn't risk public exposure of the program, which would bring consequences too terrible to contemplate. "Okay, Riley," he said through clenched teeth, "You just tell me where and when."

"Be outside the west entrance to the Bush Presidential Library in thirty minutes. And have your phone with you," Riley instructed.

"I'll be there," Coffman said.

"I'll call you in thirty. And Coffman," added Riley.

"Yeah?"

"If I see anyone but you at the library, I'm taking Ceterus public," Riley said and then hung up the phone. He turned to Amie and let out a deep breath. "I guess that went about as well as expected."

"You got him to meet us. That's all we needed," Amie said, looking down at her watch. "We better get going," she said, starting the car and pulling away from the curb.

"Need a refill, hon?"

Isaac looked up from his paper to see an elderly waitress holding a full pot of coffee. He glanced down at his cup. "Just a warm-up."

He was returning to the sports page when his cell phone vibrated, rattling the nearby silverware. He stared at the waitress until she left and then picked up the phone. "Yes."

Samuel's typically deliberate tone was gone. This was urgent. "Riley's meeting the F.B.I. at the west entrance of the Bush Presidential Library. You need to get over there now."

Isaac looked at his watch to mark the time. "Got it."

"Riley knows everything," Samuel warned. "He can't get away again. This is our last chance."

That Riley knew everything was bad news, but it really didn't matter. He had seen Isaac kill Alexander at the canal. Whether Riley knew about their plan or not, he had to be taken out. "Understood," Isaac said. "I'll take care of it."

"Yes, of course." Samuel's voice grew calm again. "I know you will. You know if Riley succeeds, we fail and so does the Republic."

"He won't make it out of that library," Isaac said with absolute assurance.

"God's speed, Isaac," said Samuel, and then he was gone.

Isaac took one last sip of coffee and slid from the booth. He threw a five on the table and walked calmly out of the coffee shop.

CHAPTER 38

Completed in April of 2013, the massive, 226,000 square foot George W. Bush Presidential Center was built on twenty-three acres at the edge of the SMU campus. It included a museum, the George W. Bush Institute and a sprawling, fifteen-acre park filled with native Texas plants. The library's red brick exterior and beige limestone columns mirrored the architecture of the SMU campus. The west entrance opened to a central plaza that stretched out from beneath an enormous limestone portico.

When Amie and Riley arrived at the library, the plaza was crawling with elementary students and senior citizens organizing their assault on the library. Riley led the way through the crowd and Amie followed with a mixture of relief and trepidation. She was thankful they were reaching out to the F.B.I. but Riley's concerns about Coffman were contagious. *Can he be trusted?* She wasn't sure but she was still convinced they didn't have a choice. Samuel's threat was real. Somehow, he had infiltrated computer systems across the country and there was no telling what he intended to do next. There was no way to stop him without the F.B.I.'s help. She just hoped the precautions they'd planned were enough.

They passed beneath the portico and through the dark aluminum doors into the main atrium – a cavernous space with oak-paneled ceilings towering three stories overhead. Inside the doors, a handful of uniformed guards ushered incoming guests through a security check.

"Wallets, keys and metal in the basket, please," rang the monotone voice of the female security guard who was handing out small plastic bins and directing visitors through the metal detectors.

Amie threw her shoulder bag on the conveyor belt and watched it disappear into the X-ray machine. Riley followed her through the metal detectors and past the final security guard. Amie picked up her bag and threw it back onto her shoulder. "Ready?" she asked.

"Do I have a choice?" he asked with a smile before leading the way across the atrium and down a short hallway to a bank of elevators. The elevators led to the library's research facilities, which were restricted to research fellows and, as luck would have it, SMU faculty members.

Amie pulled her SMU faculty badge from her bag and swiped it across the card reader to open the elevator doors. "Okay," Amie said. "Where to?"

"Third floor," Riley said. Amie's hand shook slightly as she reached for the button. When the elevator began its ascent, Riley asked, "You Okay?"

"Yeah," Amie said with more confidence than she felt. "Just a bit nervous."

"It'll be fine," Riley said, reassuringly as the elevator came to a stop. "No need to worry."

The doors opened to an inviting lobby with cream-colored carpet and a small sitting area by the windows overlooking the plaza. "Back here," Riley said as he led the way through a set of glass doors and into the oak-paneled reading room of the Bush Institute. They crossed the narrow room to a second set of doors that opened to a rooftop balcony.

They stepped into the warm sunlight and walked to the metal railing at the edge of the balcony. For a brief moment, they took in the panoramic view of the SMU campus and the Dallas skyline off in the distance. The moment passed and Riley shifted his gaze to the grounds below.

The balcony was perfect. From the elevated position, they could see the entire plaza and, importantly, the granite path that led to the park behind the Institute. It also provided an inconspicuous place to wait and watch the foot traffic below.

Riley turned to Amie. "This is perfect," he said.

"It is," Amie agreed.

CHAPTER 39

Brinson Coffman threw the transmission into park and stared at the western façade of the Bush Presidential Library. *What the fuck is this guy up to?* he wondered. *And why the hell won't he just do as he's told?* Coffman heaved a sigh as he got out of the car and crossed the street towards the library.

He arrived at the plaza and scanned the crowd of tourists and elementary students. "Where are you, Riley?" he mumbled under his breath as his eyes shifted from one person to the next. Seeing no one resembling Michael Riley, he entered the crowd and began a slow walk around the ellipse at the center of the plaza. The sounds of teachers organizing their screaming children filled the air and Coffman almost missed his phone ringing in his coat pocket.

The moment the phone reached his ear, Coffman heard a familiar voice. "Hello, Agent Coffman. Glad you could make it."

"Riley, where the hell are you?" Coffman demanded, his eyes darting around the plaza.

"Turn to your right," Riley said. "You see the path leading behind the building?"

"Yeah."

"Follow the path around to the park. When the path splits, stay to the left. Then take the right fork into the park."

"Dammit, Riley!" Coffman shouted. "I know you're watching me. Just get over here and let's talk!"

"Follow the path to the second wooden bridge and wait for my call." Riley ended the call and turned to Amie, who was keeping her eyes on Coffman. "This is a little more excitement than I need in my life," he said.

"Me too. I could go for a beach and a Painkiller right now," Amie replied, thinking of her favorite tropical drink. "But this way we'll know Coffman is alone and Isaac isn't around." A second later she pointed down to the plaza. "Look. He's on the move. You keep an eye on Coffman; I'll watch for anyone following behind him."

Coffman walked slowly down the path and into the park. Minutes later, he reached the second bridge and stopped – just as instructed. Riley looked over his shoulder at Amie, who was still on the other side of the balcony watching the plaza.

"He's on the bridge," Riley said. "I didn't see anyone follow him. Did you?"

"Nope," Amie said, walking over to Riley's side, where she saw Coffman standing on the bridge. "Did he use his phone or anything?"

"Not that I saw. I think he's playing it straight."

Amie wasn't so sure but, at this point, there wasn't much more they could do. "Seems like it," she said reassuringly.

Riley breathed a heavy sigh. "Then it's time for me to go. You stay here and watch." As expected, Amie started to protest, but Riley threw up his hands to stop her. "Look," he said, "there's no reason for us both to go down there. You can see everything from here. If all goes to plan, I'll be back in ten minutes. And if something goes wrong, go straight to your car. If I'm not there in five minutes, get the hell out of here. Understand?"

Amie nodded and her eyes welled. "Please be careful, Michael," she said, reaching for his arm.

Riley pulled her towards him and hugged her. "I will," he said. Then he turned and walked inside.

The white cargo van drove through the open gate and into the construction site. A variety of work vehicles were parked in and around the site so the van drew little attention as Isaac pulled into the parking garage and drove slowly up to the fifth floor. After circling the entire level to confirm it was empty, he selected a parking space at the far end of the garage and backed carefully into position.

He got out of the van and walked towards the open windows that ran the length of the garage. When the scene below came into view, Isaac knew he'd chosen the right place. From his elevated position, he had a clear view of the entire western façade of the George W. Bush Library. He stood in the window for several minutes, studying the layout of the grounds. To his left he could see the library's main entrance and the central plaza. To the right lay a pathway that led down the length of the building to the undulating landscape of the park.

Turning back to the plaza, he examined the crowds. People were moving in all directions, which made for a confusing scene and complicated Isaac's task. He knew Riley would have to cross the plaza at some point. Spotting him in the sea of people would require careful examination and a little bit of luck. Isaac looked down at his watch and saw that time was short.

He circled around the van and opened the sliding door. A plastic, hard-shell case sat beside the doorway. Isaac pulled it close and unlatched the metal clasps. The rifle was a black, bolt-action Remington 700 – known for its accuracy at a distance and widely considered the world's finest high-velocity hunting rifle. Isaac stood the rifle upright in the case and opened a separate compartment to reveal a Leupold long-range riflescope. Sliding the scope into place, he took the rifle to the garage window, where he released the twin legs of the gun's built-in bipod.

He placed the bipod at the center of the concrete windowsill and, as he pressed the stock of the rifle tight into his shoulder, he felt his pulse pounding in his extremities. Isaac knew a heavy heartbeat could shift the rifle and compromise accuracy – especially when firing at a distance. Today, of all days, he had to be accurate. *Breathe,* he told himself. Then he closed his eyes and visualized his target.

Isaac turned the rifle and trained the scope on the crowd below. Sweeping the barrel across the central plaza, he methodically studied the faces that passed slowly through the crosshairs of the high-powered lens. He examined one group after another, dismissing each in turn. *Where are you, you son of a bitch? I know you're out there.* Isaac searched the entire plaza, but Riley was nowhere to be found.

Frustrated, he swiveled the rifle down the length of the building and out to the park. He saw a handful of people walking the trail, a family taking pictures beneath a pecan tree, a couple resting on a wooden bench and...*Wait! What's that?* Isaac quickly swept the scope back to a wooden bridge near the middle of the park. The man didn't fit. He was wearing a suit and tie and standing by himself at the end of the bridge - clearly waiting for someone. When the man finally turned, Isaac focused the crosshairs on his face. It was Agent Brinson Coffman.

Just then, a dark shape flashed in the lens as another man entered the frame. Isaac shifted the rifle and tensed his index finger around the trigger. His vision blurred as the images sped through the sightline. He steadied the rifle and the face of Michael Riley appeared in the center of the crosshairs. Isaac held his breath to slow his heart rate and fix his aim. He could feel the weight of the trigger against his finger as his muscles tensed and he prepared to fire. *I got you now.*

Then, Riley slipped from view. Determined not to miss his chance, Isaac turned the rifle again. "Sonofabitch!" he swore as he peered through the scope. All he could see was the back of Coffman's head. Riley had shifted his stance and unknowingly placed the F.B.I. agent directly in the line of fire.

Fighting the adrenaline that surged through his body, Isaac forced his finger away from the trigger. A single shot from the high-powered rifle could easily take out both men. But killing Coffman wasn't an option. He took a deep breath and, keeping the crosshairs trained on the back of Coffman's head, Isaac waited for his shot.

CHAPTER 40

s all this really necessary, Riley?" Coffman asked, throwing his hands out at his surroundings.

"Someone's stolen Ceterus and is planning an attack," Riley said, getting straight to the point.

"What? Wait a second," Coffman demanded.

"We don't have a second!"

"Well, we're going to have to take one so I can understand what the hell's going on here. Slow down and tell me what this is all about."

Riley stared into Coffman's eyes and took a deep, frustrated breath. Coffman plainly knew more than he was letting on. He was putting on this charade to figure out what Riley knew – and what he didn't. With Samuel's clock continuing to count down, there was no time for games. Riley had to get everything out in the open and hope for the best.

"This is about Ceterus – the F.B.I.'s domestic spy program. This is about a group of men calling themselves the Sons of Liberty, who have stolen Ceterus, modified it, and are planning to use it in some sort of terrorist attack."

Coffman held his hands up. "Calm down, Riley. Just start from the beginning and tell me everything you know."

Suddenly, all the anger and frustration that had been building inside Riley over the past days came rushing to the surface. "I'll tell you what I know," he said angrily. "I know you didn't talk to me about Varden that day at the canal because Varden was the one who built your spy program. I know the F.B.I. has used that program to gain direct access to personal computers across the country and that what you've done is completely illegal. Most importantly, I know that members of this Sons of Liberty group exhumed Varden and cut him open to get a copy of Ceterus. Those same men have now modified your little program and infected God knows how many computer networks across the planet. Now, they're set to launch a massive cyber attack in under two hours!"

"Wait a second," Coffman interrupted. "You're saying an unknown group of terrorists have stolen a top-secret program that only a handful of people in the world know about and are going to use it to launch some sort of terrorist attack? How do you know all this?"

"The same way I learned about Ceterus." Riley reached into his pocket and pulled out the black flash drive.

Taking the drive, Coffman said, "What's this?"

"Varden left this for his friend, Shea Baggett, so in case Varden was killed Baggett could use the program on that thumb drive to keep an eye on what you guys are up to."

"So this is what you got from Varden's fountain," Coffman concluded. "Well? What's on it?"

"It's a key," Riley said simply. "A key that unlocks a back door to Ceterus and any program with a similar signature. We installed it on a computer at the library and it detected two files – Ceterus, which you know all about, and some other file that was not built by the F.B.I."

"How do you know these Sons of Liberty people are behind it all?"

"Because I found a video online where a man calling himself Samuel – as in Samuel Adams – claimed to be part of a group called the Sons of Liberty. He talked about Ceterus by name and described it perfectly. Then he said he was going to use it against the government and its corporate conspirators."

Coffman was stunned. If even half of what Riley said was true, everything he'd worked for had been compromised. He turned the flash drive in his hand. "Is this the only copy?" he asked, his first instinct being to contain the problem.

After everything they'd just discussed, Coffman's question struck Riley as utterly irrelevant. "You mean besides the copy Isaac carved out of Varden's hip?" he asked, his frustration welling over again. "You think I want another copy of that thing?" Coffman stood silently and stared down at the drive. "This threat is real," Riley urged. "You need to take that flash drive back to the F.B.I. and do something." Riley's voice grew louder with every word. "Samuel's going to attack in under two hours. You've got to do something!"

Coffman slipped the flash drive inside his coat pocket. "Okay, Riley," he said, coolly. "Let's go downtown and check it out."

"I'm not going downtown. I've given you everything you need." Riley thrust a finger towards Coffman's chest. "It's your job to do something about it." Then Riley turned to walk away.

CHAPTER 41

saac stood in the window and held the crosshairs on the back of Coffman's head. As the conversation dragged on, he found it impossible to contain his anxiety. Riley was the only witness to connect him to the events at the canal and the events to come. Without Riley, there would be no crime, no punishment. This was his chance. Right here. Right now. Riley could not leave that bridge alive.

"Come on, Coffman. Move." Isaac pleaded in a whisper. "Just one step is all I need." But the two men framed inside the crosshairs were locked in the same position.

The minutes passed slowly by, and Isaac's patience grew thin. *Stay focused,* he instructed himself as. The exchange below grew increasingly heated. Isaac's heart pounded heavily in his chest as he sensed his moment was near. *Riley will not leave that bridge alive,* he repeated to himself.

Suddenly, Riley turned to walk away. Isaac gripped the trigger and waited for a clean shot.

Then, Riley's head came into view. Isaac tightened his grip and pulled the trigger.

"Riley, wait," Coffman said, stepping forward.

Riley turned around and, in that instant, the unmistakable crack of gunfire shattered the air. Riley felt a warm liquid spread across his face. His eyes closed and something hit him hard, forcing his body over the edge of the bridge. He fell several feet and collided with the solid limestone blocks beneath the bridge.

The world went black and still. He felt nothing. Time had stopped and a state of complete relaxation washed over him. There were no sounds. He was floating gently in space for what felt like an eternity. He was slowly drifting away when he felt it – a gentle warmth rolling across his lips. The world ceased to exist as his every thought centered on the sensation that was now moving over his lip and onto his tongue. *What is that?* he wondered. *Is that blood? Am I dead?* A sound from the distance stole his concentration. Someone was screaming. *Who is that?* It was a woman. Her scream was getting louder, closer.

An instant later, all Riley's senses returned at once. The sensations that had been playing in slow motion were now coming so rapidly he couldn't make sense of them. Women were screaming, children crying, feet shuffling as people pushed and shoved their way from danger. Riley opened his eyes and saw a pool of deep red spreading across the limestone block before him. He stared at the deepening pool, his mind still suspended in a fog. *Is that blood?* He lifted his head and strained to focus on a blurred object hanging over him. His head was pounding. Slowly, his vision cleared and he saw the blood was running down from between the wooden slats of the bridge above.

The sight triggered a memory – something had hit his face the instant he heard the gunshot. He lifted a shaking hand and wiped his face, which was covered in blood and sweat. *Whose blood is that?* Riley took stock of his body. With the exception of a searing headache and a throbbing pain in his shoulder, he felt okay. The blood wasn't his, it was Coffman's.

"Coffman!" Riley yelled through the underside of the bridge causing his head to swell with pain. There was no answer. "Coffman!"

The unmistakable truth hit Riley in a flash. *Isaac.* Isaac fired that shot. Panic surged through Riley's veins. *Think!* he demanded. He had to find a way out. But tucked inside Coffman's jacket pocket was a copy of a top-secret and extremely dangerous computer program. He couldn't leave Ceterus behind. He made a decision. *Get the flash drive and get the hell out of here.*

Riley took a second to look around and take in his surroundings. The bridge lay just a few feet overhead. Through the slats of the wooden decking, he could see the shadowy outline Coffman's body near the edge of the bridge. That meant the flash drive was only feet away. *But where's Isaac?* Riley wondered. *And where did that shot come from?*

Riley trained his mind on the moments before the shooting. He was walking across the bridge when Coffman called out. Riley had turned just as the shot was fired. The bullet hit Coffman, who must have fallen forward into Riley and pushed him off the bridge. That meant the shot was fired from behind Coffman. Isaac had to be somewhere between the bridge and the main SMU campus – probably on a rooftop. Regardless, the bridge was obviously within range and Riley was sure Isaac was still watching the park through the lens of a high-powered scope. Riley would have to move quickly.

The park was completely deserted, leaving it eerily quiet as Riley mentally rehearsed his plan. *You'll be fine if you move fast,* he told himself. Staying beneath the cover of the bridge, Riley slowly got to his hands and knees. He looked up at the bridge to see he was directly below Coffman's body. Inching to the edge of the bridge, Riley squatted down and placed his hand on the underside of the bridge to steady himself. Blood and sweat rolled down his face as Riley slowly counted to three. *GO!*

He sprang to his feet and hurled his upper body over the top of the bridge where he grabbed Coffman's belt with one hand and the shoulder of his jacket with the other. Pulling as hard as he could, Riley threw his body backwards. In one quick movement, Coffman's body slid to the edge of the bridge and began to fall as another shot rang out in the distance. The bullet slammed into the bridge a foot from Riley's arm. The wooden deck splintered and showered down into the ravine as Riley and Coffman's bodies fell backwards and crashed into limestone rock below.

"Sonofabitch!" Riley yelled in the shock of fear and adrenaline. He rolled Coffman's body over with a heavy push and frantically searched his coat pockets. Grabbing the first object he felt, he pulled out Coffman's cell phone. He dropped it to the ground before throwing the coat open and searching the inside pocket. His fingers swept the bottom of the pocket and found the plastic flash drive.

Riley stuffed the cell phone and flash drive in his pocket and looked for a way out. The library was the safest place to be, but using the path overhead was out of the question. Riley got to his hands and knees and studied the terrain. The bridge spanned a ravine that snaked its way along the edge of the park towards the library. The ravine was flanked by a large berm that appeared tall enough to give him some cover. If he could get to the ravine, Riley was sure he could make it to the building.

He crawled along the stone buttress to the other side of the bridge and peered over the edge. The bottom of the ravine was several feet below and covered in tall native grass. *Now or never,* Riley thought. He gripped the edge of the limestone and positioned his feet like a runner in the starting blocks.

"One," he said, pulling his body forward to test his grip, "two," his body swayed forward for a second time. "Three!" Riley hurled himself out from beneath the bridge and down into the ravine. A rifle shot cracked and dirt flew into the air on top of the berm. Riley's reflexes twisted his body in mid-air to prepare for the hard landing. The tall grass brushed his face and a second later he hit the ground hard in a cloud of dust.

Riley scrambled to the bottom of the ravine and laid flat in the dirt. He held his breath and listened for another shot. But all was quiet. He rolled over and peered through the tall grass. The top of the berm was well over his head and completely blocked Riley's view of campus. There was no way Isaac could see him. Riley jumped up and ran along the ravine. His legs churned as he followed its curved path down the length of the park. He was relieved to be on the move but the relief vanished as soon as it had arrived. Just ahead, the ravine turned sharply away from the library.

Riley stopped at the edge of the ravine and crouched low in the grass. The only way to get to the safety of the library was to cross a thirty-yard stretch of open ground. With Isaac watching from somewhere in the distance, it was impossibly far. "Shit!" Riley yelled, frustration welling up inside him. For all he knew, Isaac had guessed Riley's plan and had trained his rifle on the obvious escape route. Riley couldn't risk it.

He searched for options. Further down the ravine, a concrete drainage pipe oozed heavy silt into a small creek. He was wondering where the pipe went when the distant sound of sirens broke his concentration. They were getting closer by the second. Riley had to make a quick decision – stay and try to explain this to the local police or dive into the drainage pipe and see where it led.

The decision was easy. Riley ran down the ravine to the mouth of the pipe. Throwing his head inside, he pulled himself through the mud and into the cool darkness of the concrete pipe. Though he wasn't claustrophobic, Riley instantly looked for the other end of the confined space. Thankfully, a faint light filtered down at the far end of the pipe about thirty yards away. Riley rolled onto his stomach and began a slow crawl through the mud towards the light.

He was completely covered in silt and cobwebs when he reached the other end. The pipe connected to another concrete space that was nearly large enough for Riley to stand. He got to his feet and tried to brush the mud from his pants. The sounds of the city streets echoed from above. Giving up on his pants, Riley looked up and saw the underside of a manhole cover. He reached overhead and pushed the manhole cover up and onto the sidewalk above. With some effort, Riley squeezed through the manhole and pulled himself from beneath the city streets. Sitting on the sidewalk with his feet dangling into the storm drain, he pulled out Coffman's phone and the slip of paper with Amie's new cell phone number.

"Dammit!" Isaac said, gritting his teeth and looking through the scope at the bloodstained bridge. He was slowly sweeping the rifle from the bridge to the library when he heard sirens in the distance.

With each passing moment, the sirens grew louder and Isaac's hope of eliminating Riley faded. In a matter of minutes, police would have the entire SMU campus cordoned off. His time was up. He'd missed Riley again. "Son of a bitch!" he said, retracting the rifle's legs. He returned to the van's cargo door and locked the gun back in its case.

Isaac hopped inside the cargo bay and slid the door firmly into place. Reaching the driver's seat, the scene at the bridge played over in his mind. Coffman's death was a terrible accident. Isaac had been too quick to pull the trigger. It was a costly mistake that would make the mission more difficult. His only solace was in remembering Samuel's words: *The mission is bigger than any one man.*

The sound of approaching sirens pierced the memory and Isaac snapped to attention. Thrusting his hand forward, he started the engine and jammed the accelerator to the floor. The tires squealed as the van sped down through the lower levels of the garage. The sirens were screaming when he reached the ground level. The police were closing in fast on his position.

Isaac's heart raced. He quickly pulled the van into a nearby parking space and turned off the ignition. He took his foot off the brake and slumped down in the seat. Looking in the rearview mirror, Isaac glimpsed the flashing lights of two SMU Campus police cars speeding by the garage. He took several deep breaths and closed his eyes to focus his attention. The sirens were fading into the distance.

Isaac had to move. He started the van and drove slowly to the garage entrance. To his left, a dozen emergency response vehicles had collected outside the Bush Library. To his right, the road was clear. Isaac turned down the vacant road and slipped unnoticed from the campus.

CHAPTER 42

Grace Iaucone sat at the nurse's station at St. Joseph's Hospital in suburban Maryland and charted the latest readings from the bank of monitors on her desk. There were eight monitors in all – one for each room in the hospital's Intensive Care Unit. Thankfully, two patients had been discharged from the ICU earlier that morning, which reduced the patient load from eight to a more manageable six. Still, four of the six remaining patients were in critical condition, their lives sustained by a collection of hoses, wires and machines that ran twenty-four hours a day.

Grace looked up from her paperwork to the clock on the wall. Her shift began more than eleven hours earlier and she was thankful it was almost over. The day had been long but relatively calm and she took a moment to look around the ward. The nurse's station offered a three hundred and sixty degree view of the unit. Grace was able to see each patient through the glass walls that fronted each patient's room.

She glanced into room six where the nurse gently repositioned the ICU's newest patient. Two days before, Mark Eldridge had been driving his son home from soccer practice when he slowed for a red light. The car came to a stop and Mark heard a metallic tapping on his driver's side window. He turned to the window and saw an unknown man aiming a shotgun directly at him. Mark glanced at his son in the rearview mirror and made a snap decision. He slammed the accelerator to the floor and the car lurched forward. The sudden movement surprised the assailant, who aimlessly pulled the trigger. The shotgun blast tore through the car door and ripped into Mark's left lung. The assailant dropped the shotgun and disappeared into the city streets.

When the paramedics arrived, Mark was barely alive. They rushed him to St. Josephs where, after several emergency surgeries, he was stabilized enough to be moved to the intensive care unit. Now, forty-eight hours later, Mark Eldridge remained in stable, but critical condition.

Grace looked at the monitor for Mark's room. It displayed readings from the various machines keeping him alive during his recovery. Grace was charting the current readings when an alarm sounded through the nurse's station. Her eyes shot up from the paperwork and scanned the row of screens. The alarm was from the heart rate monitor in room four. Grace shook her head and sighed. Mr. Neuhoff, who was in the ICU recovering from a brain aneurism, often pulled the leads from this chest as he slept. Each time, an alert sounded at the nurse's station.

"Susan," Grace said, catching the attention of the passing ICU nurse. "Would you check on room four? I think Mr. Neuhoff has pulled one of his leads again."

"Right away," Susan said and walked briskly towards the room.

Another alarm sounded, calling Grace's attention back to the monitors. A flashing red alert indicated the ventilator in room six had completely shut down. Grace's heart skipped a beat. Without the ventilator to gently force air into his damaged lungs, Mark Eldridge would slowly suffocate. Grace fought her instinct to rush into the room and restart the ventilator. Each nurse in the ICU had a clear set of duties and she knew the nurse assigned to the patient would respond quickly.

As expected, the nurse rounded the corner and rushed into the room. Grace watched through the glass as she pressed the ventilator's touch screen.

Seconds later, she looked at Grace through the glass, her eyes conveying the urgency of the situation.

"Need a new vent in six," she said in a booming voice that briefly overpowered the alarms ringing out at the nurse's station.

Grace sprang from her chair and rounded the corner to a nearby hallway where rows of equipment were prepped and stored for emergency situations. She grabbed a ventilator and ran back down the hall. Though ventilator failures were rare, she'd experienced them in the past. She arrived in room six knowing that if the equipment was replaced quickly, there would be no lasting damage to the patient.

Grace wheeled the new machine into the room and powered it up. She handed the ventilator tube to the nurse behind her, who hooked it to the tracheal tube running from the patient's mouth to his lungs.

"Go!" the nurse said and Grace hit the button to start the flow of oxygen. She stared at the LED screen, expecting to see an instant reading of the patient's condition. Nothing happened. She pressed the button again, but the ventilator refused to respond.

For a moment, time stood still. Grace looked down at the helpless face of Mark Eldridge. He lay there at rest – eyes closed and completely oblivious to the chaos and the slow death of asphyxiation hovering over him. His skin was a ghostly white and his lips, parted by the width of the tracheal tube, had turned a light shade of blue.

Suddenly, the rush of events surrounding her snapped Grace back into action. Her twenty years of training took over.

"Bag him!" she ordered and the nurse unhooked the ventilator, connected a respirator bag to the tracheal tube, and began manually pumping oxygen into Mark's fragile lungs. Grace ran to the nurse's station and picked up the phone. The line was answered in an instant.

"Operator," came the sharp answer.

Grace's tone was urgent but professional. "Code Blue – ICU, room six." Code Blue was the highest state of patient emergency and, once declared, a strict protocol directed each member of the ICU staff what to do.

"Code Blue – ICU, room six," repeated the operator to confirm the order and then hung up. A second later, the announcement rang out over the hospital's intercom system: *Code Blue – ICU, room six...Code Blue – ICU, room six.* Before the code was repeated for the third time, the ICU's Rapid Response Team was rushing to the scene.

Doctor Crespi was the first to arrive, followed closely by a nurse pushing a crash cart that resembled a rolling mechanic's toolbox. "What do we got?" Crespi demanded, pressing the end of his stethoscope to the patient's chest.

Grace stood in the nurse's station and listened to the succinct description of the patient's condition when another alarm sounded. "I need labs in here!" Crespi yelled from inside room six as Grace frantically scanned the monitors to see what had caused the latest alarm.

When she saw the red flashing alert on monitor four, Grace covered her mouth with her hand. "Oh my God," she said softly. It was the same alert she'd just seen in room six – only this time, the ventilator in room four had shut down. One ventilator failure was rare but two failures at one time was unheard of. Seconds later, she saw Susan running to room four with a backup vent in tow.

Grace felt a knot tighten in the pit of her stomach. She started a short prayer but was interrupted by the sound of yet another alert. Another patient's vital signs were crashing. In her twenty years of nursing, she had never heard of a catastrophic emergency like this. Every patient connected to life-sustaining equipment was crashing at the same time.

She knew there was no way the ICU staff could respond to three emergencies at one time. They needed help. She was reaching for the phone when the nurse from room four ran to the desk.

"The vent won't come on-line!" she said in a panic. "We have a Code Blue in four!"

An announcement over the hospital's intercom stole Grace's attention. "Code Blue in rooms 306, 315 and 330," said the operator in a trembling voice. Grace stood, eyes wide open and watched blankly as doctors and nurses flooded the halls running in every direction. Orders of every kind were being yelled across the ward so that there was no way to distinguish one from another. Staff members were desperately running replacement machines from the storage hall to the rooms. Standing in a sea of absolute chaos, Grace had a moment of clear revelation: *Someone has done this intentionally.*

"Grace, get in here!" yelled Dr. Crespi, dragging Grace from her thoughts. She looked into room six where she saw Crespi leaning over Mark Eldridge and performing manual chest compressions.

"Grace!" yelled Susan, still needing instruction on the Code Blue in room four.

Grace turned abruptly to the nurse, who was frozen with panic. "Call it in!" Grace commanded and then she dove into the fray, trying to help anyone she could.

CHAPTER 43

Amie pulled into the parking garage at Mockingbird Station – a popular, mixed-use development that was just across the highway from the George W. Bush Library. As she circled down through the concrete ramps, a sense of relief washed over her. The sound of Riley's voice had relieved the terror she'd felt after hearing the rifle shot and seeing Riley disappear over the side of the bridge. In that moment, Amie was certain she had lost Riley forever. Even after hearing his voice and his calm reassurances that he was okay, the pain in Amie's stomach wouldn't stop until she saw him.

She arrived on level B-3 and found a parking space near the center of the crowded garage. Putting the car in Park, she shut off the ignition and was turning to get out when a dark figure suddenly appeared at the passenger door. Before Amie could react, the door was open and a man was jumping into the front seat. Amie's eyes were wide with fright when she looked over to see the muddied face of Michael Riley.

"Sorry," Riley said, seeing Amie's fearful expression. "I saw you park and figured I'd just..."

Before Riley could finish his explanation, Amie grabbed him and pulled him close. The relief she had felt when Riley called her was nothing compared to the feeling of having him next to her and knowing he was truly safe. Her eyes welled with tears as she held him tight.

"You scared me, Michael," she said, her voice muffled against Riley's neck. When she slowly released him from her embrace, Riley's battered appearance struck her for the first time. "Oh my God," she said, wiping the tear from her face. "What happened? I heard a gunshot and you disappeared. Is Coffman dead?"

Riley looked nervously around the parking garage, half-expecting to see Isaac closing in on them. Seeing no one, he told Amie every detail of what happened.

"My God," Amie said, covering her mouth. "I can't believe they killed an F.B.I. agent. What the hell is going on?"

"I have no idea. Assuming Isaac was doing the shooting, he wouldn't have taken the shot if

Coffman was part of the plot, would he? He would've made sure Coffman was well out of the way before pulling the trigger."

"Maybe," Amie said, weighing the options. "Or maybe he just missed."

Riley replayed the moments before the shot in his mind. Both he and Coffman had moved just as the shot was fired. Now that Riley thought about it, Coffman's death could have been a complete accident. "Maybe you're right," Riley agreed. "He must have been shooting from a distance and..." Suddenly, an unfamiliar ring filled the cabin and Riley felt a vibration in his pocket.

"What's that?" Amie asked.

Knowing exactly what it was, Riley didn't answer the question. Instead, he reached into his pocket and pulled out Coffman's cell phone. He held it out for her to see as the phone rang for a second time.

"Who is it?" she asked urgently. Riley looked at the display, which read: Andy Dyll – Director DITU. He turned the phone for Amie to read. "That's the head of DITU!" she said. "I'll bet he's the guy who hired Varden to build Ceterus." Riley stared down at the phone as it rang for a third time. "You going to answer it?"

Riley was unsure what to do. The last time he had called the F.B.I., the conversation had led Isaac directly to the Bush Library and to Riley. But the facts remained the same. Samuel's attack was imminent and, without help, there would be now way to stop it. Plus, Coffman's death had shaken Riley's theories on the F.B.I.'s involvement. If Isaac had shot Coffman, maybe Coffman wasn't involved in the plot. The phone rang for the fifth time. Knowing he had to do something, Riley answered the call and the speaker crackled to life.

"Coffman?" came an agitated and unfamiliar male voice. Riley and Amie exchanged glances. "Coffman? You there?" Amie looked back at Riley, her eyes sending a clear message: *Say something.* "We're getting reports up here that."

"This isn't Agent Coffman," Riley interrupted with more confidence than he felt.

The man on the other end paused for a beat. "What? Who is this?"

Before saying anything, Riley wanted at least verbal confirmation it really was Andy Dyll on the other end. "Who's this?" he demanded.

"This is F.B.I. Agent Andrew Dyll. Who am I talking to and why do you have my agent's phone?"

"This is Michael Riley and..."

"Riley!" Dyll interrupted. "We've been looking all over for you! Where's Agent Coffman?"

"Coffman is," Riley hesitated, "he's dead." The silence that followed was deafening. Not knowing what to do, Riley continued. "I think he was shot by a man named Isaac – the same man who dumped Christoph Varden's body and killed Dennis Lavine."

"What're you talking about? How do you know?"

"Because I was standing right next to Coffman when he died." Now that he had started talking, Riley felt an urgency to get to the point and tell Dyll what he knew. "Look, Mr. Dyll," Riley began, "we know about Ceterus. But so do others. A group calling themselves the Sons of Liberty have stolen it and used it to develop a virus designed to carry out a massive cyber attack on government and corporate networks. He's planning to attack banks, airports, hospitals --"

"What did you say?" Andy interrupted. "Did you say hospitals?"

"Yes," Riley said, sensing something was wrong. "Why? What's happened?"

Andy left the question hanging in the air as the pieces fell together in his mind. The F.B.I. had presumed Riley knew out about Ceterus and that he might even have a copy. That Riley had connected the attack on the nation's hospitals with Ceterus was terrifying. "There may have already been an attack," Andy finally said.

Riley felt his stomach twist. He looked down at his watch. "That's not possible!" he shouted. "We've still got time! He's attacked a hospital?"

"We're not sure. We're receiving reports from hospitals across the country about equipment failures."

Amie couldn't believe what she was hearing. *Samuel has done the unthinkable.*

"This is only the beginning," Riley said softly, looking off into the distance.

"Look, Mr. Riley, I've got to know everything. And I've got to know it now." Andy demanded.

The abrupt tone cut through the fog that had settled over Riley. He took a deep breath and launched into an explanation of Varden, Ceterus, the video, and Samuel. "From what Samuel said in the video," Riley concluded, "he's going to launch a new attack every twelve hours until the government comes clean about Ceterus. If that's true, we've got some time before the next attack."

"Time for what? How can we stop him in less than twelve hours? We don't even know what his next target is." Andy said, with building frustration.

"We don't need to," Riley said, plunging ahead. "Varden left something behind – something he called the Ceterus Key. It's a kind of back door into Ceterus."

"Wait a second," Andy interjected. "Varden built Ceterus for the F.B.I. If he built a back door, we'd know about it."

"That's just the point," Riley argued. "Varden thought the F.B.I. might abuse Ceterus. He built the Key so he could keep an eye on what you're doing. And he had to keep it a secret so you wouldn't close the back door and lock him out."

Everything Riley was saying made sense. Andy knew it was just like Varden to create a back door to his own program. Ceterus had been designed to infiltrate systems and disappear without a trace. Once deployed, the F.B.I. had no way of getting it back. But now, a ray of hope shone through the clouds. *The Ceterus Key may solve all our problems,* Andy thought. "Do you have a copy of this Key?" Andy asked.

"Yes," Riley said as he turned the black flash drive in his hand.

"Good. Tell me where you are and I'll send some agents to get you."

If Riley was going to work with the F.B.I., he wasn't going to do it in Dallas where Isaac was waiting around every corner. "No," Riley said bluntly, "I'm not meeting anyone here. Every time I've tried to meet with the F.B.I., Isaac and Lord knows who else have tried to kill me. I can't just sit here and wait for Isaac to show up again. I'm coming to you."

"We," Amie interjected. Riley looked up at her. "We are coming to meet you," she said in an uncompromising tone.

"Is that Doctor Hawkins?" Andy asked, completely unaware she'd been there the entire time. "She's in as much danger as you are, Riley. You both need to come in."

Amie pressed the mute button on the phone. "I know you're trying to protect me, Michael," she said softly. "You need me. I can help."

Riley stared into Amie's deep brown eyes. Agent Dyll was right – Amie was in danger. And given what Riley was about to do, he doubted he'd survive without her help. He reached for her hand and held it tight. "Okay," he said. He pressed the mute button again and spoke to Andy. "You're in D.C., right?"

"Yes."

"Okay. We're coming to you."

"Hold on, Riley."

"And don't send any of your agents to greet us at the airport. We'll call you when we're ready to talk." Without waiting on Andy's reply, Riley ended the call and powered the phone off.

Amie looked over at Riley. "Looks like we have a plane to catch," she said. "Come on." Amie turned and opened the car door.

"Where are you going?" Riley asked.

Amie looked back over her shoulder. "We're going to buy you some new clothes," she smiled. "We can't take our first trip together with you looking like that."

CHAPTER 44

You can go on in, Mr. Dyll." said the receptionist as Andy entered the executive suite. This was the second time Andy had been in the Director's office in as many days and, while he knew it was part of the job, he preferred to keep a slightly lower profile than this.

"Thanks," he said, passing the receptionist and stopping in front of the heavy oak door. He paused for a moment before knocking lightly. Special Assistant to the Director, Edward Ross, opened the door before Andy had a chance lower his hand.

"Come on in, Andy," boomed Director Louis Webster from inside the office. Andy stepped into the spacious office to see the Director pouring a fresh cup of coffee. "Coffee?" the Director asked, lifting the silver carafe.

"No, thank you, sir."

The Director set the carafe on the table. "Have a seat," he said, motioning to the seating area in the corner of the room. Andy crossed the room and sat in one of the armchairs facing the oak coffee table. The Director joined him a moment later and sat on the couch across from Andy. He took a quick sip of coffee. "Okay, Andy," he said, resting the cup on the arm of the couch. "I've heard about Coffman."

Andy looked down at his feet. "Yes, sir."

"A real tragedy," said the Director. "I'm truly sorry."

"Thank you," Andy said.

"You know we'll take good care of his family." Andy nodded. "We've got to get to the bottom of this damned thing," the Director continued. "So tell me: what's the good and the bad on Ceterus?"

"Well sir," Andy began, "as you know, in its short life, Ceterus has been exceedingly successful. It has provided intelligence that has directly led to the disruption of three separate terrorist plots, and it has helped us identify a dozen suspected terrorists operating within the United States. These suspects are now under constant surveillance and are, effectively, neutralized. In short, Ceterus is the most powerful counter-terrorist tool ever developed."

"But there's a catch," said the Director, knowing where Andy was headed and spurring him to get to the point.

Just then, Edward Ross sat down in the armchair next to Andy, holding a yellow legal pad and pen. Andy glanced at the notepad and briefly wondered what parts of this Top Secret conversation Ross planned to write down. "Well, sir," Andy began, "I've talked to Michael Riley." The Director lowered his head and looked at Andy over the top of his reading glasses, his brow raised in anticipation. "As we suspected, he knows all about Ceterus and what it does. It seems, Christoph Varden left behind a copy of the program, which Riley and his friend Amie Hawkins found at Varden's house."

"So not only do they know about it, but they've got a copy of the damned thing?" the Director asked.

"Yes, sir. And that's not all," Andy continued. "You know how Ceterus was designed to infiltrate systems and go completely undetected." The Director nodded and Andy went on. "Riley claims that Varden built a second program – a sort of back door into Ceterus. Varden called this second program the Ceterus Key, which was designed to allow Varden to monitor the F.B.I.'s use of Ceterus."

"Why would he do that without telling us?" Edward Ross interjected. The question surprised Andy, who presumed Ross was simply there to take notes.

"Apparently," Andy said after a beat, "Varden didn't trust the F.B.I. quite as much as he led on."

"The whole thing's blown wide open then?" the Director asked, hoping somehow that the answer was *no*. Andy looked over at Ross, who'd stopped taking notes and was hanging on every word.

"Sir, that may be the least of our worries. Riley claims that a group calling themselves the Sons of Liberty are the ones who dug Varden from his grave to obtain a copy of Ceterus. As you know, we suspect whoever exhumed Varden killed him in the first place."

"Wait a minute," the Director held up a hand. "How does Riley know this?"

"He claims to have seen a video on the Internet where the leader of this group described Ceterus by name and threatened to use it against the government and U.S. corporations. But," Andy said, anticipating the Director's next question, "Riley hung up on me before I could ask him where the video was posted."

"Okay," the Director said. "Any specifics on how this Sons of Liberty group intends to carry out the attacks?"

"Riley has a theory, sir, that the group modified Ceterus and has already used it to conduct today's attack against the hospitals."

The Director's coffee cup hung in mid-air. "Hold on, Andy. Riley thinks these guys are the ones shutting down the hospitals?" News about mass equipment failures at hospitals across the nation was still coming in. It was obviously an attack of some kind but until now, the Director hadn't heard a single theory about who was responsible.

"That's his theory. Riley also said the group is threatening to launch a new attack every twelve hours until the government admits it has been using Ceterus to conduct large-scale domestic spying."

"Shit," said the Director.

"Yes sir."

The Director leaned forward, placing his elbows on his knees and looking Andy directly in the eye. "The truth about Ceterus can't get out, Andy. You, more than anyone, know that."

Andy's pulse quickened at the veiled implications of the Director's statement. The Data Intercept Technology Unit had developed Ceterus. As the Director of that unit, Andy would be sitting at ground zero if the truth ever came out. But, as the Director of the F.B.I., Louis Webster would be sitting right next to him.

Webster hadn't risen to the top of the F.B.I. without dodging some bullets along the way, and his instinct for self-preservation was now on heightened alert. The Director was asking Andy, point blank, to bury the truth. While Andy had his own instinct for self-preservation, he felt a rising internal conflict. By modifying Ceterus to launch terrorist attacks on the United States, Samuel and the Sons of Liberty had forced Andy to look at Ceterus through a different lens. While he certainly didn't want to go to jail, Andy wasn't sure what to do with this new perspective. For now, he decided it was best to toe the line.

"The Ceterus Key could be the answer to all our problems," Andy replied. "If it does what Riley says, we can use it to locate the new virus and stop these attacks."

"That's good news. What about Ceterus?" the Director asked.

"There's no reason we couldn't use the Key to pull Ceterus off the grid completely. It never happened."

The Director leaned back, took a sip of coffee, and studied his cup with a furrowed brow. Finally, he leaned forward and set the cup down on the coffee table. "We have to keep a tight circle around this, Andy. I want you to handle the fieldwork yourself. You'll obviously need backup, but keep the purpose of the mission on a need-to-know basis. I'm guessing you anticipated I'd put you in the field and I know you didn't come in here with nothing. So let's hear it."

Andy shifted in his chair. His plan was slightly unorthodox, and he wasn't sure if the Director would approve. "Well, sir, the way I see it, winning Riley's trust is the key to this entire operation. He has a copy of Ceterus and the Ceterus Key. There's no way to know if he's made other copies or where he may have hidden them. For this to work, we need to get every copy in his possession. We'll need to build trust fast so he'll open up and tell us what we need to know."

The Director was nodding his agreement. "Okay. Go on."

"Before he hung up on me, Riley said he and Amie Hawkins were coming to D.C. and he's promised to call me when he lands. We'll track his flight and keep an eye on things, but I think we should avoid the temptation of having a hundred agents waiting at the airport. That'll destroy any trust and probably scare him off completely. Instead, I'll head to the airport and follow him until he calls. We'll play his game, lure him in, and find out what we need to know."

The Director was nodding his agreement. "Okay, Andy," he said, standing up and thrusting his hand out over the table. Andy stood and shook the Director's hand. "I trust your judgment," said the Director. "Now get it done."

Edward Ross looked up from his notes at the Director. "Sir," he said, catching the Director's attention.

"What is it, Ed?"

"Since I'm read into the case, might I suggest that I join Andy in the field and help keep an eye on Riley?"

The Director didn't hesitate. "Any objections, Andy?"

Andy knew that Ross was once an extremely talented field agent. He also knew he could use the help. "That'd be great," Andy said.

CHAPTER 45

saac sat alone at a table in the back corner of the bar and slowly turned the highball glass in his hand. The lone ice cube stirred in the bottom to cool the whiskey. He lifted the glass to his lips and, savoring the whiskey's burn, remembered the phone call that ignited the fire raging around him. *"We both know the world will never be free,"* Samuel had said, *"if the path upon which we find ourselves remains unchanged."*

Where others had been content to sit and do nothing, Isaac had acted. He had killed Varden and he felt no guilt over it. Christoph Varden had stolen the most basic American freedoms and given it to the government. Varden was a traitor. By betraying his country, he had committed the one crime the Founding Fathers agreed must be punished by death. Killing Varden had been an act of pure patriotism.

Isaac lifted his glass in a silent toast to himself and the satisfaction that there was one less traitor in the world. The whiskey was still warm in his throat when his thoughts shifted to Michael Riley.

He was another matter altogether. Killing him was a matter of self-preservation, not patriotism. Isaac had wished a thousand times that Riley hadn't gone jogging that morning – that he hadn't witnessed Alexander's murder. But he had. That meant that Michael Riley could link Isaac to Varden, Ceterus, and the entire conspiracy.

Isaac had gone to the Bush Library knowing it was his best and probably last chance at Riley. In the blink of an eye, he'd missed his mark and killed Coffman, who was the crucial link to tracking Riley in this city of over one million people. The image of Coffman lying dead on the bridge flashed before his eyes and Isaac took a sip of whiskey to wash it away.

He was setting his glass down on the table when he felt a vibration in his pocket. *Can't be my phone,* he thought, certain the one man who knew the number would not be calling. Then, he felt it again. He pulled out the phone and looked at the display. His heart raced as he accepted the call.

"Isaac," came a familiar voice. Isaac felt the weight of his despair begin to lift – he was saved. He had not been abandoned. Samuel was there.

"I'm sorry," Isaac began.

"Do not apologize," Samuel insisted. "What happened was a tragic accident. I am not calling to punish you. I am calling to redeem you." Isaac sat breathless, hanging on Samuel's every word. "I need you to go to Washington, D.C."

Riley stood behind Amie in the center aisle and waited for the long procession of passengers to find their seats. Up ahead, a man helped his wife wrestle her bag into the overhead compartment. Watching the man shove the bag into the bin, Riley suddenly felt uneasy. He had never boarded a plane without any luggage. If he had been traveling for any other reason, he may have felt liberated. As it was, heading to D.C. empty handed was just another reminder that Riley was completely unprepared for what was ahead.

Soon enough, the man had forced the bag into place and the line began moving again. Half way down the aisle, they arrived at their row and Amie stepped aside. "You can have the window," she said.

"Thanks," Riley said, as he squeezed into the row and fell into his seat.

Amie sat next to him and watched Riley while he fumbled for his seat belt. He'd been quiet on the ride to the airport, spending most of the time staring out the window and only discussing the events to come in vague generalities. Amie didn't get the feeling he was holding anything back, but rather that Riley's plan was likely to include a certain element of improvisation. With the commotion of the loading process occupying the other passengers, Amie took the opportunity to raise a lingering concern.

"How do you know," Amie said and then stopped herself to ensure no one was listening. She leaned in close to Riley and began again. "How do you know Andy isn't in on this?"

Riley shrugged his shoulders. "I don't. There's really no way to know whose side anyone is on. You had it right when we were down at the library. This is too big for us to handle alone. We have to involve the F.B.I., but that doesn't mean we have to trust them."

When she first learned the Sons of Liberty had succeeded in manipulating Ceterus, Amie saw no other option than to call the F.B.I. But so much had happened since then, she wasn't so sure anymore.

At this point, the only thing she knew for sure was that she would stay with Riley and see this through to the end. Just then, a large man in a three-piece suit wedged himself into the aisle seat and Amie knew their conversation would have to wait. So she leaned close to Riley, rested her head on his shoulder, and closed her eyes.

Riley leaned his head into hers and gently caressed Amie's face. He couldn't believe she'd risked so much to help him. He had always respected Amie's mind and her friendship. But now, there was more. Over the past days, Riley had developed feelings that he thought had been laid to rest years ago with the death of his wife. He had never expected to feel this way again. And now, Amie's life was in his hands. Riley didn't know what would happen when they arrived in D.C., but he knew he would do anything to protect her.

He leaned back in his chair and looked out the window. He was thinking over the events to come as the plane took off and pushed its way through the clouds. The plan was simple enough, but who could he trust? Riley had been wresting with this same question since the morning at the canal. And now, he and Amie were headed straight into to the lion's den.

Riley closed his eyes and tried not to think about it. Somewhere over the skies of Tennessee, he finally fell asleep.

CHAPTER 46

F.B.I. Agent Andy Dyll checked his watch as he walked past the ticketing counters at Reagan Washington National. Riley's plane wasn't scheduled to land for another fifteen minutes, which left Andy plenty of time to get into position. He casually entered the airport's central mall, where soaring steel I-beams and graceful yellow arches created a feeling of stepping into Victorian England. The mall had two levels that were filled with the same shops and restaurants seen in airports around the world. An expansive balcony ran the length of the upper level and overlooked the arrival gates below. Andy walked to the edge of the balcony, rested his arms on the railing, and watched the crowd below.

Situated in the heart of Washington, D.C., Reagan Washington National was a popular airport for businessmen, members of Congress, and tourists alike. Tonight, as expected, the airport was busy. Though the crowds would make it more difficult to keep an eye on Riley, Andy wasn't concerned. After all, Riley wasn't some foreign operative or terrorist. He was just a law professor who was in the wrong place at the wrong time.

Still, Andy had to be careful not to be seen. Riley had asked the F.B.I. not meet him at the airport. If Andy was spotted, it would jeopardize his ability to gain Riley's trust. He had to play Riley's game or, at least, make Riley believe he was playing the game. Andy had to stay in the shadows and follow Riley, but the playing field wasn't level. Andy had a distinct advantage that went well beyond his years of training.

For more than a decade, the F.B.I. had been developing programs to collect information from mobile devices. They had smuggled their program onto smart phones through a regular software update released by the major phone manufacturers. Leveraging these programs, the F.B.I. could perform GPS tracking on any cell phone – even those that were turned completely off. Over the years, the program had been perfected to allow the F.B.I. to track individuals through a classified smartphone application, which now appeared on Andy's screen.

On its surface, the map looked like any other GPS application. It displayed an outline of Reagan Washington National in gray and a red dot in the center that indicated Andy's position. Andy glanced at the map and then turned to look at the listing of arrivals on a nearby monitor. *They should be here by now,* he thought, looking back at his phone. There was nothing to do but wait. Minutes later, a blue dot appeared at the edge of the screen. The dot showed the precise location of Coffman's phone, and that meant Riley and Amie had just landed in D.C.

Waiting for the passengers to arrive in the terminal, Andy pulled two small pictures from his jacket pocket. He looked down to see the faces of Michael Riley and Amie Hawkins, which he had come to know well. The flight manifest showed 125 passengers aboard the plane, all of which would soon spill into the terminal and blend in with the other travelers. Andy would need to spot Riley quickly or risk losing him in the crowd. Having refreshed his memory, Andy tucked the pictures back in his pocket and waited.

Slowly, a stream of passengers emerged from the jet way and fanned out into the airport. Andy focused his gaze at the entrance as, one after another, the passengers filtered into the airport: an old man in a wheel chair, a harried businessman, a husband and wife with three small children in tow, a large man in a three-piece suit. Then, he saw them.

Riley and Amie stepped into the terminal and slowed as they studied the signs overhead. Riley pointed to one and then grabbed Amie's hand as the two of them walked beneath the balcony and disappeared from Andy's view.

Andy drifted to the nearby staircase and descended to the ground floor. He circled to the gate and looked up to read the sign Riley had pointed to: *Ground Transportation*. Andy followed the signs down the escalator and out to the street where a tangled mass of people, busses, and cars jockeyed for position. Andy looked quickly from one person to the next. To his left, he caught sight of Riley as he slid into the back seat of a cab and closed the door.

"Shit," Andy said under his breath. He waited calmly on the sidewalk until the cab pulled away from the curb and entered the heavy stream of cars leaving the airport. With the taxi just out of sight, Andy darted to the parking garage across the street and jumped into his unmarked car. He pulled out his phone checked the map. Riley and Amie were headed north towards the George Washington Parkway. Andy threw the phone in the passenger seat, started the car and headed after them.

He caught up with the taxi as they crossed the Arlington Memorial Bridge. Keeping a safe distance, Andy followed the cab along the Potomac River and into town. The taxi turned onto 22nd street and slowed before pulling into a circular drive that ran beneath a brick portico. Andy drove slowly down 22nd and peered at the gold lettering above the portico: *The Ritz Carlton*. Andy spotted a gas station across the street and pulled in. He adjusted his rearview mirror and watched Riley and Amie get out of the cab and walk casually into the hotel.

Andy parked the car on the side of the gas station and waited five minutes before he walked across the street and stepped through the gold trimmed doors into the foyer of the Ritz Carlton.

"Welcome to the Ritz Carlton," said an impeccably dressed bellman in an accent that Andy couldn't quite place. "How may I help you?"

Andy's eyes darted around the lobby but there were no signs of Riley. "I just need to talk to the receptionist," he said, walking past the bellman through the opulent lobby. He arrived at the marble reception desk and was greeted instantly by an attractive Asian woman.

"Welcome to the Ritz Carlton," she said, her long, dark hair hanging perfectly over her shoulder. "How may I assist you?"

"I need to know about a man and woman who just checked in," Andy said. The receptionist was visibly surprised by the question. Before she could protest, Andy pulled out a black leather case and flashed his F.B.I. badge and identification card. The receptionist's face went from surprise to concern. Andy glanced down at her nametag. "Nicole," he said in a low but forceful tone, "I need to know if a Michael Riley or Amie Hawkins checked into this hotel." Nicole stood frozen in place. "No one is in danger," Andy said, trying to calm Nicole's fears, "but this is a matter of national security. Do you understand?"

After a long moment, she shook her head slightly, "Yes."

"Good. I need you to tell me if they've checked in."

Nicole reached for her keyboard and began typing. "Yes. They just checked in."

"What room are they in?"

Another pause before Nicole shifted her gaze back to the hidden computer screen. "Four seventeen," she said softly.

Andy rapped his knuckles lightly on the counter. "Thank you, Nicole. Best if you don't tell anyone that I've been here." Nicole shook her head and Andy turned back into the lobby. He found a chair in the corner where he could see the elevators, and made a phone call.

CHAPTER 47

Riley slid the plastic key card into the door handle and the electric lock buzzed its acceptance. The room was well appointed with a king bed, flat screen television, mini-bar, and a desk by the windows along the back wall. Riley held the door open and Amie stepped inside. When the door closed, Amie pointed to the rest room. "I'll be right back."

Riley glanced around the room and was again reminded of how strange everything felt. When checking into a hotel, he typically found a place for his bag, unpacked a few of his things and hung his shirts in the closet. But there was no bag and there were no clothes, which again reminded him of how this was anything but a typical trip.

He walked to the window and opened the shades to look out over the city. When they had woken up on the tarmac in D.C., both he and Amie's stomachs were in knots. They decided they needed a place to calm down and go over the plan one more time. The Ritz Carlton seemed as good of a place as any. "May as well go out in style," Riley had said with a smile.

He stared out of the window and as he walked through the plan over and again, the bustling city below faded from view. He wasn't sure how long he'd been standing there when he felt a hand slide gently across his lower back. "We're going to be okay." Riley turned to see Amie standing at his side.

He reached for her hand and turned back to the window. There were a million things that could go wrong and there was no way to predict what would happen. The F.B.I. had built a program to conduct mass surveillance on American citizens. Ceterus was illegal as hell and if word got out, someone would be going to prison. Congress would be forced to do something drastic, which could even mean the end of the F.B.I. Riley knew there were people inside the Bureau that would never let that happen. The F.B.I. would have an even bigger problem if the world made the connection between Ceterus and the recent terrorist attacks. That was Riley's only leverage, and he would have to use every ounce of it to get out of this.

Riley put his arm around Amie and pulled her close. After a long moment, they sat on the bed and walked through their plan over and again.

Finally, after playing out every scenario they could imagine, a heavy silence settled into the room.

"Guess we better make that call," Riley said, staring into Amie's brown eyes. She nodded and Riley dialed Andy's number.

"Riley?" came Andy's voice after one ring.

"We're here."

"Good. Where are you? I'll come and meet you."

"I'm sure you know exactly where we are, Agent Dyll."

Damn right I do, Andy thought. "This is your game, Riley. I'm just playing it."

"We'll meet you at the Lincoln Memorial in one hour."

"And you'll bring the Ceterus Key with you?"

"That's why we're here," Riley said.

"Okay."

"We'll give it to you, and then we walk away. That's the deal."

"Deal," Andy said. "I'll see you in an hour." Then the line went dead. Andy looked down to confirm the call had been disconnected and instantly dialed another number.

"This is Ross."

"Lincoln Memorial in one hour," said Andy.

"We'll get a team in place," Ross said. "I'll meet you there."

Isaac answered the phone on the first ring. "Hello?"

"Have you arrived?" asked Samuel.

"Yes. I'm here."

"Good. There is no time to waste. Riley will be at the Lincoln Memorial in under an hour."

The Lincoln Memorial, Isaac thought, *how fitting.* "I'm on my way."

"We must be careful this time, Isaac. I believe Riley will be carrying a copy of the Ceterus Key, but I am not certain. The Key is the first priority. We must secure the Key before you kill Riley."

"I understand. Will the F.B.I. be there?" Isaac asked, his voice laced with concern.

"Yes. But so will I."

Isaac was shocked. Samuel had always been in the shadows – an omniscient but invisible force. But tonight, the man who had brought purpose and direction to Isaac's life would be there in person. Confidence welled inside him. If anyone could protect Isaac and give him the opening he needed with Riley, it was Samuel. "I'll be at the Memorial in ten minutes," Isaac said with a renewed sense of purpose.

"Remember: we must have the Ceterus Key before you kill Riley. We must get it before the F.B.I."

"We will," Isaac said.

CHAPTER 48

Y ou can let us out here," Riley said and the cab pulled quickly to the curb. He paid the driver and stepped out at the corner of 23rd and Constitution. Amie had decided it would be safer to walk the last couple of blocks to observe the people moving in and around the Lincoln Memorial. They hoped to catch a glimpse of what the F.B.I. had in store, though they knew it was unlikely. Riley and Amie were no match for the trained F.B.I. agents.

They cut through Gorla Park and mingled with the tourists and locals. Having already discussed their plan in detail, they walked the moonlit sidewalk in silence and kept an eye out for anything that seemed out of place. But everything appeared normal. It was the normalcy that was so unnerving.

They reached the far end of the park where a white glow filtered down through the trees, creating a patchwork of light on the grass. Riley led the way through the evergreens where they saw the source of the light sitting majestically on the nearby hilltop.

The sight of the Lincoln Memorial at night had always affected Riley. Sitting atop its pedestal, the magnificent edifice glowed white like a beacon of hope – much like the man it was built to honor. Inspired by the Greek temple of Zeus, the structure was surrounded by thirty-six limestone columns – one for each state in the union at the close of the Civil War. Inside, a towering sculpture of Lincoln peered through the colonnade towards the Capitol Building and kept a watchful eye on the workings of modern day government. Lincoln sat with one hand relaxed – open to new thoughts, ideas and perspectives – while the other hand was clenched in a fist, resolved to do what was right regardless of the consequences. Tonight, Riley felt he could use some of that resolve.

They reached the sidewalk at Lincoln Memorial Circle and Riley stared up at the imposing building. He wasn't admiring the Memorial's architecture or the man it was built to honor. Instead, he studied it like a tactician preparing for battle. They had selected the Lincoln Memorial because there was only one way in, which meant, once inside, Riley and Amie would be assured of seeing whatever came at them. If they kept their eyes forward, Lincoln would have their back.

"Come on," Riley said, seeing a break in the traffic. They darted across the road and arrived at a waist-high retaining wall that encircled an open lawn on the north side of the Memorial. "Up here," he said as he hopped up on the wall and stepped onto the grass. They crossed the lawn and entered a dark thicket of trees. Stepping over roots and sweeping branches aside, they arrived at the base of a white, stone wall.

Amie looked up through the branches and saw the Memorial towering overhead. "You think they're already here?" Amie whispered.

Riley cleared the branches out of the way as they followed the length of the wall towards the front of the Monument. "I'm not sure," he said. "We got here pretty fast. But it's the F.B.I. we're talking about. They could be anywhere." They reached the end of the wall and Riley peered around the corner. "I'm hoping we can see something once we get up there," he whispered, motioning to an outcropping of smaller bushes near the Memorial's front stairs. He looked back at Amie, whose face glowed in the soft light filtering down from above. "You ready?"

Riley's eyes exuded a quiet confidence that quelled Amie's fears. They'd gotten this far together. Now, standing on the edge of the unknown, there was no one else Amie wanted by her side. "I'm ready," she said, squeezing Riley's hand.

They ran from the cover of the trees and across an open stretch of grass to a cluster of large bushes. Riley crouched down to wait for Amie, who was right behind him. Using the cover of the bushes, they moved quietly towards the marble stairs leading up to the Memorial. Reaching the last bush, they stopped to survey the entrance.

"You see anything?" Amie asked.

Riley's plan was to approach the Memorial from the side and find a safe place observe the entrance. He had hoped to hide and look for any signs of danger before exposing themselves on the grand staircase leading up to the Memorial. The bushes, he'd thought, would provide the perfect vantage point.

"I can't see a damned thing," he said. "I can only see the top of the stairs."

"Me too," Amie said, shifting her position. "I just see a bit of the entrance."

Riley nodded and they sat in silence for a second, unsure of what to do next. Even if they could have seen everything they'd hoped to, Riley wasn't sure what they'd be looking for. It wasn't like the agents would be standing there with F.B.I. signs around their necks. They'd be disguised to look like everyone else. Riley didn't like the idea of flying blindly into the storm. But now, it seemed they had little choice.

"I guess we just have to take our chances," he said, reluctantly. "We'll need to get to the top of the stairs as quick as we can. Once we're inside, we'll be okay."

Amie agreed. "Let's do it."

Riley stepped into the central plaza at the base of the marble staircase and looked around nervously. A dozen or so tourists dotted the fifty-eight steps leading up to the Memorial, but none of them appeared to take any notice of the two fugitives who had just stepped out from the bushes. Amie shot Riley a wary glance and then they headed up to the Memorial.

Climbing the stairs, they passed an elderly man with his grandson, a gaggle of teenaged girls, a young couple holding hands, and a few lone photographers who were ever-present around the Capital. Riley studied each in turn as they walked past, looking for eye contact, waiting for something to happen.

"Maybe they're not here yet," Amie said as they continued their climb.

Riley craned his neck around. "I doubt that," he said, tentatively. "They've got to be here somewhere."

They reached the top step and saw the enormous statue of Abraham Lincoln staring down at them through the colonnade. Riley quickly surveyed the Memorial, which was divided into three sections. The central chamber was the largest of the three and housed Lincoln's statue. On either side, two smaller chambers were created by rows of massive ionic columns that soared more than six stories up and supported the translucent marble ceiling above. Riley estimated around twenty people were milling quietly around the Memorial.

"Where should we wait?" Amie asked over the quiet echoes of conversation.

Given why they were there, Riley knew there was no safe place to wait. The best they could do was find somewhere in the open where they could see what was coming. "Over here," he said, leading Amie across the pink marble floor to the base of Lincoln's statue. With Lincoln at their back, they looked out over the National Mall and the white dome of the Capitol in the distance.

Riley breathed a heavy sigh. They had finally arrived. Everything they'd gone through – witnessing Alexander's murder, breaking into Varden's home, running from Isaac, and narrowly escaping with their lives at every turn – everything came down to the next few minutes. Riley felt the tension of the moment building inside. He cast his eyes nervously around the chamber as visitors floated by: a handful of women speaking Chinese and taking pictures; a woman across the room leaning on a column looking at her phone; a man setting up a tripod and camera near the entrance; two veterans standing at the far side of the statue and staring up at Lincoln. The F.B.I. could be anywhere.

Riley fixed his gaze back on the woman. She was young, slim, and wearing a black pantsuit. Everyone else in the room seemed to fit. She did not. She was just leaning against the column and staring intently at her phone. Riley was reaching to get Amie's attention when a piercing *CRACK!* echoed across the chamber.

Riley's heart pounded as he tore his eyes from the woman to locate the source of the sound. Spinning towards the entrance, he saw the photographer's tripod had fallen over and crashed to the marble floor. His eyes darted around the room, searching for the photographer. When he finally saw him a pulse of fear seared down Riley's spine.

The photographer was running directly at them. He was yelling something incomprehensible and then, out of nowhere, a gun appeared in the photographer's outstretched hand. With the sites trained on Riley, the man reached to his jacket and ripped away a strip of Velcro fabric. Behind the fabric, three bright yellow letters were emblazoned on the jacket: F.B.I.

"Stop! F.B.I.!" boomed the agent's voice.

In that moment, Riley knew all was lost. He and Amie had information to expose everything the F.B.I. had done. They knew too much. For it's own survival, the F.B.I. could never let them get away.

Amie screamed, "Michael! Look out!"

"F.B.I. – I said don't move!" yelled the dark haired agent who was charging at full speed. Suddenly, a flash of light and the concussion of gunfire filled the marble chamber.

Riley turned and threw his body over Amie. They fell through the air as another sharp crack exploded from the agent's gun. Amie crashed hard on the ground. Riley landed on top of her, shielding her from the gunman's fire. Screams and frantic footfalls mixed with the echoing gunfire as tourists scattered to safety.

Riley could hardly breathe as the final shots faded off into the night. Then, like thunder rolling off into the distance, the Memorial fell silent once again. Riley's eyes were clenched, his arms held Amie tight.

"Mr. Riley?" the man said urgently. "Mr. Riley!" Riley slowly opened his eyes. When he lifted his head, the site before him was utterly confusing. He had expected to see the barrel of the gun pointed directly at him. Instead, the agent was aiming at something on the other side of the Lincoln statue.

"Are you alright, Mr. Riley?" asked the agent, his eyes fixed on his target.

Riley wasn't sure if he was alright or not and he quickly took stock of his body. "Yes," he said weakly. "I'm fine." He turned to look at Amie, who was motionless on the floor beside him. "Amie?" he asked anxiously. There was no response. Panicking, Riley quickly checked to see that she was still breathing. "We need some help here!" he yelled as he searched her body for any visible injuries. When his hands reached the back of her head, he felt something warm and wet. *Oh God, no!* He slowly pulled his hand from beneath her head to see his fingers glistening with a deep crimson.

Riley looked up at the agent, whose eyes were still pinned on his target. "We need help here! Somebody do something!" Riley yelled.

A man with sandy blonde hair and an F.B.I. jacket appeared beside Riley. Seeing the blood on Riley's hand, the agent pulled a radio from his belt. "This is Agent Dyll. I need paramedics to the scene now!"

"She's bleeding," Riley pleaded. "Please do something."

"Paramedics are on their way, Mr. Riley. They'll be here any second." For the first time, Riley heard the sirens in the air and noticed the columns at the front of the Memorial were flashing blue and red. A moment later, a team of paramedics carrying heavy orange equipment bags ran into the Memorial. Riley moved aside as a female paramedic arrived and immediately checked Amie's pulse.

Agent Dyll grabbed Riley's arm and helped him to his feet. Arriving with the paramedics were teams of men with *F.B.I.* embroidered on the front of their bulletproof vests. Riley hardly noticed them. His eyes remained on Amie and the paramedics huddled around her. Moments later, they lifted her to a gurney and wheeled her quickly towards the exit. When the team rushed past Riley, the female paramedic paused. "She's going to be okay," she said sympathetically. "Her head hit the floor. She's got a slight concussion and a fairly nasty cut on the back of her head. But it'll be okay." She patted Riley on the arm and ran off.

The site of Amie being wheeled away was infuriating. Riley spun on Agent Dyll. "What the hell are you guys doing?"

Before Andy could answer, the plain clothed agent who had posed as the photographer interrupted. "Come with me, Mr. Riley."

"Who the hell are you?" Riley shot back.

"Would you please step over here?" He placed his hand on Riley's back, guiding him around the base of the statue under the watchful gaze of Abraham Lincoln. "I'm Agent Edward Ross," he said. "Sorry if we gave you a scare. This wasn't what we'd planned but, as you'll see, I didn't have much of a choice."

They approached the edge of the pedestal and a pair of black combat boots emerged from around the corner. Each step Riley took revealed more of the man lying motionless on the ground: his black boots, black combat pants, silver belt buckle, black tactical shirt. Riley's eyes traveled up the man's body until they finally rested on his face. There, in an expanding pool of deepest red, lay Riley's tormentor. Isaac was dead.

CHAPTER 49

Do you know this man?" Ross asked. Riley stared silently down at the man who had made his life a living hell. The blood from Isaac's chest wound expanded across the floor and soaked into his blonde crew cut hair.

Riley finally nodded. "Yes," he said looking up at Ross. "This is the man who's been trying to kill me; the guy I saw down at the canal. His name is Isaac."

"I doubt that's his real name," Ross said, writing a note in a small notepad he'd taken from his jacket pocket.

The confusion that had settled around Riley began to lift. What had been an utterly chaotic scene of gunfire, sirens and paramedics was now relatively calm. "Where's Amie?" he said, looking towards the Memorial's entrance.

Agent Andy Dyll put a hand on Riley's shoulder. "She's safe, Mr. Riley. There are a hundred F.B.I. agents around this building. She'll be all right down there. You can see her in a minute. We've just got a few questions first. For starters, are you sure you're okay?" he asked.

"Yeah. I'm okay. What happened?" Riley asked, blankly.

"He was waiting for you around the other side of the column," Ross said without looking up from his notepad.

Riley turned back to Isaac's body, still lying on the ground. Then he looked up at the white column standing just to the right of the statue. Riley's stomach churned. He turned to look at the fallen tripod and the place where Ross had been standing. *He was just waiting for you around the other side of the column,* Riley repeated in silence.

He looked at Ross, who had stepped away and was talking quietly to another agent. A tingling sensation ran up Riley's spine as his eyes snapped back to Isaac's body. What should have been an overwhelming feeling of relief did not come. Isaac was there, his blood pooled around him. But something was wrong. Something was terribly wrong.

Riley scanned the scene desperately. *It has to be here somewhere.* He looked at Isaac's hands, his belt, and then the span of marble floor between his body and the column he'd hidden behind. Nothing. *Where's the weapon?* Riley asked himself. There simply wasn't one. No gun. No knife. Not even a piece of rope.

Riley's pulse quickened. It wasn't just the missing weapon. There was something else. Something he couldn't quite place. He replayed the scene slowly in his mind and as he did, the realization took shape like a ship coming out of a fog. *Oh my God.* Riley turned and called out to Agent Ross. "You said he was just waiting around the corner?"

Ross broke off his conversation with the other agent. "That's right," he said before turning to Agent Dyll. "Andy, would you look after Mr. Riley for a moment? I need to update the Director." With that, Agent Ross passed through the colonnade and disappeared down the grand staircase.

Riley's mind was racing. He looked back at Isaac and everything became clear. "There's no gun," he said urgently, turning back to Andy.

"What?" Andy asked.

"There's no gun," Riley repeated, pointing down at Isaac. "No knife. No anything."

Andy glanced down at the body. "Riley, what are you talking about?"

"Agent Ross said that Isaac was *waiting around the column*."

"Right," Andy agreed. "So?"

"If he didn't have a gun or some other kind of weapon, how did Agent Ross know Isaac was waiting for *us*?" Riley paused while Andy thought it over. "How did Ross even know who Isaac was? There's no way for him to have known unless he'd seen him before!" Riley said, emphatically.

"Riley, calm down." Andy demanded in a low voice.

"Ross *knew* who Isaac was!" Riley pressed. "And there's only one person who knows that."

Andy made the connection and immediately shook his head. "You don't know what you're talking about, Riley. Edward Ross is a legendary Agent. He's risked his life countless times for his country."

"Think about it!" Riley demanded. "Ceterus is a top secret program. No one knew about it outside the Bureau. Samuel's got to be in the F.B.I. How else could he have known about Ceterus? And about Varden?"

Andy saw Riley's logic but searched for another explanation. "The guy's dressed in all black military gear for God's sake," he said, pointing at Isaac. "Are you telling me he doesn't look suspicious?"

Riley didn't hear the question. He needed indisputable proof that Samuel and Edward Ross were one and the same. Then, it came to him. Riley threw his hand into his pocket and pulled out Coffman's cell phone.

"What're you doing? You can't call anyone about this," Andy said firmly.

"I'm not calling anyone," Riley said, pulling up the phone's browser. "You need to see something." Riley held the phone out as a video of a darkened server room filled the screen. Seconds later, a voice echoed from the phone's speaker. *My name is Samuel. One hundred and fifty years ago Abraham Lincoln warned us of a gathering storm,*"

Samuel's haunting voice filled the chamber and Andy's mouth fell open.

"You know that voice," Riley said, pressing stop on the video. Andy's expression was blank, as if he were looking into a great abyss. "Agent Dyll?" Riley prompted.

"Yes. I know that voice," Andy said slowly, trying to accept that a legendary agent had betrayed the F.B.I. and his country. Then, without warning, Andy ran to the front of the Memorial. Riley followed him through the colonnade to the top of the marble stairs. Red and blue lights flashed from every direction and reflected off the white surfaces of the Memorial. They stood there for a long moment and stared at the chaotic sea of emergency responders below. There are too many people, Riley thought. *We'll never find him in all this.*

Andy was having the same thoughts. "Look, Riley," he said. "Edward Ross is a very powerful agent. We need to be smart. If we broadcast this over the radio, Ross will simply disappear."

"So what do we do?"

Andy scanned the scene below. "I know some agents who will help. I'll quietly spread the word and we'll find him." He turned and looked Riley squarely in the eyes. "You stay here. Understand?"

Riley held up his hands. "I understand," he said. Andy ran down the stairs and disappeared into the crowd.

It was finally over. Isaac was dead and Samuel had been identified. Any minute, Andy and the other agents would have Edward Ross in custody. With the terrorists' mastermind chained to a desk in some basement interrogation room, the attacks would stop. With time, the F.B.I. would learn how Ross had managed to infect the nation's computer systems with his new virus. Whether the F.B.I. had learned the lessons Ceterus had taught, Riley would never know.

For now, he didn't really care. He only wanted to find Amie and tell her that everything was over. Riley scanned the scene below for the team of paramedics. He'd just spotted an ambulance in the distance when Coffman's phone began to ring. Riley was relieved to see Amie's number on the caller ID. "We know who Samuel is," he said the instant he answered the phone. "It's Edward Ross, an F.B.I. agent who…"

"How very clever of you, Mr. Riley." Riley stopped cold. The voice was deep. Mechanical. Familiar. It was Edward Ross. Riley's eyes raked frantically over the crowd of agents, police and emergency responders.

"You won't find me, Mr. Riley," said Ross. "And you don't need to."

"Where's Amie? What've you done with her?"

"Ms. Hawkins is just fine. I'm taking good care of her."

"Where is she?" Riley demanded.

"You'll see her very soon. I'm going to tell you exactly where she is. But first, you must do as I say. And if you don't, well," Samuel let out a long sigh "you won't see her again." Riley turned in place, his mind racing for options. "I know what you're thinking," Samuel continued. "You want to cry out for help. But you see, I can't allow you to do that. You will have to do this all on your own."

"How do I know Amie's okay?"

Seconds later, Riley heard Amie's muffled scream. "Michael!"

"Now," said Ross, "you will stay on the phone with me and walk calmly down to the reflecting pool in front of the Memorial. You will then go to the corner of 23rd and Independence and catch a cab. When you get in the cab, I will give you the next instructions."

Riley looked at the scene below and noticed the heavily manned police barrier. "What if they don't let me through the barrier?"

"Then you will hand them the phone and I will get you through. Now, get moving."

There was no other option. Riley started down the stairs. "Remember," Ross said, stopping Riley in his tracks, "I'm watching your every move."

"I understand," Riley said.

CHAPTER 50

Riley reached the bottom of the stairs and melted into the chaos. He fully expected one of the dozens of F.B.I. agents swirling around the scene to stop him but no one seemed to notice as he casually ducked under the wooden police barrier. As instructed, he walked down to the reflecting pool where the image of the Washington Monument stood perfectly still in the cool water.

"Well done, Mr. Riley," said Ross. "Now, cut across the park to 23rd and Independence."

Riley looked out across the park towards 23rd Street. The tourists who had previously dotted the area were now collected at the edge of the police barrier, leaving the park completely empty. The eerie silence amplified Riley's every step as he made his way across the grass. Just ahead, the squad of steel soldiers at the Korean War Memorial cast a ghostly appearance under the moonlit sky. Riley looked into their faces, which reflected the same fear of the unknown churning in Riley's gut.

Moments later, he reached the corner of 23rd and Independence and put the phone back up to his ear. "Now what?" he asked anxiously.

"Now you find a cab."

Riley looked up and down the street. "There aren't any cabs here," he said, his words laced with frustration and anger. Just then, a yellow taxi pulled up 23rd street. "Wait. There's one," Riley said, throwing his hand up in the air to hail the driver. The cab pulled to an immediate stop.

Riley jumped in the back seat and closed the door. "Where to?" asked the driver, glancing at Riley in the rearview mirror.

Ross heard the driver's question. "Tudor Place and Gardens," he directed. Riley repeated the destination to the driver.

"What's at Tudor Place?" Riley asked Ross as the car pulled away from the curb.

"Roll down your window, Mr. Riley," Ross ordered, ignoring Riley's question.

The instruction took Riley by surprise. "Why?" Riley asked, looking reflexively out the window.

"Because I want you to throw your phone out of the window."

"You want me to what?" Riley asked in disbelief.

"The F.B.I. and your friend Agent Dyll can track that phone, just as I have."

Riley hesitated. The phone was his only connection to Amie. If he threw it out the window, he would have no way to know that she was okay. And, as Ross had anticipated, he would have no way of contacting Andy Dyll or the F.B.I.

"Throw it out now, Mr. Riley!" demanded Ross.

Riley looked around the car in a panic. There must be something he could do – some way out of this. His eyes darted to the front seat and he saw the driver wearing a Bluetooth headset in his ear. *Of course!* Riley thought. *The driver's got a phone.* With that, Riley rolled down the window and tossed Coffman's phone into the middle of Ohio Drive as the taxi sped past the chaos around the Lincoln Memorial.

Riley turned to the driver as he rolled up the window. "Sir, I need to use your phone." The man stared straight ahead. "Hey man!" Riley shouted. "I need your phone. This is an emergency! A man has kidnapped a friend of mine and I need to call the police!"

This time, the driver glanced at Riley in the rearview mirror. He'd heard Riley's request, he just wasn't responding. "Hey!" Riley yelled. "What the fuck is going on?" The man smiled and a heavy weight fell into Riley's stomach. The driver knew exactly what was going on – he was working for Ross.

An orange glow filled the taxi as it passed beneath the street light at the corner of 31st and Q. Riley slid close to the door and caught a glimpse of the green information sign as it passed by the window: Tudor Place Historic House & Garden. They were close.

Riley had spent most of the short drive pleading with the driver, trying desperately to convince him Samuel was nothing more than a terrorist. It made no difference. "We're all victims here," Riley had declared in desperation. The driver glanced in the mirror and let out a chilling laugh. At last, Riley accepted his fate and rode the rest of the way in silence.

The car slowed as they neared the Tudor Place gate. Riley sat up, expecting the car to stop. Instead, the driver turned right onto a darkened side street and Riley's view was suddenly restricted to the reach of the car's headlights.

As the taxi crept along, Riley's stomach tightened into a knot. He had naively convinced himself Amie would be waiting for him at Tudor Place. He realized now how ridiculous that was. Ross was determined to launch a new attack every twelve hours until the government admitted it was spying on the American people. He would force the F.B.I. to confess it had gained access to their most intimate details. That is, unless the F.B.I. used the Ceterus Key to cover up what they'd done. But the F.B.I. didn't have the Ceterus Key. Riley did.

"Get out," the driver said abruptly.

The taxi had stopped in a quaint Georgetown neighborhood. "Where am I supposed to go?"

Riley asked, looking for anyone who may be lurking outside.

"The gray townhouse on the corner. Go downstairs and ring the bell."

Riley glanced at the driver, whose eyes remained straight ahead. Then, Riley reluctantly grabbed the handle and opened the door. He had just stepped onto the street when the tires squealed and the cab sped off down the road. Within seconds, it had turned the corner at 30th Street and disappeared.

The wind carried a slight chill as Riley stood alone in the street and looked at the gray townhome on the corner. The house itself was completely dark and quiet. Shadows from the neighboring trees danced on the front of the three-story façade. A split stairway led up to the front door and down to the basement below. Riley strained to see the bottom of the stairs in the faint light from a distant streetlamp.

He had no idea what awaited him at the bottom of the stairs, but it didn't matter. Amie was in there somewhere and Riley had to find her. He stepped onto the brick sidewalk and peered cautiously over the metal gate at the top of the basement stairs. Seeing nothing but blackness, he turned and looked down the street once more. With the exception of a black cat walking lazily by, the street was completely deserted.

Turning back to the stairs, Riley placed his hand on the gate and gave it a push. A high-pitched screech shot from the rusty hinges and Riley instantly grabbed the gate and silence its alarm. He stood frozen in place, his eyes darting from left to right, his ears strained to catch even the slightest sound. But he only heard the leaves rustling high in the trees.

Riley took a breath and slowly descended into the darkness. The landing was cold and dank. As Riley drew close, the faint outline of a black door appeared. Feeling along the doorframe, he found the doorbell. He stood with his hand hovering over the button for a long moment. Finally, he let out a nervous breath and pressed the button. But there was no bell, no sound. There was no indication the button had done anything until finally, an electric buzz sounded and the lock released with a heavy click. Riley reached for the knob and opened the door.

The interior chamber was completely dark. Riley stepped cautiously inside and strained to see any detail of the room. It was small – perhaps five feet by seven – with no furniture. There was a solid concrete wall before him and a heavy gray door to the left. Uncertain what to do, he stepped hesitantly towards the gray door and gave it a push. The solid metal structure didn't budge.

I've got to be missing something, Riley thought. Scanning the tiny room, he turned slowly in place until he faced the front door, which was still wide open. Riley paused. *Maybe,* he thought. Then he stepped back to the door and closed it, plunging the room into total darkness.

Instantly, the lock's heavy bolt slid back into place. "Holy shit!" Riley said, pulling desperately on the knob. Just then, a blinding white light filled the room. The intense light was disorienting. Riley shielded his eyes and tried to get his bearings. The room was surrounded on three sides by thick concrete walls. To the left, a heavy steel door with no knob blocked the entrance to the basement's interior. Above the door a security camera kept watch over the confined space. Seeing the camera, Riley looked directly into the lens for several long seconds.

Another electric buzz and the metal door's lock clicked open. Riley stepped forward and pushed on the door. The precision hinges swung open with ease and the light from the entry room carved a long rectangle on the darkened floor of the interior room. Riley eased forward and stepped across the threshold.

As his foot hit the ground, the bright lights of the entryway switched off, leaving Riley in the dark once again. He kept his hand on the doorframe to steady himself while his eyes tried to adjust.

"Come in, Mr. Riley," came a distant but clear voice out of the black. It was Edward Ross. "And please do close the door."

"Where's Amie?" Riley asked defiantly into the void.

"Close the door and I'll show you," Ross said.

CHAPTER 51

Riley felt his way into the room and closed the metal door behind him. With another electric buzz, the deadbolt fell into place. A desk lamp flickered on at the far end of the room, instantly drawing Riley's attention. When his eyes adjusted, the sight before him filled Riley with a rage so intense his skin began to burn.

Amie sat roughly in a chair, her hands bound with a thick layer of duct tape. Her eyes were red from crying, her cheeks wet with tears. Her dark, long dark hair was tangled and loose strands stuck to her face. A strip of silver duct tape covered her mouth. A thin line of blood ran from beneath the tape and down her chin. Riley focused on Amie's eyes, which silently pleaded for his help and his forgiveness. It was an image Riley knew he would carry for the rest of his life.

"What have you done to her?" Riley asked, his voice shaking with rage. He searched for Ross deep in the shadows of the room.

"I had to be certain she was telling the truth," Ross replied from somewhere in the void. "I had to be sure there's only one copy of the Ceterus Key and that you have it." Ross stepped into the hazy edge of the light. "Come in," he directed. "We have a seat for you right over here." Another light clicked on, illuminating an empty office chair to Amie's left. Riley looked at the chair and then back at Ross, who pulled a pistol from beneath his F.B.I. jacket and pressed it to Amie's temple. Amie's tearful eyes cast about, trying desperately to find Riley somewhere in the dark.

Riley looked quickly around the basement, which was littered with discarded furniture and equipment. Tangled heaps of cables and wires spread out across flimsy plastic tables and onto the floor. Computer monitors had been thrown on the floor, their screens cracked and broken. Hard drives and server equipment were smashed and thrown haphazardly around the room. *What the hell is this place,* Riley wondered. The answer came to him in an instant. *This is where Ross built his virus. This is the source of the attacks.*

"Come along, Mr. Riley," said Ross. "We have things to do."

Navigating around the mass of wires and equipment, Riley made it to the empty chair on the other side of the room. He had started to sit down when Ross suddenly spoke. "Ah. Ah, Mr. Riley. Aren't you forgetting something?" Riley stopped and looked into the light towards the voice, confusion evident on his face. "The Key, Mr. Riley," prompted Ross. "You forgot to give me the Ceterus Key."

Riley hesitated. The Ceterus Key was the only thing he had to bargain with. "Why are you doing this?" he asked, stalling for time.

"To save my country," Ross said forcefully. "And to answer the call made more than a century ago. All those years ago, Abraham Lincoln knew the government would conspire with corporations to strip away our freedoms. The moment I heard about Ceterus, I knew Lincoln's Prophecy had come true. Don't you see, Mr. Riley? Our government has betrayed us. They've slipped into our bedroom window and taken our most valued possession – our privacy. Now, they're trying to slip back out of the window like the cowardly thieves they are."

"So you think the best way to protect our freedom is to assault our most fundamental right?"

"Okay, professor," Ross said, intrigued. "Tell me: what is our most fundamental right?"

"The right to life," Riley said, his anger rising. "You and your so called Sons of Liberty are murderers!"

Ross let out a condescending laugh. "You are so naïve," he said, shaking his head. "Those are the precise thoughts that led us to this moment of crisis."

Ross lowered the pistol to his side and leaned close to Amie. "The flaw in your reasoning is right here," he said as he extended his disfigured hand and gently brushed the silver tape covering Amie's mouth. Amie closed her eyes and turned away in disgust. Ross's hand continued gently down her arm to her hands and across the thick layer of duct tape binding them together. "You see, don't you?" Ross said, brushing his hand back across Amie's cheek. "Ms. Hawkins has life. But she does not have her freedom. You say that life itself is the supreme right. But as Ms. Hawkins demonstrates, life without freedom is no life at all."

The sight of Ross touching Amie was sickening, but Riley had to keep him talking. He wanted to get the focus off of Amie and quickly changed topics. "How did you know Varden had implanted a copy of Ceterus under his skin?"

"Oh, Mr. Riley," Ross said, as if Riley had disappointed him, "I presumed you had figured that one out already. Ceterus wasn't some sort of routine F.B.I. surveillance program. It was unprecedented. And unprecedented programs get the Director's attention. As the Director's Special Assistant, I was there from the beginning. I sat across from the *great* Christoph Varden as he explained how he was going to *save his country*. I couldn't believe what I was hearing. Varden wasn't there to save his country; he was there to destroy it. As I listened to his traitorous plan, I never believed the F.B.I. would allow it. But I was wrong. The Director was willing to pay any price to prevent another 9/11."

Ross had become increasingly agitated and began pacing back and forth in front of Amie. "In the following months, I met with Varden a dozen times," Ross continued. "And in every one of those meetings, Varden brought one of his little black notebooks. He was compulsive about his note taking. When it was time to act, I knew all the information I needed would be somewhere in those notebooks. Simple, old-fashioned bribery took care of the rest. Lupita Suarez." Riley's face went blank. "Varden's housekeeper, Mr. Riley," Ross said, addressing the question left hanging. "She knew Varden kept his notebooks in a secret compartment in his library. It won't surprise you that $100,000 can purchase a lot of information."

"They must be paying F.B.I. agents a lot these days," Riley said.

Ross laughed out loud. "Oh it wasn't my money. It was yours." Riley looked at Ross, completely bewildered. "And yours, Ms. Hawkins," Ross said. "In fact, I suppose some of the money was mine, too." Ross gazed up at the ceiling, momentarily distracted. "Do you know how big the F.B.I.'s annual budget is?" Ross asked suddenly. "Eight billion dollars. And that's just the publicly reported numbers. In an ocean of money such as that, no one misses a few dollars here or there – especially if you're the one who provides final spending approvals on behalf of the Director. So, you see," Ross threw his hands out and turned around the room, "it was your money that paid for all of this."

"So you used F.B.I. money to pay Isaac and Alexander?"

"You miss the point, Mr. Riley. Isaac and Alexander were zealots. You don't have to pay zealots. You simply need to give them," Ross paused, thinking of the right word, "direction; that, and the means to do exactly what they wanted to do in the first place. I merely demonstrated what Ceterus could do and they became all too willing to help."

"Who were they?" Riley asked.

"Patriots. They were patriots. But I can see that isn't what you were asking." Ross said, reading Riley's face. "They were members of a militia movement dedicated to action, not just words. It took me some time to find them. Most militia members are all talk. I was actually getting quite discouraged, but then I found Isaac. His belief that Lincoln's Prophecy was real made it all too easy. I simply took Lincoln's words and interpreted them to suit my own ends."

"So you never believed in the Prophecy?"

"No, Mr. Riley," Ross said in a patronizing tone. "Though I imagine Abraham Lincoln would be disgusted by what his government has done."

Ross's mind appeared to wander and Riley stalled for more time. "So why kill Isaac if he was such a dedicated patriot?"

"Isaac had served his purpose," Ross snapped. "I told him you were coming to D.C. and he was quite eager to follow." Ross breathed a heavy sigh. "It was easy, really."

"What about Agent Coffman? Was he another one of your zealots?"

"No. Coffman was an idealist, not a zealot. But he wasn't one of mine," Ross said, shaking his head. "No. Coffman believed in Ceterus. More importantly, he believed in the F.B.I. That's why, since the moment you met him that day at the canal, he tried to cover up the very existence of Ceterus. With Varden dead, you were the only civilian who knew the F.B.I. was conducting illegal surveillance operations. Naturally, you became the center of the cover-up. Coffman's orders were to find out what you knew and contain you. But Isaac," Ross began pacing the room again, "Isaac just couldn't let you go after you witnessed Alexander's death. He needed you and I needed him."

The pieces were falling rapidly into place. "So whenever I talked to Coffman, he would report it to the Director, and you passed everything on to Isaac."

Ross shrugged his shoulders casually, as if the whole conversation was starting to bore him. "It was what had to be done," he sighed. "The F.B.I. was desperate for you to come in so they could get the Ceterus Key and complete their cover-up. When I learned the Ceterus Key also detected my little virus, I knew I had to get to you first. And here we are. Now, enough of this," Ross said, looking down at his watch. "It's time you gave me the Ceterus Key."

Riley pressed on. "Why not just let them remove Ceterus? Wouldn't that be better than turning it against your own country?"

Ross snapped. "I believe in God, Mr. Riley!" he roared in anger. "I believe that you do not obtain forgiveness until you confess your sins. Allowing a cover-up would leave an indelible stain on this country." Ross was pacing back and forth, his face flushed. "No, Mr. Riley. Confession that is the only path to forgiveness. They must confess!" Without warning, Ross thrust his gun out and pressed the barrel hard against Amie's temple. Amie whimpered through her taped mouth and closed her eyes tight. "Now give me the fucking Key!"

"Alright!" Riley yelled. "Alright! I'll give it to you!" Tears streamed down Amie's face as Riley reached into his pocket and pulled out the black flash drive. "Here!" he said, holding it out towards Ross.

"Put it on the table," Ross demanded. He pointed to a white folding table a few feet in front of Riley. With his eyes locked on Amie, Riley stood and placed the flash drive on the table beside a computer terminal. When Riley returned to his seat, Ross stepped over to the table and slipped the drive into his coat pocket. "Thank you," he said, his voice calm once again.

Ross glanced at his watch and shook his head. "I wish our government would take me seriously. Perhaps another demonstration will get their attention."

Amie whimpered beneath the duct tape. "Don't do this," Riley pleaded.

"I suppose the hospitals weren't enough of a spectacle," Ross said. "How about," Ross rolled his eyes to the ceiling, "airplanes," he concluded. "A mid-air collision should make them admit what they've done." Ross spun towards the computer but then hesitated. He only had one functional hand, which he needed to hold his gun and maintain order. He couldn't type the necessary commands into the computer.

"After all you've been through," he said, looking Riley in the eyes, "I think you deserve the honors."

Riley shook his head. "I won't do it," he said firmly.

Ross circled around the table and stood next to Amie. He pressed the cold barrel hard against her temple.

"Okay! Okay!" Riley yelled, as he stood with his hands in the air. He walked to the table and sat down at the keyboard. "What do you want me to do?"

"I'm going to give you a series of instructions to type. If I find you haven't done exactly as I've instructed, I promise both you, and Ms. Hawkins here, will wish you had." Ross shifted his gaze from Amie back to Riley. "Do we have an agreement?"

"Yes," Riley said instantly. "Tell me what to do?" Ross began dictating a series of complex commands, which Riley slowly typed. *There's got to be a way out of this,* Riley repeated to himself. *Think, dammit!* Riley furtively searched his surroundings for anything that could help. The only things within reach were a pile of cables and a stack of discarded hard drives.

"And now," Ross said, after Riley typed the final command, "we're ready for our demonstration."

Riley looked at Amie, who was only feet away. Her eyes were wide open, the force of the gun barrel wrinkling the skin around her temple.

"All you need to do is press enter," Ross said. Amie's eyes pleaded with Riley. "Do it!" Ross demanded. "Do it or she dies!" Ross pressed the gun even harder, forcing Amie's head to tilt sideways.

Riley's finger hovered over the key. Sweat collected on his forehead as images from his past flashed uncontrollably through his mind: a hospital room, a doctor telling him his wife had died, his wife's face as she lay breathless in the casket. Riley squinted to force the memories away. He had already lost one woman in his life. He would not lose another. Slowly, his finger lowered towards the button.

BOOM!

Riley spun from the keyboard. The ear-shattering sound had come from the front of the basement. Ross turned the gun on Riley.

"Press the fucking button! Press it now!" he screamed, stepping closer to Riley.

Riley looked to the front door and back at Ross. There were men shouting in the foyer and then something rammed hard into the metal door.

"Push the fucking button!" Ross screamed, edging closer. Another step and Ross could reach the keyboard himself.

Suddenly, from the corner of Riley's eye, he saw Amie move. Her hands and feet still bound, she lunged from the chair and flew through the air. Her body collided with Ross like a battering ram. The unexpected blow sent Ross stumbling. Instinctively, Riley grabbed a heavy hard drive from the table and swung it over his head. Bringing it down with every ounce of force he could manage, he made contact with the back of Ross's head.

Ross pulled the trigger wildly as he fell towards the ground. The crack of gunfire filled the basement. Riley dove on top of Ross and they crashed to the ground. Ross swung the gun across his body, hitting Riley just above the eye. Riley faltered as a blinding pain shot through his skull. Ross had the advantage and rolled on top of Riley.

BOOM! The deafening concussion of another explosion ripped through the room.

Riley opened his eyes to see Ross hovering him, his gun aimed directly at Riley's head. Riley threw his hands out to shift the gun's position.

Crack! Crack! Two shots rang out. The weight of Ross' body pressed heavily against Riley's outstretched arms. Then, all at once, the struggle was over and Ross collapsed on top of Riley. Pinned beneath Ross' weight, Riley looked to the front of the room. Andy Dyll stood ten feet away, a smoking gun extended in his hand. Then Riley felt the warmth of Edward Ross' final breath against his skin.

CHAPTER 52

Within seconds, agents poured into the basement and confusion swirled around the room. Riley rolled Ross' lifeless body to the floor and scrambled over to Amie. Then he gently removed the tape from her face to reveal her bloodied and swollen lips. He unwrapped the tape that bound her hands and feet.

Amie and Riley embraced for a long time, words useless in conveying the rush of emotion. Slowly, reluctantly, Riley released her from his grasp and was looking deep into her brown eyes when a thought suddenly struck him. *Oh shit.*

He turned from Amie to look around the room. Agents were scattered throughout the basement, some huddled together talking, others had started rummaging through the mountain of evidence. Quietly, Riley stepped back to Ross's body. Kneeling down, Riley reached for his coat pocket.

"Looking for something?" The voice was startling. Riley looked up to see Andy Dyll standing over him.

"I...I was..." Riley stuttered to explain himself but stopped when Agent Dyll pulled his hand from his pocket and held up the black flash drive.

"I think it's best if the F.B.I. takes care of this," Agent Dyll said as the drive disappeared once again into his pocket.

Riley wasn't sure what he would have done with the flash drive, but it didn't matter now. The F.B.I. had Ceterus and they had the Key. It was over.

After being treated for cuts and bruises, Riley and Amie were escorted to an unmarked car and placed in the back seat. Seconds later, Andy Dyll opened the door and fell into the driver's seat. He found his passengers in the rearview mirror. "You guys like to make things complicated," he said with a incredulous grin. Then he started the car, and wove through the police barricade and into Georgetown.

They were passing Tudor Place and Gardens when Riley broke the silence. "Agent Dyll?" Andy looked up into the rearview mirror. "How'd you find us?"

"Ross was driving an F.B.I. car when he abducted Ms. Hawkins. Every F.B.I. car has a GPS tracking system."

"But we were parked blocks away," Amie interjected. "There are hundreds of townhomes around there."

Andy smiled and nodded. "There are," he agreed. "But once we found the car, we knew you probably hadn't gone too far."

"Yeah, but how'd you find *that* townhouse?" Riley repeated.

"Electricity bills," Andy said, plainly.

"What?" Amie asked.

"It's a technique we've used in drug cases for years. You see, marijuana needs constant light to grow. So grow houses use a lot of electricity. When we've narrowed our search for a particular grow house to a certain area, we pull the electricity bills of the surrounding blocks and look for anomalies." Andy looked in the mirror and saw that Riley and Amie weren't following. "We guessed that Ed Ross and his terrorist friends would need a lot of computing power to pull this thing off. Running all those servers and the air conditioners needed to keep them cool takes a lot of electricity. We pulled the records. That one came up hot."

Andy looked back in the rearview mirror. Riley and Amie were leaned against one another with their eyes closed – exhausted and emotionally drained. "I tell you what," he said, "How about we start our discussion in the morning?"

"It's a date," Riley said, his eyes still closed.

Minutes later, the car pulled to a stop. "Hope this'll do for the night," Andy said. Riley opened his eyes to see a beige brick wall emblazoned with gold lettering: Ritz Carlton.

"I knew you'd tracked us from the airport," Riley said in resignation.

Andy shrugged. "What can I say?" A bellman opened the door and Riley turned to get out. "Oh, Riley," Andy said. Riley turned to the front seat. "We'll have agents around the building tonight. They'll make sure you get to the office in the morning."

Riley nodded and got out of the car. Minutes later, Amie pressed a button and the elevator doors closed. Riley stared down at the floor as the elevator climbed upwards.

"What's wrong?" Amie asked.

"I don't know what I would have done with it, but I wish I'd gotten to the Ceterus Key before Agent Dyll."

Amie smiled. "Well," she said, drawing Riley's attention as she reached down the neck of her shirt. "We could always use this one."

Riley's eyes opened wide. "Is that," he hesitated looking at the red flash drive in Amie's outstretched hand. "Is that what I think it is?"

"It might be," Amie said.

"Where the hell'd you get that?"

"I might have made a copy of it when we were at the lab on campus."

"And it's been in your bra this entire time?" Riley was shell shocked.

"Yep. But there's some even better news," she said as they stepped off the elevator and walked to her room.

"What's that?" Riley asked.

Amie slid the card key into the door. "We have all night to think about what to do with it," she said and then she pulled Riley into her room and closed the door.

EPILOGUE

How do I look?" Riley asked, holding his arms out and examining his blue pinstripe suit.

"You look perfect," Amie said, encouragingly. "You'll do great."

"Thanks," Riley said, though he wasn't so sure.

"Mr. Riley," came the deep voice of a uniformed Capitol police officer. "They're ready for you."

"I'll be right here when you're finished," Amie said.

Riley squeezed her hand and then walked through the heavy wooden door and into the chamber. At the far end of the room, a white marble wall stood behind two rows of oak-paneled benches. The chamber was empty, except for the fifteen members of the Senate Intelligence Committee. The Committee members waited patiently as Riley walked down the blue-carpeted aisle and stood behind the oak table at the front of the room.

A heavy silence hung in the air before the Committee's chair, Senator Jason Cassady, finally spoke. "Welcome, Mr. Riley," he said warmly. "Please have a seat. I know I speak for the entire Committee when I tell you we are truly thankful that you're here with us today."

"I'm glad to be here, Senator," Riley said, settling into the leather chair and adjusting the microphone.

"Before we go on the record, I think it's important that you understand the Committee's mindset on these hearings."

"That would be appreciated, sir."

"As you can see, this is a closed door session," the Senator said, motioning around the empty room. "You and Ms. Hawkins remain the only two civilians in the country who have any idea of the events surrounding Christoph Varden and the F.B.I. Our job as a Committee is to learn what happened and, after careful deliberation, determine the best way forward. Our concern is not only for the F.B.I., but for this entire country.

"Rest assured, we fully understand that you and Ms. Hawkins were inadvertently drawn into a series of events that were not of your own doing and were outside your control. You and Ms. Hawkins are not under investigation here. The F.B.I. is the subject of our inquiry." The Senator looked down and shuffled the papers in front of him.

"The F.B.I.'s motives in creating Ceterus were clear," he said, looking back at Riley. "Their aim was to protect this country from external forces that mean us harm. But at what cost? That is the fundamental question here. How much are we willing to trade in the name of security? Those are the questions that must be answered, not only by this Committee, but by generations to come. There is nothing more essential to answering these questions than knowing how far we've already gone so that we may, if required, change our course before it's too late. Do you understand?"

"Yes, sir," Riley said. "I understand."

"Good. Then let's get started, shall we?"

Riley stood and raised his right hand.

"Do you solemnly swear that the testimony you will give in these proceedings will be the truth, the whole truth and nothing but the truth, so help you God?"

"I do."

Made in the USA
San Bernardino, CA
28 October 2016